KLONDIK

McCoy blasted his right fis
powered his left arm around
the man bellowed.

"I should break your damn neck right here!" McCoy barked.

He eased off the choke hold, and just as the man turned toward him, McCoy slammed the derringer down across the side of his head, blasting him into unconsciousness.

McCoy stripped the laces out of one of the gunman's boots and tied his hands behind his back. Then he used the man's hat and brought a hat full of ice-cold water from the stream and sloshed it in the man's face.

By the time McCoy retrieved his black flat-crowned hat with the bullet hole in it, the gunman was conscious.

"Why the hell you tie me up?" he shouted.

McCoy grabbed him by the throat and pressed his thumbs on his windpipe. "Why the hell you try to kill me?"

SPUR

KLONDIKE CUTIE

DIRK FLETCHER

LEISURE BOOKS   **NEW YORK CITY**

A LEISURE BOOK®

April 1993

Published by

Dorchester Publishing Co., Inc.
276 Fifth Avenue
New York, NY 10001

Printed in the United States of America.

SPUR

KLONDIKE
CUTIE

DIRK FLETCHER

Prologue

St. Michael, Alaska Territory, May 10, 1898

It wasn't the first whorehouse in a tent that Spur McCoy had ever seen. He was in St. Michael, Alaska Territory, a woebegone sketch of a fishing village turned into the gateway to the Klondike gold rush. His boat up the Yukon didn't leave until dawn the next day.

The young redhead nuzzled against his bare chest and sucked on his man breast.

"I love to eat man tit," she said between slurps. "The man smell is just terrific."

He had met her on the ship he came up from Seattle on, but there was no place for even a quick coupling on the crowded coastal steamer. So she had insisted that he come to her every night in her new one-woman fancy-lady tent until he sailed up the Yukon.

"I told you, you won't find any pussy on that next boat, the *Pacific Queen*. No staterooms, no room to wiggle on deck or in the cabins, let alone room for a good fucking."

She sat astride his naked body on the bed set up in her tent and grinned at him, her big breasts bouncing as she pretended to be riding him like a bronco.

"You ready to ride me again, lover? I need your big whanger pounding into me again. Damn but it feels good after some of these wimpy little dicks I've had to handle lately. Why are these gold rush men all proud of their little whangers?"

She reached down and aroused him again, bringing him to his full hardness and then sliding down to position herself over his weapon. She guided him to her wet red lips, and groaned in delight as he slid upward into her waiting vagina.

"Oh, Christ, but that is wonderful!" she whispered. "So damn, fucking good!" When he was fully inserted so their pelvic bones ground together, she let her hands down to the bed beside his shoulders and began a series of grinding and jolting movements from side to side that had him aroused before he wanted to be.

"The fourth time is always the best for me," she said. "Delsey likes the fourth fuck." She lifted now, and brought up her knees higher and began to ride him like he was a young heifer in heat and she was the rampaging range bull.

"You still there, cowboy?" Delsey asked. Sweat beaded her forehead. Her breath came in huge gasps now, and McCoy grinned knowing that he could last longer than she could. After three go-rounds he knew he could.

"Come on, McCoy, give me an even race. Move your damn hips a little."

He began to punch upward with each of her downward thrusts, and she laughed and nodded and he saw her surging toward a climax.

"Oh, damn!" she bellowed, and half the other couples in the tents near them must have heard. There were a few calls and a shriek or two in answer to her outburst.

Delsey shuddered and then exploded into her climax. It was stronger than the previous three, and she rattled like a narrow-gauge railroad train on a new-built trestle.

"Oh, God, oh, God, damnit to hell!" She couldn't talk then; a high, shrill keening spilled from her throat as she jolted again and again as one climax after another tore into her small form and shook her like a mouse in a tomcat's jaws.

At last she tapered off and wiped sweat from her forehead, then looked down at McCoy.

"Damn you, you won again." She pretended to slap him, but her hand barely touched his cheek. She bent and kissed his lips instead and his hips began to respond, driving her higher and higher over him until he gave one bellow of victory and exploded inside her with ten hard spurting thrusts that brought a smile to her face.

"At least you didn't beat me by much," she said.

Ten minutes later they still lay on the bed, resting.

"What's it like up there at Dawson?" McCoy asked.

"Don't have the foggiest idea. We came up here on the same boat, remember? Takes a month to get up the Yukon from here and you ain't getting no pussy all that time. So we rest up and see if we can break your record of seven, right?"

"Seven, yes. But remember, you'll have to carry me on your back to the dock tomorrow morning."

Delsey grinned. "I can do that, or drag you by your whanger. That really works as a good handle."

He pinched one of her breasts and she grinned at him.

"I don't know what it's like in Dawson. I've done some men coming back down. They say by the time they got there the best claims were already staked. They came down the river from Lake Bennett. A couple came down on one of the boats that broke up the ice. I don't know what another twenty thousand men are going to do up there."

"I'm just interested in finding one man," McCoy said. "I've seen more gold camps than I want to remember and most of them look alike. High prices, low wages, mostly out-of-work men, and a few who get filthy rich."

"You get filthy rich and come back and marry me. Hell, we fit together good."

"True, but I'm not going up to find gold."

"That's what they all say." She reached to a small table and picked up a bottle of whiskey and two shot glasses. "One more shot and then we'll go for number five. I can't let you get too soft or you might never come alive again. I've seen it happen."

McCoy thought about the month-long trip up the Yukon and held the glass while she poured. He was going to be sore as hell tomorrow, but he'd have a whole month to heal up.

Then, up in Dawson, it would be business first, pleasure afterwards.

He thought about the assignment. Not one he was thrilled with. All this travel and work to find one man. The U.S. Government wanted him bad because the British Government wanted him bad. He had killed someone and raped a woman, and there was going to be hell to pay. The sod couldn't have been in Canada for more than a month or two.

The British had tracked him to Quebec and lost him there. Then someone claimed to have seen him heading for Vancouver, B.C. The latest telegram McCoy received from General Halleck said that the British had information from the Duke's household that the errant son had given his father an address of General Delivery, Dawson City, Canada. The household servant hadn't heard what name the son was using, but odds were it wasn't Walling.

It wasn't much to go on, but it was all they had. McCoy's job was to find the man and bring him to justice with the Royal Canadian Mounted Police, who were also on the alert.

"Hey, you still here?" Delsey whined. He looked down, and she had him ready for action and he hadn't even felt her.

"You're good," he said. "Damn good."

"So, prove to me how good *you* are. Remember, don't overdo. This is only number five and it isn't midnight yet."

McCoy nodded, set her on her hands and knees, and showed her that he was more than good for his fifth time.

Chapter One

Spur McCoy stood on the gently swaying deck of the *Pacific Queen* and stared at the bustling tent town that St. Michael, Alaska Territory, had become in the only two years. It was no longer a sleepy village, and the small dock, the mud flats, and the few frame buildings were all pulsating with activity, ready to charge into the future and bulging with thousands of men and foodstuffs and equipment, all heading for the Klondike gold fields in Dawson City in the Yukon region of Canada.

So was McCoy, but not to hunt gold. He was manhunting.

The captain of the ship, John Nizelry, bellowed at a well-dressed gentleman standing only a yard away.

"Blast ye, Henderson. I told you no handguns on board 'less I got them locked up in me cabin. Cause too much deadly kind of trouble that I won't put up with for a whit. Hand over your piece or get to the dock. One or the other."

Captain Nizelry was a thickset man with a whiskey-ripe nose, eyes given to bloody lines shredding the whites, and deep down, a liver half-eaten away. "Hand over your piece now, Henderson, otherwise I'll chuck you over the side."

Henderson snorted, drew the revolver, and held it pointed at the deck. Henderson was a head shorter than the captain, and wore clothes of a gambler, with a curl-ended mustache and a fancy red checkered vest.

"Would you be putting me off now, Captain? I think not. Unless you want to do it with five holes in your scurrilous old hide. Now back away and let's cast off. The ice in the Yukon broke yesterday and it's two hours past dawn, our sailing time."

Spur McCoy, leaning against the rail of the *Pacific Queen* ten feet from the squabble, saw the fear in the eyes of the old sea dog. McCoy moved with the silence and grace of a big cat up behind the gunman. He slammed his right fist into Henderson's right hand, jolting the six-gun to the deck, where it landed on a seabag without enough of a jolt to discharge.

"What the devil?" Henderson roared, and spun around. He met the good right fist of Spur McCoy as it landed squarely on his jaw; then another McCoy fist plowed into the gambler's belly. Without pause, McCoy powered a killer uppercut with his right hand that smashed into Henderson's chin, lifted him an inch off the deck, and dumped him into a coil of hemp rope on the wooden planks.

Henderson tried to get up, clawed at the sea-wet hemp with one hand, and then passed out.

Captain Nizelry stared at McCoy a moment, then guffawed and held out his hand. "Be damned, never seen a man put down so quickly, and with so little wasted effort. I thank you, sir. 'Tis a pleasure to shake the hand that put Henderson on his ass."

McCoy took the hand and nodded. "Figured you was in a bit of a tight spot there, Captain. I checked both my guns, figured he should do the same."

"Rule on my boat. Some captains don't do it and get into trouble. Friend of mine lost his ship to a gang of no-good pirates just last year six hours out of port here."

The captain waved at two seamen who had watched the small fight. "Dump this swab on the deck and throw his goods after him. His gambling money ain't no good on my ship. Tell the man at the plank to let on another paying customer. We lift the anchor in five minutes."

McCoy watched the seamen work to get the 150-foot stern-wheeler underway. Almost any vessel that would float was heading north for the gold fields now that the ice breakup had come cracking and charging down the winter-frozen Yukon River, which was about a hundred miles to the south. St. Michael was the closest bit of habitation to the great river's mouth.

As the heavily loaded stern-wheeler eased into the Pacific Ocean and headed south, Captain Nizelry turned the wheel over to his first mate and leaned on the rail beside McCoy.

"I'm beholden to you for that fancy bit of fist work back at the dock. I understand you're some kind of a lawman."

"Yes sir. Name's Spur McCoy and I'm a Secret Service agent for the United States Government."

Captain Nizelry grinned. "Good and proper! Proud to have you on board. You get a bunk in a cabin?"

"I did, with only seven other men. I hear it will take us a month to beat our way upstream to Dawson City."

The old captain nodded. He lit his pipe, puffed it a moment, then nodded again. "Yep, about a month, if'n we don't bottom out on a shallow spot. We got ourselves thirteen hundred and fifty-five miles to sail. I ain't bottomed out yet, but there's a time for every man on this crazy river."

Nizelry paused, rubbed his sun darkened face, and looked up from his bloodshot eyes. "I'd guess you're hunting a man up there. Gonna be a chore. By the time we get there, the pack will be down from Lake Bennett in their homemade boats. Could be over thirty thousand people in that wild tent town by that time. Hope you brought along enough victuals to eat for a time."

"I was warned about that. Doesn't look like your ship here is one of them luxury liners with fancy china and crystal on the dining table."

Captain Nizelry chuckled. "You heard right. Every passenger provides his own food for the trip, and there ain't no ports to stop at to eat on shore." He tamped down his pipe, then looked up over the fire.

"Course, me being beholden to you and all, I'd be obliged to offer you some food now and then if'n you run low. Captain's table and all that. Say, Sunday dinner in my quarters."

McCoy grinned and held out his hand. "Might

hold you to that. I'm not partial to my own cooking for long."

The captain laughed and handed McCoy a magazine. It had a drawing on the cover of a wilderness filled with a forest of green trees and a rushing stream.

"Fella give me that today. Said it's the story of how the Klondike gold field got discovered. Don't know if'n it's gospel or not, but made a nice story. Read it through if'n you want."

McCoy took the magazine, thanked the captain, and went below to his cabin and the bunk next to the top. His sleeping area was two feet wide, and the space between the bunks on the other wall was another two feet. Only one man at a time could dress or undress in the cramped quarters. Cooking would be done on deck.

McCoy heaved into his bunk and closed his eyes. He'd be well rested on the day they landed in Dawson. He lay there for a half hour to get used to the confined space, then lowered into the slot between the bunks and went topside to read the magazine the captain had lent him. He'd heard that reading material and news of any sort were in desperately short supply in Dawson. He'd be sure to give the magazine back to the captain.

He found a suitable spot in the sun on deck and leaned back against the bulkhead. He could hear the diesel engine deep in the bowels of the ship pounding away. The engine turned a long shaft that went to the big paddle wheel on the stern that drove the craft up the river.

He settled back to read:

THE KLONDIKE GOLD RUSH . . . How It Started, by the Man Who Was There.

Yukon Region, Klondike River, August 1896.

Robert Henderson, a tall, icicle-thin prospector with a thick mustache and ragtag clothes, floated down the Yukon in his pole boat and saw a white man he knew sun-drying salmon on tall racks on the banks of the Klondike River where it dumped into the mighty Yukon.

Henderson was well acquainted with the man, George Carmack. ·He was a squawman, and thought of himself as half Indian, living by trading, logging, and catching and drying salmon in the sun with members of his wife's tribe, the Siwash. Carmack looked up and waved and Henderson poled into the shore landing near him.

"You'll never get rich catching salmon," Henderson called.

"Suits me," Carmack said. He was shorter and stockier than the bean pole Henderson, and had heavy jowls and close-set eyes over a drooping mustache in the Oriental fashion.

"George, next time I see you, I think you'll turn into an Indian."

"Fine by me. You still chasing gold dust?"

"Not chasing, Siwash, found. Stopped by to tell you. Up and over the ridge from the Indian River. Brought out seven hundred and fifty dollars worth of the yellow. Heading back that way. Figured by the code of the Klondike, I got to tell you about my strike."

Siwash George looked up at him and preened his long mustache. "How much a pan?"

"Usual, ten to fifteen cents worth. Enough to keep a man hunting for more."

Siwash George turned over a fillet of salmon he had cooking on a small fire. The pungent odor of the quickly cooking fish made his mouth water. He broke off a piece of the thin section and chewed on the salmon as he thought about gold.

George Carmack worked at catching and drying the salmon with his two Siwash tribe brothers-in-law, Skookum Jim and Tagish Charley. His wife, Kate, a tall, sturdy daughter of the tribe's chief, stood swishing a branch to keep the flies off the salmon.

George waved his hand. "I got it good here. Why leave?"

"Millions in gold, Siwash. You should come." Henderson shrugged. His piercing dark eyes and hawklike face lost interest. "So I told you. Come along or not."

George ate another bite of the salmon, broke off a new piece from the slab on the fire, and gave it to Henderson, who only nodded and ate it. This was the custom in the rugged wilderness of the Yukon: men shared food when they had it. Many men had died of starvation and the cold in this region.

Siwash George squatted by the fire a moment, then nodded. "Yes, I'll come. Might as well bring my two brothers along as well."

Henderson looked up quickly. His usually expressionless face showed a touch of anger. He ate another bite of the salmon, then shook his head.

"I didn't mean to invite the whole damned Siwash tribe along to stake claims," Henderson said softly. But George and the two Indians heard him. The two Siwash looked at each other and frowned.

Henderson left soon after that, and Siwash George said he'd find him in a couple of days. When Henderson was out of sight working upstream on the Klondike, the Indians yelled at Siwash George.

"What the matter dat white man?" Skookum Jim shouted in his pidgin jargon. "Him kill Siwash moose, Siwash caribou, ketch gold from Siwash river. What for he won't let Siwash stake claim? No damn good!"

Siwash George wasn't happy either with Henderson's quick remark and remembered it.

The next morning, Siwash George and his two Indian companions poled up the Klondike River heading for the spot Henderson had named Gold Bottom. But they turned in at another stream before they got there that they called Rabbit Creek. All of the talk by Henderson about the gold had made them curious.

"Might as well stop and do some panning," Siwash said, and they did, swirling a pan or two as they went.

Skookum Jim shouted a while later. Sure enough, gold.

"Ten cents a pan," Siwash George said, fingering the small splash of gold dust. "Not good enough," Siwash George said, and they moved on. They worked some more spots, then turned up a fork of the creek toward Gold Bottom. After a hike through tangled underbrush and mosquitoes, they found the right spot.

A column of thin, blue smoke helped them hone in on the place at Gold Bottom.

Henderson looked up and waved. He had left his partners at the site when he went for supplies, and now they had dug out a deep gash in the frozen ground to reach down to the gravelly bedrock where the richest placer gold might be found in an old streambed.

"Try a pan or two," Henderson invited. The three men all worked two pans for gold dust and found some color, but nothing to get them excited.

The two Indians were plainly uneasy around the white men and Henderson in particular.

Siwash George shook his head. "Nope, Henderson. Don't think we'll stake here. Seen a spot over across the ridge I want to try."

Henderson shrugged. He wasn't that anxious to have more men working his find. He sucked on a pipe and eyed Siwash George.

"You be sure to let me know if you hit anything over there better than what we have here. Hell, I'll pay one of your Indians to come over and tell me the good news."

Siwash George nodded. "Sure, easy. Ain't that far." So the promise was made and the two men shook hands. Siwash George left soon after that with his kinfolk.

George Carmack and his brothers-in-law headed back over the hills and the thick brush going toward Rabbit Creek. The hills weren't that high or steep, but the going was slow as they struggled around and over fallen logs, past spiky clumps of devil's clubs, and floundered through the lush growth of tangled underbrush in the rain forest.

At last they got over the top and down the other side to the swampy flat spotted with clumps of matted grass that had grown up over the decades and served as unsure stepping-stones across the muck.

They slipped and fell often, and soon their boots and pants were soaking wet as they battled the homeland of a million mosquitoes.

When they finally reached the headwaters of

Rabbit Creek, they began working down toward the spot where they had found the color. The heavy going took its toll on them, and they paused for a rest at a fork in the creek among some birches.

After a break, they walked on downstream a quarter of a mile and made camp. Before they got a fire going, Skookum Jim spotted a wandering moose, and promptly shot it to supplement their food supply.

Siwash George Carmack had hunkered down to the stream for a drink of the pure, fresh water when he uttered a scream of disbelief. He reached out to a rim of bedrock jutting along the bank and picked up a gold nugget as big as an acorn.

He stared at it for a moment, then screamed in delight. The others came to look; then they all gaped at the raw gold just under the water spread thick between slabs of rock like golden cheese in a sandwich.

The three men grabbed pans and shovels and began to work the gravel round and round in their pans. Minutes later, when Siwash George had washed away the gravel and swirled the final pay dirt in the pan, he found he had a quarter of an ounce of fine gold dust.

"Great snakes!" Siwash George screeched. "That's four dollars worth in a single pan! We're rich!"

Skookum Jim finished washing out his pan, and they had another quarter of an ounce of pure gold dust and a few flakes.

"By thunder! Dat goot!" Tagish Charlie shouted, and the three of them jumped up and began doing a war dance around the two pans of gold.

The three screeched, bellowed, howled, and

roared, jumping around like half-crazed monsters in a crazy, wild dance. It was part Scottish hornpipe, part Siwash mating dance, part Indian fox-trot, and a lot of screaming in wonder and glory.

At last Siwash George fell on the bank and stared at the gold in the two pans.

"Four dollars a pan!" he bellowed into the woods. The Indian brothers sat down near him, grinning and panting, exhausted but so excited they could barely stay sill.

"We're rich, boys," Carmack said. "We'll never dry another salmon as long as we live!"

They moved across the creek to a better camp spot and made a fire as darkness closed in on them. They talked long into the night, puffing on their pipes and watching slabs of the moose meat roast slowly over a bed of coals.

The next morning, they staked their claims. By Canadian law, each claim was 500 feet long following the creek and extended from ridge line to ridge line across any small valley. Tagish Charley asked what good the ridge lines were.

"This little creek's been running through this valley for hundreds of thousands of years," Siwash George told him. "It could have left gold in any of a dozen different streambeds, and even some high on the banks. Might be gold all the way to the ridge. So it's all part of the claim."

Carmack had made the discovery, and by law was entitled to two claims. He staked the Discovery Claim and One Below. Skookum Jim paced out his claim as One Above the discovery claim. Tagish Charley took Two Below as his claim. Any other claims staked on that creek would be numbered from the Discovery Claim either above or below.

"Now we have to record our claims," Carmack told his two brothers-in-law. They struggled back into heavy packs, left the rest of the moose meat to rot, and moved out toward the mouth of the Klondike.

On their way downstream in their boat, they met a dozen men who were tired, wet, and discouraged. Carmack told them all about his good fortune, and the men raced upstream to find Rabbit Creek and stake our their own claims.

It was the code of the Order of the Pioneers to tell everyone a miner met about his strike and good fortune and point out the way to get there. A gold discovery in the Yukon was never kept a secret.

As Siwash George Carmack and Tagish Charley began their trip down the Yukon River to Fortymile, Skookum Jim hurried back to the Rabbit Creek to cut some firewood and set up a close watch over their four mining claims.

At Fortymile, Siwash Charley Carmack tried to tell the miners in Bill McPhee's saloon about his find, but too often they had been tricked by "Lying George" and they didn't believe him now. He had two whiskeys and roared at the men in anger, then took out his shotgun shell full of gold dust and flakes and poured it into a blower pan on the gold scales which sat on the bar.

The men now crowded around.

"Won't work, Carmack. That's some dust that Ladue gave you to trick us with," one old-timer yelled.

But the men up close shook their heads. Placer gold had a fingerprint all its own, and this dust and flakes and the sheen of black sand were unlike any that they men who knew gold had ever seen. Slowly the truth broke through to the men.

The next morning, Siwash George went across the Yukon River to the Royal Canadian Mounted Police post and recorded the four claims on Rabbit Creek. Then he picked up some supplies and headed back up the river, poling his craft along the slower water at the edge of the mighty Yukon.

During this time and in the busy days to follow, Siwash George never thought to send a man over the ridge line to tell Robert Henderson about his good fortune.

Somehow the promise was forgotten. It may have been partly because of the angry statement Henderson had made about the Siwash Indians. Henderson continued to work his claim at Gold Bottom drawing out eight to ten cents a pan, not knowing about the big strike until it was too late for him to get rich.

Before the sun set on Fortymile, the small village was missing a lot of the first disbelieving miners. Men in twos and threes slipped out of town and moved upstream the forty miles toward the Klondike River mouth. In three days, Fortymile was deserted.

The saloon owner and promoter, Joe Ladue, who had been the lifeblood of Fortymile, left as well, moving everything he owned the long trek upstream to the mouth of the Klondike.

Across the Yukon River from where Henderson had met George Carmack smoking fish, there was a wide gravel beach and a stretch of frozen swamp behind it over a mile long. On this open stretch, Joe Ladue began to built the settlement of

Dawson. Ladue was a round and jolly Frenchman who knew nothing but retailing and at the same time had a passion for the wide-open spaces. He loved the wilderness, and had always dreamed of being in on the big gold rush when it happened in Alaska or Canada. He didn't want to prospect; he wanted to mint gold by selling goods and services to the miners. Now he saw his big chance.

He quickly staked out a land claim of a square mile fronting the river on the frozen swamp and wide beach and cut it up into city lots. He built a log cabin before winter, opened a saloon, and moved his sawmill to the new city of Dawson, where he put two men to work sawing logs into building lumber for his new town.

It was still September of 1896, but already Dawson was growing. Ladue sat on his porch wondering if this was the big strike and if the boomtown would quickly build up. He desperately wanted to start and own and run Dawson, a gold rush town. He would know for sure come next summer and the thaw.

Spur McCoy finished reading the article and closed the magazine. He couldn't imagine so much gold in one spot. It had created a monstrous rush of miners and men who thought they could be gold miners. The gold fields stretched mostly across the snow-covered slopes of southern Alaska, into Canada, and down to the series of lakes and rivers that eventually led to Dawson City.

It was a man-killing task just to get to Dawson, he'd read, and by the time most of the Klondikers got there all of the worthwhile mining claims had already been taken.

He closed his eyes, imagining that first day when Siwash George Carmack came up with four dollars worth of gold in that first panning. He'd have a month on the river to think about it. He also had a month to figure out exactly how he was going to track down the gambler and killer who had murdered a man in England and was said to be heading for Dawson. His boss in Washington, D.C., had said it was top priority. The British Government was hot to find this one. Now the Secret Service was also.

The Service had been instructed to do all it could to help, since the fugitive had passed through Alaska and thus the U.S. had some responsibility. Spur had been telegraphed and assigned to follow this man wherever he went, spending as much time as it took to capture him. Spur McCoy would then turn him over to the Royal Canadian Mounted Police if he were in Canada, or return him to Washington, D.C., if the man was caught in the U.S.

McCoy thought of the thick packet of information he had about the man. His name was Arthur Walling, the third son of a Duke in England who'd run to the New World to escape the hangman's noose for murder. He probably was using another name now, and while McCoy had a good description of the man, he didn't know what name Walling was using. He figured that with some twenty thousand residents who would be in Dawson City by the time he arrived, he might have a tough time finding his man.

He'd work closely with the Royal Canadian Mounted Police in Dawson, since he would be in a foreign country. He was sure they would cooperate. He stood and went to lean against the rail, watching the endless sea of green evergreen trees that paraded up and down one mountain after another. There would be nothing boring about this trip upstream to Dawson, he was sure.

Chapter Two

Dyea, Alaska Territory, August 22, 1897

Bryce Jeferies stood on the sandy beach at Dyea, Territory of Alaska, and stared at the mass of men and goods that crowded the miles of wet shoreline around the bay. He could see stacks of wooden boxes and more stacks of cardboard that stretched down the muddy, rocky shore. He could still smell the stench of the hold where he had spent a week packed in with dozens of other men like stalks of wheat in a field.

He turned, and a breeze from the sea washed away the stale body odor and brought the tang of salt air. Jeferies was on his way to the Klondike. Nothing would stop him. He was 22 years old, had a cargo of 5,000 fine cigars, and was determined to get them over the pass ahead and down to Dawson.

He was sturdy enough for what came ahead. He stood five feet eight inches tall, average for the day, and had a muscular upper body and strong legs. He had dark hair and a well-trimmed black beard. Brown eyes showed under heavy brows, and he knew he could take care of himself because he had done some bare-knuckled boxing down in Seattle.

He took a deep breath and looked at Dyea again. This was the quickest way. He had missed the last boat that could have made it up the ice-choked Yukon River to Dawson, 1355 miles from the tiny port of St. Michael, before the river froze solid. Now the overland route was the only way to Dawson until the ice broke up in the Yukon River next spring.

He knew the odds and the dangers. He had heard all about Chilkoot Pass and the Royal Canadian Mounted Police's weigh station at the summit.

Bryce looked around at a thousand other men who seemed just as determined as he was. He had seen the first steamer come into Seattle from the Klondike gold fields July 19, 1897. Sixty-seven men poured off the freighter lugging sacks and jars and boxes of gold dust that had weighed in at just over a ton. *A ton of gold!*

The men wore the rags of clothes they had left Dawson in, some with gold dust still in the mud on their boots. They were bearded, with long hair, and telling tales of such a rich strike that every man in Seattle wanted to fly to the north.

At once Bryce had made arrangements to get up the coast of British Columbia to Alaska and the tiny port of Dyea. He talked to the miners, found out what he would need, bought his supplies, and worked on plans for a boat he could build. Dyea was the landing place for those going over the Chilkoot Pass into Canada and the lake country with the headwaters of the Yukon River.

The secret had been speed, still was. He had to get his thousand pounds of food, his merchandise, and enough equipment to build a boat, and get it on a coastal steamer. There was no certainty when winter would move in and close down the pass. Then no one could get across it until spring.

But he would make it. He had his food supply and his merchandise and tools and clothes and other essentials all assembled in lightweight wooden packing boxes so they came to exactly 60 pounds each. He would carry the 20 boxes with a pair of wide straps around the box and then around his shoulders.

Standing there on the dock at Dyea on August 22nd, he knew he had planned everything down to the last detail. First he had to move his 20 boxes of food and supplies up to the timberline on the mountain. He would have to do the job himself. He couldn't afford to pay a dollar a pound for some other man to pack his goods.

There were more than two thousand men in the small town by that time, and most of them were shepherding stacks of boxes and moving them slowly toward the mountain.

Packing one box up the pass would be easy, but with 20 it took planning. Bryce did what most of the men on the trek did, moved one box six miles and set it in a spot he wouldn't forget. Then he walked back to his stack, took another box, and carried it forward to his cache. After 39 six mile trips he would have moved his boxes six miles.

The first day he made two round trips before it got dark. He made one more round trip after dark, then opened one box and took out blankets and fell on them exhausted. He had walked 36 miles that day and was just getting started.

As Bryce looked at the remaining 17 boxes, he thought of giving up and sailing back to Seattle. He realized that by the time he had carried the boxes all the way to the headwaters of the Yukon River, 30 miles away, he would have walked 1170 miles, half of it with a 60-pound pack on his back. Bryce shrugged, pulled the blankets around his aching shoulders, and went to sleep.

The next morning he could barely move. He had blisters on both feet, and his shoulders were so sore he could not lift his arms for half an hour. After a quick fire and a cup of coffee and some hard rolls, he put a pad on his shoulders, strapped on the first 60-pound box, and staggered to his feet.

That day he moved four boxes forward. The first part of the trail led up a wooded river valley in several easy grades toward the base of the mountain ahead. He tried not to look at the snow- and ice-coated barrier. If lugging these boxes was this hard on nearly flat ground, what would it be like climbing up a 45-degree angle over steps that had been cut out of the ice?

That night he went to bed as soon as he had cooked himself some supper. Food was plentiful in the small town. He bought some potatoes and a slab of moose meat and stuffed himself. Another cup of coffee and he was so tired that he fell asleep before he could even wash his camp dishes.

At first, Bryce worried about someone stealing some of his goods. But quickly he realized everyone was in the same situation. If a man stole something, he would only have that much more to carry up and over the slope. He worked hard the next two days, making the 48-mile walk again. He had five boxes left. If he tried hard enough . . .

The next day he awoke early and had his first box halfway to his cache before the sun came up. He jogged back to the shore and strapped on the second.

Before he quit that night, Bryce was out of the little town and six miles into the woods, beside a brightly chattering stream with his 20 boxes of goods, all six miles up the trail.

To Bryce, it seemed as if 2,000 men were plodding along unaware that anyone else was around. Soon he realized it was a defense mechanism. If you made no friends, you wouldn't be obligated to help anyone. A 600-mile hike toting along a ton and a quarter of goods was enough of a job for a dozen men, let alone just one.

He made his second six miles during the next five days and found himself farther along, working up a steep canyon. At the end of his 12-mile mark was a bustling little settlement called Canyon City. It looked to Bryce as if some men had given up the trek, and used their thousand pounds of goods to open small shops and set up tents. He found two places to eat, three to gamble, and even a fancy lady plying her trade. Bryce waved at her, and that was all the energy he had left after his 48 miles of pretending that he was a pack mule.

Soon he had his goods at Sheep Camp. It was in a round valley at the end of the steep canyon and near the timberline. No trees grew above

Sheep Camp and firewood became a premium. He had climbed into the snowbelt, and at Sheep Camp hundreds of tents were pitched in the snow. Beside them were the inevitable stacks of boxes of food and merchandise.

He saw one couple, a man and a woman, packing a piano up the slopes. They had their 2,000 pounds of food and a piano that they had disassembled and placed into boxes and carried up the hill. He wondered if they would ever get it to Dawson.

Sheep Camp was set up more like a town, with places to eat and with one frame building that served as a hotel where you could buy a spot on the floor to sleep if you could find a space.

A small meal of bacon, beans, and tea cost two dollars and a half. Bryan fixed his own meals.

He looked up in the fading light at the jagged looming mountains all around him. To the north he saw one that had a deep notch in it. That was his destination—Chilkoot Pass.

By this time his shoulders and feet were tougher. He had learned how to carry the load with the least strain on his body. His sturdy legs were building new muscles. His black beard now had grown longer, but he didn't take time to trim it.

Bryce talked with a few men and found out that four miles ahead they would come to a settlement called the Scales. This was where the Mounted Police would weigh each man's goods and food and give him permission to move across the border—or turn him back because he didn't have enough food. Once over the border they would be in the Canadian Yukon region.

September had come, and now and then a few

flakes of snow sifted down on the men. It seemed to urge them on to greater effort.

Bryce made six four-mile round trips a day through the snow and ice to get his goods to the Scales. The fourth day he had only two boxes to take and when he had them moved, he stood in line to have his goods weighed.

The Royal Mounted Police turned down the man just ahead of Bryce. The man had only 600 pounds of food and 600 pounds of goods to sell.

Bryce shivered at the thought of starting over, but he passed the test and moved his boxes to one side as he eyed the long black line of men struggling up the 45-degree trail on the final ascent to the pass. It was only 1500 feet to the top, Bryce had been told.

He had learned that there were 1500 steps cut into the ice and it would take six hours to climb to the top. He checked the sun, shouldered one of his boxes, and trudged into the long line to get to the steps.

When he came to the wide notches cut into the ice, he couldn't believe it. They were a foot high and the first dozen almost knotted up his toughened legs. Then he warmed to the task and commanded his legs to work. Once a man fell out of the line, he had to go back to the end to begin again or hope that someone else fell out near enough that he could jump into that space.

Step, step, step. Bryce started counting. When he got to 300 he gave up. The top was nowhere to be seen. The angle of the slope was still at 45 degrees. He could lean over just a little and touch the ice snow ahead of him.

At last he made it to the top. He wanted to stop and look at the view, but the man behind

him growled and he walked 50 yards to the left
to an open spot and dropped his box. He sat on
it, panting from the exertion. Only 19 more trips
up the ice steps. Now Bryce knew for certain that
he wished he had never come. He also knew there
was no turning back now.

This was the adventure of a lifetime. He heard
that women and children had made the trip ahead
of him. He wasn't going to let them outdo him.

He looked for the way down, then remembered
the stories he had heard and followed a dozen
men heading for the "chute." It had at first been
a narrow groove where men slid from the top
down to the bottom of the steep slope on the
seat of their pants.

After hundreds and then thousands of men had
jumped in the chute, kicked out their feet, and
slid the fifteen hundred feet down the mountain,
the ice- and snow-covered chute had grown deeper and deeper. In some places it was cut ten feet
into the year-round ice mass by the "cheechakos"
thundering along down the chute to the bottom.

Once there, Bryce learned to get up and out
of the way quickly before the next man came
barreling down the slide to the stopping-place.

He checked the sun. No chance to make another trip today. He didn't want to be caught on
the ice steps in the dark, at least not after only
one trip. The dark might be easier if it was less
crowded. He would see. He ate some hard crackers mixed with melted snow and a half-dozen
dried apricots. Then he curled up in his blankets
behind his stack of boxes and went to sleep.

It took Bryce ten days to get his other 19 boxes up the ice steps to the summit. Once there
he dug into one box and took out a hammer

and nails. He went to work on three of the other boxes and took pre-formed wooden slats off them and quickly assembled the runners for a sled.

The wooden boxes fit snugly into the runners to form the sled body. By the time Bryce was done, he had a sled six feet long and 20 boxes wide. Soon all 20 boxes were loaded on the sled and he began the trip down the far side of the pass toward the string of frozen lakes below.

Bryce knew what was ahead. He would pull the sled to the large lake, Lindemann, then he would continue on to Lake Bennett, which was where most of the stampeders would stop to build their boats.

He had never tried to build anything before. For this task he had carefully drawn plans and a list of materials. Mostly what he needed would be lumber, but there were whipsawers around Lake Bennett who would rent their rigs or do the sawing themselves. First he needed two partners who would go in with him on the cost and labor of building the boat.

The partners would have to be men he could trust with his life, men he could get along with during the boat building and the float down the Yukon for 500 miles to Dawson.

It took him a week before he found the men he wanted. One was a preacher heading for the gold country to prospect. The second was a carpenter who wanted to ply his trade in Dawson and let the others dig into the ground.

It was the end of September before they made their pact. Then they quickly bought the first timbers to fashion the keel and side stringers of their boat. Next they had to build a sawing pit. This was an elevated platform ten feet high where the log or timber was placed.

One man stood on the platform above and pulled and pushed the saw while a second man below on the two-man saw did his work from that angle. It was a grueling task. They sawed out slabs from the logs they hauled in. It was backbreaking work and they changed off every 15 minutes.

Time was no factor. They would not find any water to try to float a boat in until April. That meant they had seven months in which to build their boat and ready it for the float downstream.

After they had the craft built, they could use it as a makeshift house during the winter.

It took them nearly a month to saw enough lumber to finish their boat. It was a 24-foot flat-bottomed scow, the kind generally favored as easy to build, steady in the currents, and the simplest to pilot down the river. It was designed so it was deep and wide and would almost exactly fit the food and freight they had to carry. By April much of the food they had brought would be gone.

Bryce looked out the next morning and sighed. Another day of sawing the thick logs. At least by this time they had learned how to do it, and had decided to saw lumber in exchange for food when they had enough done for their own boat.

That way they could conserve their own food supply for whatever might come ahead. Bryce pulled on a second pair of gloves. His first pair had been worn out until they couldn't be patched anymore.

Within two months after Bryce arrived at Lake Bennett, there was a whole town assembled. Mounties said there were over 10,000 men, women, and children at Lake Bennett that winter of

1897-98. Some said it was the largest tent city in the world.

Tents and a few cabins lined the lakeshore in a double row. Merchants were quick to set up their businesses. There were hot-bath emporiums, barbershops, saloons, restaurants, lawyers, doctors, dentists, and promoters all getting rich off the sudden inactivity of 10,000 people.

Usually a pall of wood smoke hung over the tent city as thousands of fires kept the inhabitants somewhat warm and cooked their food. For men with money, there were boats for sale. But the boats cost between $250 and $600, and few of them were ever sold.

Most men formed partnerships and built their own boats.

The boat builders were strung out on Lake Bennett's shoreline along its entire near-side length, 26 miles. From nearby forests the lumbermen's axes rang out as long as the snow wasn't too deep, and whipsawing lumber went on until the snow covered the men and their saw pits.

During the early days, Bryce and Preacher Tom worked the saw, and they left Percival, the carpenter, at their campsite, where he crafted the beginnings of their boat. They had picked a spot 20 feet from the high-water mark of the year before and set up their tent. If the water came as high as it had last year, they could roll the boat into the water on a set of four round poles and be ready for the ice breakup.

There were the beginnings of boats as far as they could see along the shore. Many different kinds of craft were in various stages of being completed. None would be done before the snow flew, but most of them would have a good start before the spring rush.

It was a long winter. At last the snow did come in earnest, so thick and fast that they couldn't see ten feet in front of them. They huddled in the tent and took turns knocking the snow off the top so the thin canvas wouldn't collapse.

When the snowstorm stopped after two days, their tent was a cave and they had to tunnel out to find the light and a brilliant sunshine. One thing the snow blanket did was to keep the tent a lot warmer. Now a candle inside would heat up the air enough so they could melt snow and take impromptu sponge baths in comfort.

The three men became good friends during their enforced company. The preacher had been a Baptist, but couldn't refuse the call to the gold fields. The carpenter had left his wife and three children in Omaha and promised to come back rich. He would stay in Dawson for two years, working as a carpenter and charging four times his usual rates. When the boom began to wane, he'd be on the next boat down the Yukon with his sack of gold nuggets and gold coins paid for by his labor. He would go home a rich man, but not from mining.

They worked on their boat every day they could. More snow came. It was going to be a long winter.

Chapter Three

Vancouver, British Columbia, January 20, 1898

Mary Elizabeth Cromwell sat on the edge of her bed in Vancouver, British Columbia. Soon now she would find him. It would be a surprise for him. After all these months of waiting and hoping, she would find her intended in the Klondike and they would be married and all would be well. That was all she really wanted to do, to be married to Walter Livingston.

Walter had asked her to marry him, then took off for the Yukon from their Toronto home last May. He'd gotten into the Klondike before the river froze over and was working on a claim. He was partner with another man and they were digging out real gold dust!

She couldn't imagine.

That's why she wanted to go to the Klondike and see for herself. Her mother had forbidden her to go. Her father had died years ago, and she had been independent ever since. Now she was grown up at 18 and eager to get on with her life. That meant finding Walter just as soon as she could.

Her mother was well fixed and Mary Elizabeth had no qualms about leaving her alone in Toronto with her friends.

In the three months since then, she had worked her way across southern Canada. She had a knack for singing and dancing, and had reached Vancouver and chanced into a good position here at the Variety Hall. Her best friend and roommate was Janice, who'd gotten her the job.

In the act they called her the Vancouver Blue Bird because she sang so well. Now all she was doing was waiting for the boat to Alaska. There she would catch the first steamer up the Klondike River after the ice broke up in the spring.

Mary Elizabeth had started calling herself Liza and liked the sound of it. She was a small package at barely five feet two, and weighed a trim 95 pounds. She had long dark hair, large deep brown eyes, and a classic nose over wide-set eyes. She had a regal bearing and was small-hipped and big-breasted. She blushed when she thought of how excited Walter became when he saw her bare breasts.

Liza at first look seemed slight and frail, but she was tough as old saddle leather, fit and sturdy both physically and mentally. She was tenacious with a driving desire to succeed and to find Walter. She'd had eight years of lower school in

Toronto and was as educated as most women of the day.

She soon discovered that the Variety Hall where she worked wasn't really a music hall; it was simply a saloon with a stage. It was mainly for drinking and gambling. It was the largest saloon in town, and the only thing it didn't have was a house of ill repute upstairs. The performers on stage didn't have to sell drinks or mingle with the customers. They were on stage or in the small dressing room.

Liza was making seven dollars a week at first, and after she started to sing in the act, her boss raised her to ten dollars a week.

She saved all of the money she could. One day she went to the steamship line to ask about passage. The clerk told her it was too early, the boat wouldn't leave for three months yet. She went back to the boardinghouse.

The first night she sang in Vancouver she had been nervous. Her boss, Old Brassie, had made a big production of it. After two dancing numbers, Old Brassie went on the stage and held up his hands to quiet the drinkers and gamblers.

"Now we have a treat for you folks. A new singer for your entertainment. Here she is, direct from the wonders of Toronto, the little songster we call the Vancouver Blue Bird!"

Everyone clapped, and Liza walked on the stage feeling shy now that she was singing in such a big hall. Luke pounded the piano, hammering out the little introduction they had planned, and she launched her Vancouver singing career with the old standard "Charlie." Before she was into the third verse, the men were singing along with her on the chorus. They quieted for the verse, and when she ended the song they cheered and clapped until she promised to do the same song again.

She sang it three times before they let her move on, and by the time she had finished her third song, there wasn't room for another person to stand in the jam-packed saloon.

She became an instant success and something of a star at the Variety. She and Janice had worked hard on their little shows. She had brought the dancers into her singing act, and it worked well.

Soon they were doing skits with costumes that she and Janice cut out and stitched together. She was learning more about performing each day, and after two more months considered herself a seasoned veteran. She had thoughts of singing when she got to Dawson City in the Klondike.

It rained a lot in Vancouver, more than she was used to. Soon the performing became routine and the weeks dragged.

Liza showed no one, not even Janice, the two diamond rings that she had sewed in the hem of one of her skirts. That was her nest egg, her bank account to get to Dawson City as soon as spring came. She had a pint fruit jar that she hid under her mattress at the boardinghouse. Slowly the dollar bills began to build up in it. She took them to the bank and traded them for gold pieces. In Vancouver at that time, both Canadian and U.S. money circulated. She asked for American 20-dollar gold pieces.

By February she was getting anxious about moving on north. She left early for work one day and checked at the steamship company to talk with the agent. The same man she had seen before stood behind the counter.

"Well, if it ain't the Vancouver Blue Bird. I see your show every Friday night. You sing wonderfully."

"Thank you, sir. It's what I'm doing until the spring breakup. Any idea when it will be this year?"

The agent laughed. "If I knew that I'd be several thousand dollars richer. A lot of people bet on the exact day and hour and minute when the breakup comes. It'll be sometime between April fifteen and June first."

"So when should I go north to St. Michael to catch the paddleboat into Dawson City?"

"You and about a thousand others will be waiting. Let's see, on average the breakup is around May eighth. Doesn't always come all at once the length of the Yukon. You need to get to St. Michael early and book a reservation on the boat. Then they can't put you off.

"Most of our boats that go to St. Michael take about a month to get there. Y'see we stop at every little port along the way, up through the inland passage, then around the edge of Alaska and out around the Aleutian Islands and through the straits at Unmak Pass.

"I figure you best to leave here about the first of April. Let's see, we'll have a ship leaving Vancouver on April 3rd that should do it. We'll be swamped with passengers by then. If'n you want to pay the fare now, I'll guarantee you a berth for the whole trip."

Liza blanched at the price of the ticket. "A hundred and fifty dollars? You must be mistaken."

"No, miss. It's a trip of almost two thousand miles, right up to the top of the world. At least you won't need to take all of your own food. You can get off the boat twice a day during port calls and eat at small cafes. That's the best way."

The next day, Liza sold one of the diamond rings for eighty dollars to a jeweler in Vancouver and went back to the boardinghouse to count her money. She had heard that the fare up the Yukon River on the stern-wheeler was another $100. That meant she'd have to sell the other diamond ring just before she left. It should bring $100.

When she counted the money in her fruit jar, she found that she had saved well. From her new pay of eleven dollars a week, she had hoarded almost $60. In two more weeks she'd have enough cash to buy the ticket.

That night when she sang her solo at the Variety Hall, someone tossed a coin. She quickly bent and picked up her long skirt, holding it out to catch any more coins. This showed off her slender legs, and the men hooted and cheered and threw more coins.

Right then she decided that she would hold out her skirt every night for the men to throw coins into. That first show she counted up two dollars in coins, and on the second show she caught another dollar and a half. Yes! Soon she would have enough money for the trip to St. Michael.

The weeks flew past. Liza confided to Janice that she was going to go to Dawson City as soon as the weather permitted. At first Janice wanted to go along, but then she decided she had a good situation there in Vancouver. She could dance for another few years, then get pregnant and make some man marry her.

"Dearie, I think I'll just stick it out here for a while. Them gold camps ain't what I'd want to live in. I'll stay here and dance my feet off and then do some man in bed enough to get me in a family way and have a wedding."

Near the end of March, Liza bought her ticket. There were two other women who would be in the tiny cabin with her, but the agent said that was normal. Most of the men would sleep on the deck or in the hold with the cargo. Already the first boat was half booked.

Liza gave Old Brassie, her boss, a week's notice that she was leaving.

"Liza, you can't go. Aren't you happy here? We're making money. You make twice as much as a workingman makes now. You want a raise?"

"Mr. Brassie, it isn't that. I need to go to Dawson City to find my intended."

"I'll give you a raise to . . . to twenty dollars a week! Nobody in Vancouver has ever earned that much as a singer."

Liza frowned. "If you can afford to pay me twenty dollars, how come you've been only paying me eleven?"

"Good business."

"Which means you must be making fifty dollars a day off our singing and dancing. And you pay all six of us only ten or eleven dollars a day. You offer me fifty dollars a week and I'll consider staying. You'll still be making tons of money."

Old Brassie took off his hat and rubbed his balding head. He stared at her and shook his head. "I'll have to think about it. Damn but you are a hard one, Liza."

Liza grinned. "Hey, it's just good business."

Old Brassie offered Liza 30 dollars a week the day before her boat was due to sail. She turned him down, sold her second ring to a jeweler, and got $95 for it, which she sewed inside her warm jacket. She had her other money safely tucked inside her high-topped shoes.

After a tearful farewell with Janice, Liza boarded the *Coastal Queen* and was shown her cabin. It was smaller than she had imagined. There were three bunks against one wall, one atop another. Once she slid into the bunk, there wasn't room enough to sit up. Beside the bunks was a three-foot-wide area where they stacked their suitcases and boxes. One small stool was provided for sitting.

The other two girls were prostitutes who said they'd heard a girl could earn a fortune in just one year in Dawson City. They were going to try. They assumed that Liza was a lady of the night as well, and Liza never told them otherwise.

She lay awake for hours listening to the two women tell stories about their work in Seattle and San Francisco. They asked her about some of her wild times, but she said she came from a smaller place and most of the men were a lot calmer and sedate in their lovemaking.

The first day was a lark, but after that it grew harder. They didn't stop every day at a port, so sometimes the girls had to eat from the cheese and crackers and fruit that they had stocked up on before the trip.

Most times they trooped off with forty other passengers and crew from this mostly freight-hauling ship and ate clam chowder and fried fish and whatever else was on the local cafe menu.

Liza had never seen an iceberg before, and when she spotted the first one she was amazed. They passed close to a spot where a glacier came right down to the water. They saw huge chunks of ice break off and fall into the sea. She was surprised how little of the huge slab of ice remained above the water.

They made the long, cold run around the Aleutian Islands, and then on the third day of May 1898, they docked at St. Michael, Territory of Alaska. It was little more than a fishing village, but with the influx of men charging for the Klondike it had boomed into a respectable town of tents and new buildings.

The three women marched over to the Yukon Steamship Company office and asked about a trip up the river.

The agent who talked to them was mostly Indian from the looks of his long dark hair and sharp nose.

"You're early, ladies, but if you want to buy your ticket now, you'll be able to get on the first boat. We're putting on two more boats this year, but you'll be on the *Belle*, a proud little sternwheeler. The ticket price is a hundred and ten dollars."

"They told us it only cost ninety-five to get to Dawson City," Liza shot back at him.

The agent grinned. "That was last year, missy. The new price is a hundred and ten, take it or stay in town."

All three paid the price with gold and paper money, mostly in U.S. funds since they were in the Territory of Alaska, part of the United States.

"Be a notice on the town bulletin board in red ink when we get ready to leave. You won't be able to miss the breakup. Always a big celebration that day. We leave that evening, right at sunset so we can catch the outgoing tide."

Clutching their tickets, the three women went out to the street and looked for a hotel. Instead they found a tent that had a large sign that boasted: "For Women Renters Only." When they stepped inside, they found four women. One came forward.

"You ladies just off the boat?" a henna-red-haired woman asked. She looked more like a fancy woman than any Liza had ever seen. The three of them nodded.

"Fine. You need a place to stay. My name's Maud. I run this feline hotel. Price is a dollar a night and no men inside. You want to work, fine by me, but you do it outside my hotel. A week in advance."

The three women looked at each other, shrugged, and gave the henna-haired woman the money. She tucked it in her purse on a string around her neck and led them through a tent flap down an open space with smaller tents on each side. She stopped at a flap and flipped it open.

Inside the girls found an eight-foot tent. Two bunks were double-decked. There was one chair and a wooden box for a dresser.

"Here it is, room for three. Take care and I'll see you in a week."

"Where is the best place in town to eat?" Liza asked.

"Skagit Joe's about a block upstream. Not fancy, but good food and reasonable."

"Will our things be safe here?" one of the other girls asked.

Maud looked at her and touched her purse. "Ain't nobody had any complaints. I catch one of my ladies stealing anything, I'll whip her back raw with a leather strap and you can count on that. But I'd suggest you take any cash money and valuables you have with you. Damned hard to identify stolen money."

The three prowled the small village. It had rained that morning and seemed to be threatening again. The street was still muddy. A few horses and wagons moved around, but there didn't seem to be much of anywhere to drive. The docks and the inlet there on Norton Sound seemed to be the town. If there was much inland it couldn't be seen.

There were a lot of men on the street. Most of them walked from one end of the settlement to the other, then down to the dock, where they watched the ships.

Here and there, the women saw signs advertising the ice-breakup pool. Closed bids were being taken at two dollars a try. The idea was to forecast the breakup of the ice down the Yukon River to the sea by the day, the hour, and the minute. The notice said that a fast boat would bring them the news just as soon as the ice broke up and the ship came out the mouth of the Yukon River 100 miles to the west and slightly south of St. Michael.

"Does that mean we're in the wrong place?" one of the prostitutes wailed.

"This is the closest town to the Yukon River mouth," Liza said. "Let's try that cafe over there."

Time passed slowly for the three women, who became friends. Soon Liza admitted that she was not a fallen woman, and the other two said they didn't mind, she could still be their friend.

A week after they arrived, on May 10, 1898, a small steamer sailed into St. Michael with its steam whistle echoing around the small town, which had now grown to more than 5,000 souls.

"Breakup!" the people began to scream and chant. Watches were held for the exact minute that the steamer touched the dock in St. Michael. That would be the winning time for the pool that had by that time grown to over $3,000.

Liza and the two girls raced to the dock, and were caught up in a throng who had the same idea. A man at the dock announced the exact time: 1:47 P.M. May 10, and there was a sudden silence by the crowd. Then one man at the back of the group screamed in delight. He was the winner.

The *Belle*'s crew doubled its work getting ready to embark. The steamship agent stood at the gangplank warning everyone that the first sailing was sold out and they would have to wait. Fistfights broke out over who owned certain tickets. Liza and the girls hurried away to get their meager belongings ready so they could board the boat.

They had spent part of the waiting time preparing a supply of food. The trip would take nearly a month working upstream against the strong flow of the current for 1,355 miles. There was only one or two small villages along the way. Each person was required to bring along a month's supply of food. They laid in a goodly supply of cheese and crackers, dry beans, raisins and lots of dried fruits and rice, flour, and coffee. They had heard about the food requirements for crossing into Canadian territory by the land route, but no one had said anything about such requirements on a boat.

The notice went up on the bulletin board. The *Belle* would sail at seven o'clock that evening on the outgoing tide. The three women clamored to get their suitcases and two boxes of food to the dock, and waited in line with some 200 others for permission to board the small craft.

It was a stern-wheeler, a paddleboat of shallow draft and built wide and solid. It was well after four that afternoon before they at last boarded, and found that they were in a small cabin with 20 bunks stacked four high, all of them for men except those for the three women.

They found a blanket and hurriedly walled off their three bunks against the far end of the room for privacy. Not a man on board touched the curtain during the whole trip. Liza had the impression that the other two girls were disappointed in that fact.

There were more fights on shore for tickets before the boat finally lifted anchor and sailed out into Norton Sound, and turned west and slightly south to find the channel through the various openings of the Yukon River into the Pacific Ocean.

Now began the longest part of the trip for Liza. She was in a hurry to get to Dawson City and find Walter. She had thought of him every day since she had left Toronto. Now she worried about how he was, if he had filed a claim, and how much gold he had found. She had no doubt that he would be overjoyed to see her and that they would be married the same day she arrived.

But those were only dreams. Now she sat on the deck of the *Belle* and watched the swollen river with its chunks of ice rushing along toward them and then sweeping past. Most of the ice was in small pieces, not big enough to damage the craft. Their progress was far slower than Liza had hoped it would be. She wondered if it indeed would take them a whole month to get to Dawson City. She would mark each day off in her small journal.

Chapter Four

Arthur Walling, the 24-year-old third son of the Duke of Walling, had no title and little chance of gaining one. He was the forgotten third son so far as the nobility went, and now he realized he was in the worst trouble of his life.

The vicar's daughter had just raced screaming and crying from her bedroom. She was naked to the waist, wailing and screeching like a wounded elephant. She glared at him, then spat foul words at him, calling him filthy names that would make a sailor wince.

Worst of all, her brother, on home leave from the Royal Guards, had seen the whole nasty scene in the second-floor hallway and knew at once what had happened.

The young man was Lester White-Smith, 22, a

strong and serious soldier. He rushed down the hall and covered his naked sister with his jacket, then turned to face Arthur Walling.

"You!" White-Smith roared. "You've ruined my sister. You'll make an honest woman of her or answer to my blade!" He pulled a six-inch fighting knife from his belt and advanced on Arthur Walling.

"I'm unarmed," Walling said with a sneer. "Surely even a commoner such as you wouldn't attack an unarmed man."

"Then get armed!" Lester bellowed. He ran back down the hall to his own room and came out with a six-inch dagger. He threw it so it stuck in the carpeted floor near Walling's feet.

"Now, you're armed."

Walling had often prided himself on the use of a rapier. Now he pulled the knife from the floor, hefted it, then held it the same way he would a rapier. He would use the same tactics. He held it by the handle with the blade extending outward from his hand. That way he could slash in either direction or thrust forward. It gave him three moves.

Lester White-Smith hadn't had the fencing lessons, and was more of a brawler than swordsman. He drove in quickly, his knife held like a dagger for a downward strike but little else.

Twice Walling brushed aside the charges of the younger man. The third time he tripped Lester, sending him crashing to the hallway floor. Lester leaped up snarling like an enraged wolf. The next time he charged, but suddenly changed directions.

Walling held his knife in front of him at arm's distance. He sensed the feint to one side and easily followed Lester's change of direction and his lunge. Lester White-Smith saw his opponent's countermove, tried to correct, but stumbled and fell directly onto the point of the other blade. It drove past a rib and plunged into Lester's heart. He died by the time he slumped to the hallway floor.

Arthur Walling looked at the man, knew he was dead. Then he watched the half-naked woman and closed his eyes in despair. Now he had tied it! He had no title. He was a third son of a duke, but not even his father could protect him from a murder charge.

Before Arthur could drop the deadly weapon, Martha's older brother, James White-Smith, hurried up the stairs to find out what the screaming and yelling was about. He took in the situation in an instant and charged forward.

Arthur darted down the other stairway, leaped on his black stallion, and kept a long step ahead of James White-Smith, who raced after him.

"Walling, I'll hunt you down and kill you for what you've done to my family!" White-Smith roared. No horse was saddled in the White-Smith stable, so no immediate chase was possible.

Two hours later, Arthur found his father hunting in the south valley on the estate and told him what happened. Arthur stayed in the huntsman's house that evening and all visitors for anyone in the Walling castle, including a magistrate looking for Arthur, were turned away at the front gate.

The next day at sunrise, Arthur Walling boarded a ship in the bustling London harbor that was outward bound for Canada. Its first stop was Halifax, Nova Scotia, and the next stop was in Quebec.

All the way across the ocean, Walling had been pondering the threat by the girl's brother, James White-Smith. The man could be a huge problem. The vicar must have reported the killing that same afternoon, and by now might have added the charges of rape as well. Martha's brother had not been an eyewitness to the killing, but the girl had. They would get a true bill and a warrant with no trouble. An English arrest warrant for murder could be carried to Canada by anyone seriously searching for him. A British arrest warrant for murder would be quickly honored by the lawmen in Canada.

Walling walked the decks of the small ocean freighter for two nights trying to decide what to do. It was his name he had always been most proud of. If by some chance his two brothers met with disaster, he might have become the Duke of Walling. Not now. His name could lead to his arrest, conviction, and surely his hanging.

At last he decided what to do. He had to change his name and his appearance. First, he would shave off his full beard. It wasn't that much of a beard anyway with its soft, sandy-blond color. Once he had shaved, he trimmed his mustache into a small bristle, and then hired the ship's barber to cut his longish hair neat and short. That along with a new name should put what he hoped were more than enough problems in the way of any prowling White-Smith searching for him.

Another day of walking the deck brought about his new name. He would keep Arthur, there were thousands of them. But his family name had to be changed.

It wasn't until they were coming into port that first time since leaving England that he had it. One of the deckhands nodded at him and winked.

"Halifax dead ahead, sir. They've got some of the most energetic wenches in that town I've ever bedded." He moved along on his work, but Arthur had his new name: He would be Arthur Hallifax.

His ticket was to Quebec, but he disembarked at Halifax in another effort to hide his trail. If a detective or a White-Smith did somehow track him to the ship, he would be at once thrown off the scent by riding on to Quebec.

Arthur Walling Hallifax had been gifted with 1,000 pounds sterling by his father before he left England. There would be a check for 50 pounds a month for as long as he needed it, but only when he had a new address.

Arthur Hallifax stepped off the ship in Halifax the first week in March 1898. For three days he lazed around the town, searching out the fanciest women and drinking to the Queen's health at some of the lowest pubs in town.

Then he met Lois and spent the next day in her small apartment, where she provided board and room and her lovely body.

"I've never done a real Englishman before," Lois said sitting on the bed looking at him. "Take a duke's clothes off and he looks like any other bloody Englishman."

"My father's the duke, not me. The Duke of Hallifax. You must have heard of him."

"Not likely. He don't romp in me garden too often. You ready for another fuck-fuck?"

"How much am I paying you, Lois?"

"For all of it? A tenner, I'd say."

"Pounds or dollars?"

"Pounds. Now turn over, I've got me a hankering again."

She was fat and big, the way he liked his women, with swaying breasts he could eat on all day. He caught one and pulled it into his mouth, but she eased away from him.

"You want to do two of us tonight? I got me a sister."

"Two for the price of one?"

"Two for the price of two."

He shook his head. He'd have to figure out what to do sooner or later. He couldn't live on 50 pounds a month. The 1000 pounds had been whittled down a lot already.

Lois rolled on top of him, her hips pushing against his, her big tit lowered into his mouth, and Arthur forgot all about his life's plans. He had a woman in hand.

He rolled her over and they slid slowly off the bed. Both started laughing. Lois hit the floor and he came down on top of her.

"Right here, mate?"

"Right here." He pushed her legs apart and eased between her heavy thighs, found the right spot, and jolted into her with one thrust.

Lois lifted her brows. "Damn, I guess that little thing is inside me. Kind of hard to tell." She giggled before he could hit her. "Just joking, guvnor, you know I'm joking. You got a damn pole size of a fir tree you have, and you jolly well know how to poke with it."

Arthur tried to stop but he was over the top. Damn, he wished someone would tell him how to hold back. It was now or never for him sometimes. A good fat woman like Lois got him so excited that he just couldn't control it. Some men said they could. He wondered.

Lois waited for him to rest a bit after he finished, then squirmed, and he came away from her.

"That's three. I'll get us some food, then you promised to take me to the traveling actors' show. It's *Macbeth*. I do love to see all the killing."

The next day Arthur Hallifax took the first boat he could find to Toronto. There was some portage part of the way and another ship, but he got through. He'd heard about Toronto in the heart of Canada.

He took a room, then got into a card game and challenged the best gambler in the place. Before long they were in a two-man game and before he was done, Arthur had won $300. The loser bellowed about being cheated.

Arthur left with his winnings, made sure nobody followed him, and knew he had to get out of town before the gambler had him beaten up and robbed.

He'd heard about the gold rush. The papers were full of it. There would be plenty of money floating around a gold rush camp. He asked some questions, and the next day decided to head for the Klondike and Dawson City, far to the west and north. Somebody said it was 3,500 miles to the spot.

He read a newspaper story that told of the route and how to get there. The water route in would be open only for a few months in the summer.

The next day Arthur Hallifax bought a ticket on the Canadian Pacific Railway, and soon chugged his way across the broad expanse of central and

western Canada. He had never seen such open
spaces. The land seemed to run on and on without a break for a hundred miles at a time. The
whole of England could be dropped into one of
the great valleys and lost from sight. The midday
sky seemed so high it would never reach earth.

He played some poker on the train until the
conductor told him to stop or he'd be thrown off
at the next station ticket or no ticket.

Arthur read and looked out the window; he
played solitaire and tried to learn bridge, but had
no mind for it.

After a week's travel they arrived in Vancouver,
British Columbia. He didn't think he'd ever seen
such green mountains. They were all swathed in
evergreen trees that marched from one hill to the
next.

He spent his first two days there learning all he
could about the Klondike and the big gold strike.
Yes, there was lots of money in Dawson. Gambling was legal and carried on night and day.

Anyone could get in. He inquired about the
routes of travel and the means. Quickly he eliminated the Skagway Trail over White Pass and the
Dyea Trail up and over the infamous Chilkoot
Pass.

That left the steamer up the Yukon, but the
trip from Vancouver to Dawson would take nearly two months. He asked at the steamship company.

"Dawson? We don't go there. Can get you all
the way to St. Michael. From there you get a river steamer up the Yukon. You want to be there
when the ice breaks up?"

"I'm not sure what that means."

"The Yukon is frozen solid all winter. In the

spring the ice melts and starts downstream, and then one day the ice breaks up all the way to the ocean and the travel route is open into Dawson again."

"I've decided to go," Arthur said. "When's your next boat heading for St. Michael?"

The steamship clerk grinned. "That wasn't as hard a sale as I thought it was going to be. Fact is, we have our next ship leaving on April 3rd, two days from now. A ticket is a hundred and fifty dollars."

"All I have are pound notes," Arthur said.

"They'll do fine."

That night Arthur wrote his father two letters saying the same thing in each one. He told his father he was heading for Dawson, in the Yukon region. His address would be General Delivery there, and he would appreciate his bank drafts for the support money he hadn't received yet. By sending two letters he hoped that one of them would get through and be delivered.

For the next two days Arthur spent all of his time with a gambler who taught him all the tricks he knew of how to cheat at poker. The game was made for cheating. One card could mean the difference between winning or losing.

Arthur practiced until he could use some of the tricks and not even his friend knew he was cheating. He was ready.

Arthur boarded the *Coastal Queen*, mostly a freighter, with some 40 other passengers. One of the women he recognized. She had been a singer in one of the saloons in Vancouver and he thought she was quite good. They called her the Vancouver Blue Bird. He didn't try to talk to her; it was too complicated on the small boat.

He enjoyed the trip, watching the natural wonders of the inland passage and then the swing around the rest of Alaska and through the islands and on to St. Michael. He ate ravenously in the ports they stopped at, and had a good supply of food with him when they had no small port of call.

The ship arrived at St. Michael on May 3, 1898. He nodded to the singer but said nothing. There would be plenty of time for her later. He guessed she was heading for Dawson as well. What would a pretty woman like her do in a fishing village like St. Michael besides be a whore? This girl was no whore.

They were a week in the small town. He played some cards, won enough for his ticket up the Yukon, then looked for the small singer. He remembered her: pretty, big-breasted, with a tiny waist and gorgeous long dark hair. He would find her in Dawson, but it would be nice to get an early start in getting acquainted with her.

On May 10th the ice broke and they sailed that night. There was a month's journey ahead, but he could put in the time. He was heading for the gold fields with one intent—to gamble and cheat those sourdough miners out of every last bit of gold and gold dust that he could. He'd either be a rich man when he came back down the Yukon or he'd be buried in the frozen ground of the Great North.

As he stared into the icy waters of the Yukon as the *Belle* worked slowly upstream, he had a sudden thought. Rich or dead, the choice had little importance to him. He really didn't care one way or the other.

He knew one thing for sure. He would have a good time before he had to find out what fate had in store for him in Dawson and the Klondike Gold Rush.

Chapter Five

Spur McCoy watched the waters of the Yukon. It was smaller now than when they'd entered it two weeks ago. The captain said they were on schedule and should make the trip in his allotted 30 days. McCoy had taken Sunday dinner with Captain Nizelry both Sundays they had been on the river. The captain wanted to talk as much as anything. He said it was a lonely trip and he hadn't brought a good book this time.

McCoy spent an hour each morning on the afterdeck. There he went through the exercise routine he had worked out for himself to stay in top condition. Since he couldn't do a three-mile run, he did it in place, counting a thousand steps, then resting for two minutes and counting another thousand steps. Somehow he found running in place harder than when he traveled the three miles on some country road.

He then dropped down to the deck, rested on his hands and his toes, and lowered his body to the deck and pushed it up until his arms were straight. He did that 50 times, and then sat down panting.

"Why do you do that?" a young man asked McCoy.

"So I can defend myself against ruffians like you, sir," McCoy said.

"Land sakes, I wouldn't hurt you," the youth said, joshing right back at McCoy.

"Try the exercise," McCoy invited. The boy got down on his toes and hands and did three of the push-aways before he collapsed on the deck. He sat up scratching his head.

"But you did fifty, I counted them. I did three."

"Work on it," McCoy said. "You'll get up to ten, then twenty before you know it."

McCoy did another exercise that amused the watchers. He stood with his feet together and arms at his sides. Then he jumped and spread his legs three feet apart and landed on the deck. At the same time he swung both hands so they hit over his head.

Quickly he jumped back so his feet were together and his hands came down at his sides. He did the exercise 50 times. The youth who tried the push-aways also did this one, but gave up after ten repetitions.

A half hour later, McCoy sat on the deck going over the material on the man he hunted. By now he knew him as well as he did himself. This Arthur Walling was 26 years old, the third son of the Duke of Walling, who had a castle of sorts and lands near London. The boy had no hopes of getting the title with two brothers ahead of him.

He was five feet eleven inches tall, slender, with sandy hair that was sometimes reddish, sometimes blond, and wore a full sandy-colored beard. He had blue eyes and would have the typical English accent and airs of the nobility. He was said to be a gambler and traveling as such. He should be easy to find and turn over to the Royal Canadian Mounted Police in Dawson. Then McCoy could get back to the West he knew, where they had cattle and rustlers and wide-open spaces.

McCoy gave up on the background and watched the water and the shoreline. Twice they had seen small Indian villages. The Indians came out to the ship and bartered fresh salmon for almost anything of value. McCoy had salmon for two days, when the rest of it turned bad.

Spur McCoy stood six feet two inches tall, and kept his weight at a steady 185 pounds through exercise and watching what he ate. He worked as a Secret Service agent, and his boss was General Wilton D. Halleck in Washington, D.C. William Wood was director of the agency, and each of the agents had received an appointment by the President of the United States.

The Secret Service was created just after the Civil War to watch over and protect U.S. currency. During those early years there was no law and order in many of the unorganized areas of the nation, and the Secret Service men were called upon to do all sorts of law-and-order work in many different situations. They were the only lawmen who could pursue a criminal from one state to another or into a territory. Later U.S. marshals took over much of this work.

Spur McCoy was assigned as the resident agent in St. Louis, and had the entire western half of the nation as his responsibility.

He was a Harvard graduate, and had learned to ride and shoot on a cattle drive early in his life. He had a nodding acquaintance with several of the Indian tribes on the High Plains, but these Alaska Indians were total strangers to him. He hoped he wouldn't have to deal with them.

He settled back against some sacks of supplies packed on the deck and decided to have a short nap. Not a lot else to do on this trip. Two more weeks. Lots of naps coming up.

More than eleven hundred miles away up the mighty Yukon River, on Lake Bennett, Bryce Jeferies had continued to work on the boat that would take him and his two partners down the waterways to Dawson City.

The first day they had the ribs of their boat up earlier that winter, one of the Royal Canadian Mounted Police came around with a record book. He talked with them, and found out they were a team and would be floating down the river together.

The Mountie looked over the start of their boat, examined their plans, and signed the paper.

"This craft should make it. You'll be loaded a little heavy, but by April you'll be about five or six boxes lighter. That'll help."

He gave them a registration number, 349.

"Paint that on both sides of the bow of your boat in numbers a foot high. We'll be following you all the way down the river, and remember, there are check stations for you to stop at so we can be sure we don't lose any boats."

He wrote down their names and hometowns, and told them they would find a check point every 25 miles along the river. "Like I say, you'll have to pull in at every Mountie station and sign off that you've reached that point."

Before winter really set in, the Mounties knew each man and woman and child on the shores of Lake Bennett.

There was little crime in the settlement. The Mounties had inspected the boxes of goods and made it known that absolutely no handguns of any type were allowed in the Yukon. Knives and rifles to provide food were permitted. But no fighting knives were allowed.

More snow came and work on the boat stopped. They couldn't dig down far enough to find the lumber they had sawed in the fall.

Another two months of playing cards and writing in journals for the three men in their six-foot-square tent. When nerves got on edge, one of the upset men would take a long walk in the snow. He always came back exhausted from smashing through the snow, and more than willing to forget the problem just to find his warm blankets again.

The first spring day that they heard snow melting, the men cheered. From that day on they watched the snow turn to water and run into the lake. Every day more and more of their ship's skeleton showed, until the time came when they could get back to work on it. Now they had a timetable.

The breakup of the ice in the lake would come first; then the breakup in the series of streams between lakes that led them to the true Yukon River would take place. The Mountie told them the breakup usually came anywhere from April 1 to May 1, depending on how warm the spring was.

Bryce held one of the green spruce boards against the ribs as the other two nailed it firmly in place. There was a lot of work to do yet. The green planks would dry when the sun came out, so they would have to be caulked. They were much nearer to their goal now. The boat took shape. It passed the second inspection by the Mounties.

Each day the snow receded more and the ice on the lake grew thinner. By the first of April it was so warm they could work without their jackets. Soon they would be done with the boat; then they could launch it in the lake when the ice broke up and see if it would float.

On April 7, they finished their boat. They named it *Winter's Child* and painted their large number on the side, 349.

Now the waiting continued. Bryce walked down to the lake and pushed a stick into the ice. To his delight it penetrated the ice and a chunk of ice broke off. Any day now they could get their boat into the water and check it for leaks, then do the rest of the caulking.

By April 14, most of the boats had been finished, and a few had slid into the water around the edges of the lake where the ice had given way. Bryce's boat floated properly, and they worked for two days caulking and sealing small leaks until the boat was watertight. Then they loaded their equipment and the rest of their food, and practiced working the boat back and forth on the fringes of water around the shore.

They had taken down the tent by then and lived on the boat. The water level of the lake rose as streams broke up and surges of water and ice flowed into Lake Bennett.

On April 20, Bryce had just finished frying a fish he had caught in the chilly water when they heard a loud crack and a roar and then a general rumbling.

"What's that?" Bryce yelped from his position near the bow of the boat and his small charcoal grill.

The roar intensified, and then they knew it was the breakup; the ice in the Yukon had broken from increased pressure from the water and the ice pack in Lake Bennett. The wall of water and ice surged into the narrow opening of the Yukon River, and a great cheer went up from the boat people.

Boats of every shape and description lifted anchors and headed for the Yukon Channel. Some had sails, others were rowed. All had steering paddles and tillers in the back. That year of 1898, 812 boats sailed and floated out of Lake Bennett heading downstream that first day.

Bryan's boat was one of them. The three dry-land sailors settled into their assigned places on the boat among the boxes of goods and food and let the gentle wind fill their sail and move them toward the river. The weather was warm and everyone grinned and sang or yelled at one another as they sailed down the headwaters of the mighty Yukon River.

An hour later they floated into Tagish Lake just downstream from Lake Bennett. There the wind died and the current slacked to nothing. Ahead of them Bryce could see a strange-looking flotilla of sailing craft, all becalmed.

One after another the men in the boats paddled them to shore to wait out the night and a fresh breeze in the morning. That night, thousands of men and women camped out on the shores of Tagish Lake.

With dawn someone called out loudly:

"Fresh breeze. The wind is up!" The call was repeated for five miles around the side of the lake. As quickly as they could, the landlubber sailors pushed off their craft and hoisted makeshift sails to get out of the lake and into the steady current of the Yukon as quickly as they could.

Shortly after leaving Tagish Lake, they went through a short stream, and then they met the weed-clogged Lake Marsh. A good wind helped this time, and they maneuvered through it to the outlet that led downstream to Miles Canyon and the first rapids on the Yukon.

For weeks the three partners had heard wild stories about the dangers of the rapids. There was a five-mile run of dangerous water, whirlpools and smashing boulders that had killed more than a dozen men in the few boats that went down last year. Riverboat captains stood by to act as pilots through the dangerous water for those who could pay.

Usually the Mounties would let only one man guide his own boat through, and any passengers, partners, or family in the boat would have to walk around the five miles of white water. Fewer lives were at risk this way.

Norman McCauley was a man with enterprise. He knew the danger, had seen men lose their whole outfits and boats in the waters. He built a road on wooden rails around the five miles of canyons and rapids, used a horse to pull a

large sled on wooden wheels, and charged anyone
making the trip three cents a pound for freight
and boat alike.

While still waiting for the breakup, the three
partners had heard of the railroad. They'd rea-
soned it out and decided to take the road even
before they saw the rapids. They pooled their
cash and came up three dollars short. McCauley
waved the difference aside. Before the end of the
summer he would be a rich man and he knew it.
Bryce, the preacher, and the carpenter were in
the second load around the rapids on the horse-
drawn wheeled rails, and lost only half a day.

Back in the calm water again, the Bryce boat
functioned well, and the partners were glad they
had spent their money on safety rather than risked
their lives on bravado.

"We can't get rich if we're all dead," Bryce
cracked, and the three laughed as they rode
down the mighty Yukon. For the first time, the
stampeders met the Siwash or Stick Indians, of
the same tribe as Tagish Charley and Skookum
Jim, who'd helped Siwash George Carmack dis-
cover the Klondike gold. The Indians called to
the boaters offering to sell dried salmon and to
trade for anything the white men wanted to part
with.

Bryce shook his head. "I've never seen a bunch
of people who were more ragged or dirty in my
life." Their boat didn't stop to trade for any of the
salmon.

Another few miles and they swept into Lake
Laberge. There they had to check in at a Mounted Police security point. Once that was done, the
boats had 30 miles of still-ice-filled waters to the
end of the lake.

They moved along slowly, making as many miles a day as they could and camping on the shore during the dark hours. When they left Lake Laberge they entered a treacherous part called Thirtymile River. By now they had better command of their boat and with Bryce steering most of the time, they worked their way through the twisting stretch of white water.

Next they found the Teslin River that joins the Yukon, and here another flotilla of boats merged with the others on the Yukon. These stampeders had come up the Skeena and Strikine Trails, and wintered in the Teslin area before heading downstream with the ice breakup.

Five Fingers was the next challenge. At this point the river erupted where four giant pillars of rock sprouted from the middle of the channel. This left five "fingers" of water surging past the hard rock. The Mounted Police were there to warn each boater to be sure to take the far right-hand channel, which was the best for boats to get through.

Bryce steered into it, and they shipped water and all three men got wet, but nobody was lost overboard and the tied-down boxes all stayed in place. The preacher and the carpenter and Bryce cheered when they came through the five fingers and into calmer waters.

"Now I think we'll make it," the preacher said, and they all cheered again.

The next surprise was the muddy Pelly River, which entered the Yukon at the old Hudson's Bay Company fort called Selkirk. The Pelly was alive with more stampeders who had crossed the Continental Divide from Laird and the Mackenzie. Somebody said that they were the first of many men coming overland and then down the river from Edmonton.

Bryce and his two partners camped below a trading post near Selkirk. The talk in the camp that evening was that Dawson was less than a day's float ahead of them. It would be on the right-hand side of the river.

Bryce curled up in his blankets that night wondering what Dawson would be like. He'd been working and sweating and straining and fighting harder than he had ever done in his life to get to this boomtown. Now he hoped that it would be all worthwhile. He grinned and shook his head lying there in the dark. Even if it wasn't worth it, this had been the greatest adventure he had ever known. It would be enough to last him the rest of his life.

They were up at dawn, but already half a dozen boats were in the main current and slipping downstream. One even had a sail up to make better time.

Bryce wondered what they would do if they missed Dawson and went surging right on past it. He talked with his partners, and they decided to stick closer to the right-hand side of the river, letting anyone past who wanted to go faster.

About mid-afternoon they saw wood-cutters on the shore and pulled in close enough to ask how far to Dawson.

"Dawson? Why would anybody want to go there?" one of the wood-choppers asked. "If'n you want to go, it's just around the next bend in the river."

About six bends later they decided the man was having a joke at their expense. They kept to the inside of the current, and an hour later came around another bend and saw another river pouring into the Yukon. On the right bank there was a sea of white tents that staggered all over a gravel beach and a flat space behind it more than a mile long.

"Dawson!" Bryce bellowed. "We've finally found Dawson." Bryce gave a screech of joy and steered for the bank. It was plain that there were not enough docks or wharfs for this many small boats. He could see only one real dock along the gravel beach.

Bryce angled the scow into a sturdy part of the shoreline near the biggest tents and let it ground itself. Bryce jumped out, grabbed the anchor rope and a 20-pound slab of iron they had found to use as the anchor, and pulled the boat as high on the shore as he could. It was June 11, 1898, and he had at last arrived in Dawson City. Now all he had to do was make his fortune.

He heard a steamship whistle and looked downstream. A paddle wheeler ground along the Yukon bursting upstream through the current. She hesitated, then swung toward the shore, and half a dozen small boats rushed out of the way to reveal a dock. The large stern-wheeler cut power, angled for shore, then pulled in at the dock and tied up.

On board Spur McCoy unwound from where he had been sitting on a coil of rope and stared. It was the largest collection of tents that he had ever seen. He figured there must be ten thousand tents along the shore and stretching back halfway to the timber. All types and styles and colors of tents.

He picked up his suitcase and hurried toward the gangplank. His first stop would be the Royal

Canadian Mounted Police. His two revolvers were stowed deep in his bags. He'd get them approved by the lawmen and then begin his search for the English killer.

He had been wrong about the 20,000 people he'd expected to be in town. Captain Nizelry had told him with the rush down from the northern stretches of the Yukon there would be close to 30,000 men, women, and children in the gold capital.

McCoy took a deep breath and stepped off the gangplank onto the dock. One way or another he was going to nail that killer's ears to the ice or turn him over to the RCMP. Spur McCoy didn't much care which.

Chapter Six

Spur McCoy sat back in the strap-leather chair in the rough room that served as the office of Superintendent William C. Irons, Royal Canadian Mounted Police.

Irons had eyed him coldly at first, then examined his credentials, his identification card signed by the President of the United States, and at last read the telegram authorizing McCoy to follow Arthur Walling as far and for as long as it took.

Irons grunted. "I like the way you people do business. Reminds me a lot of our own tenacity in getting our man."

Superintendent Irons was a five-ten 180-pounder with a ramrod for a back and fierce gray eyes that could stop a brawl with a glance.

He held absolute authority over the 30,000 residents of this teeming city, but had only a skeleton force to keep order. But keep order he did, and during the long rough summer of 1898 there would be only one murder in the whole area.

"You as a lawman are authorized to retain your weapons. I'll pass the word to my men. We know about this Arthur Walling. No man with that name has come into Dawson yet this year. It's our guess a man of his sort would come upstream on the stern-wheelers. No such name has appeared on any of their passenger lists so far."

"Superintendent, I don't have to tell you that the man has undoubtedly changed his name by now and his appearance. Probably no beard, short hair, and perhaps no mustache. I've heard it said that you can find any given man in Dawson in three days. What about Walling?"

Irons stared at McCoy and frowned. "That three days is when I know the man's name and occupation and he isn't trying to hide. This killer will be an entirely different manner.

"One caution. You're in Canada now. Our laws are much like yours, but you'll be working here with my authorization. I won't allow any wild shootings or Wild West antics. I've heard of you in the States, and such tactics will not be allowed in my jurisdiction."

McCoy nodded. "Superintendent Irons, I intend to obey your laws, to work under your general supervision, and to help you capture this Walling lout as quickly as possible. Your mosquitoes alone are enough to drive me back to the wide-open spaces of the American West."

Irons chuckled. "McCoy, I think we're going to get on well. We've been making inquiries about Walling since the first boat came in with the news yesterday. We have no telegraph here. We'll continue to search for him. You'll be able to go places me and my men can't without attracting attention. I was thinking mainly of the gambling halls.

"It's said this Walling is a gambler, perhaps traveling as a gambler. I might suggest any one of the several gaming houses along Front Street might be a lure to Walling."

"Would the General Delivery address on his mail be a help?"

"No, half the men in town get their mail addressed that way. There's a two-hour wait in line at the post office just to have a clerk check all of the alphabetized General Delivery mail."

"So it's a dead end there. I'll check out the gamblers. Bound to show up at the tables sooner or later. How many English accents do we have in town?"

Irons shook his head. "Not much luck there either. We have about seventy percent Americans here, but in the other thirty percent there could be a thousand men with English accents."

"Back to the gambling end for me. Where's a good place to stay in town?"

"Almost none available. I'd let you stay in the barracks with the Mounties, but that would tell everyone you were a lawman. Might try Francine's. The price is high, but she's particular about who she lets in. She might have a room. It's room and board there, which is the best way up here."

McCoy shook the Mountie's hand and said he'd keep in touch, only not so openly, and carried his bag outside and followed the directions he'd been given to Francine's. It was half a block off Front Street, a two-story building in back of a big gambling and drinking establishment.

McCoy pushed open the heavy door and went into a small entryway. A table sat there flanked by three doors. It obviously hadn't been intended to be a boardinghouse by its builder. A small bell had rung when he opened the outside door. A woman came through the center panel and stared at him.

She was in her thirties, he figured, blond, with soft blue eyes and a slender figure.

She had half-glasses perched on her nose, and she looked over them at him as if examining a new species, with interest and some curiosity but not a lot of enthusiasm.

"Francine? I'm looking for a place to stay," McCoy said. Now that was smart. Why else would he be standing there with his bag?

"I figured that. Who are you and what are you doing in Dawson?"

"I'm a businessman looking for a store to buy. I figure Dawson should have one more good year before things dry up around here."

"And you want in on the gravy."

"About right. Any law against that?"

"Not even in Canada. What's your name?"

"Spur McCoy."

"I usually don't let Irish in my front door; but you don't look like a brawler." She stared at him again. "Board and room for thirty dollars a week. No cooking in your room, no women in your room, no wild drinking parties. This is a respectable place and I aim to keep it that way."

"Yes, ma'am. I reckon I can control myself to meet those regulations."

"Good. A week in advance. You get the last room I have. That makes three of you off the boat for me today. I swear, I don't know where all of these men are going to sleep. Most don't even have tents."

She smiled then and it changed her whole personality. It was a fine smile with the corners of her mouth lifted, a row of bright white teeth showing and a dart of a dimple on one cheek.

"Oh, your room is up the stairs and first on the right. I'll show you." She went back through the middle door, which he saw led to a short hall with a stairway up one side to the second floor.

The room was ten feet square, with a window that opened on the street. It had a bed, dresser, and a pitcher and bowl on a low washstand. One chair stood near the window, which had soft filmy curtains blowing in the breeze.

She pointed to the bed. "If that one isn't long enough for you, we can change the bed." Color seeped up from her neck and she moved on. "Breakfast is at seven, lunch at twelve if you want it, and dinner is promptly at six." She went to the door and held it half open.

"Mr. McCoy, I'm pleased to have you in my boardinghouse. I hope you like it here." She smiled. "You're a most attractive man. I wonder if you realize that, Mr. McCoy." With that she turned, stepped into the hall, and closed the door behind her.

McCoy grinned as he watched her leave. She was over five-six, tall for a woman. She had a slender, lithe figure, with breasts not large but round and delicately formed, he imagined. He noted that she wore no wedding or engagement rings on her left hand.

For just a moment he'd sensed a tension between them when she looked at the bed. Then it had passed and she'd blushed and slipped out the door. It would be interesting to see how things progressed with his landlady. McCoy grinned. It would be one hell of a lot of fun to see how long it would take him to get her interested in him.

He unpacked, left the six-guns in the bottom of his bag, and put the hide-out .45 two-shot derringer in his corduroy jacket inside pocket. He'd had a pocket sewn in that wouldn't show with the weapon under his arm.

His Western boots seemed appropriate for the dirt and mud streets. He wore dark brown trousers, a white shirt and dark tie. He'd look somewhat respectable, obviously not a miner, but not dressed so fancy he would attract any undue attention.

He went out to Front Street and walked its length. More than a dozen places to gamble that he saw, probably half a dozen more that he missed. There were several places that had revues and singers and dancers on stages. He'd investigate those once it got to be eight o'clock.

He had noticed the daylight the first time he hit Alaska back at St. Michael. Now in June it was light for 18 hours a day. In another month it would be virtually daylight all night as the sun made its weak circle around the North Pole. He had to forget his old ideas about daylight and darkness. Here it was day and then "after supper."

He went to the nearest good-looking gambling establishment and stepped inside. It was the Monte Carlo, thrown together in haste from green lumber cut at the local sawmill, which now worked 24 hours a day to keep up with the demand.

The three-story Monte Carlo had a dark little saloon where neckties, coats, and hats were in the majority. McCoy worked through the crowd to the gaming room behind it. This room was only a little larger than the saloon, and featured half a dozen different gambling games.

McCoy wandered over to the poker tables and surveyed the 20-odd men playing cards. None of them wore a sandy-colored beard. Only one man had a beard, about half had mustaches. At the first game he heard some of them talk when they bet and two sounded British, but one was fat as a goose, and the other one almost short enough to be a midget.

McCoy walked past the other games, but found no one who seemed he might be the errant son of a duke. He went back outside to Front Street, and decided that he'd go back for supper at the boardinghouse. It would give him another contact with Francine, the owner, and he'd see how the food was going to be.

As he walked down Front Street, he was amazed at the number of men who were in the town. More and more small boats would land at the waterfront every day. He heard someone say that more than seven thousand boats were coming up the Yukon, and another five thousand men were expected to come in on the paddleboats from St. Michael.

Even now men with nowhere to go and nothing to do wandered up and down Front Street. Most of the good claims were gobbled up and gone. These men had no money to buy a claim from someone. They walked from one end of town to the other in their hip-high rubber boots.

Superintendent Irons had told McCoy that by the time the last boats arrived there would be from 30,000 to 35,000 people in the city. He expected a lot of them to be moving back down the Yukon on the stern-wheelers before long.

"Too many men, too few claims, too few creeks to claim," was the way the tough RCMP superintendent had put it.

Into this mass of humanity had blundered the English killer who McCoy had to find. At least he wouldn't be trying to be a miner. He'd have a much narrower range of activities.

McCoy slipped into the boardinghouse just off Front Street, and cleaned his boots on a boot scraper and then washed them down as a small sign asked him to do on the porch railing.

He found the dining room at ten minutes until six, and already half a dozen men waited at the table. Francine nodded at him, and precisely at six she sat down at the head of the table and rang a small bell, and two young girls brought in the food.

It was good and there was lots of it. Nine men sat around the big table. Tonight they had a beef stew and slabs of moose roast along with freshly baked bread, jam, and coffee and rice pudding for dessert.

Four of the men ate quickly and left. Two others tarried over their coffee. None of the borders were women. McCoy made ready to leave as the other two men did, but Francine motioned for him to stay.

"I need to talk to you, Mr. McCoy," she said softly before he reached the door. He paused, letting the other two men leave. When they were out of the dining room and the door was closed, Francine turned to McCoy.

"I wondered if you'd like to share a brandy with me in my rooms."

McCoy watched her, trying to read some meaning into her words. He couldn't. They were a simple invitation to come for a brandy, nothing more. Anything else would be speculation.

"I'd enjoy that a great deal, Miss Francine," he said. He held out his arm, and she took it and nodded toward the door at the far end of the dining room. He opened it and she went through first. At once the plain decor of the boardinghouse changed.

Now they were in a short hall with a carpet on the floor. Two doors opened off it. She turned the knob at the first and went in. He found it to be a sitting room, with a sofa and two overstuffed chairs, family pictures on the wall, and four theater posters proclaiming attractions on the stage.

He studied the pictures on the posters. They were of Francine. She was known in the posters as Francine Miller.

"So you were on the stage?"

"Yes, when I was much younger, and much more foolish."

"It must have been an exciting life. Boston, New York, Chicago."

"Yes, but also there were unexciting Little Rock, Shelby, Columbus, Ferristown, and Farmington. It was more work than glamor."

"But exciting?"

"Yes. Exciting." She sat down on the sofa and pointed to the place beside her. When he sat down she moved so her thigh touched his. Francine turned and looked at him.

"I'm sorry, I don't have any brandy. That was a line from a play I used to perform in."

"I really don't want any brandy anyway," McCoy said.

"Oh."

He bent his face toward hers. She didn't move. His lips came closer to hers and then she leaned forward to meet him. They kissed, but only their lips touched.

"Oh, my!" Francine said. Her eyes opened as he leaned back. She watched him, then smiled. "Mr. McCoy, would you mind doing that again?"

He kissed her again; this time his arms went around her and he pulled her toward him and the kiss lasted longer. When his lips left hers, she nodded.

"I was trying to decide if I liked it. Yes, I do. Now that I like your kisses, I'd like a few more." She turned toward him and pushed her breasts against his chest as their lips met. This time her arms came up around his neck and her fingers played with the hair over his collar.

One kiss turned into another and by the time she pulled away he had felt her heart beating rapidly.

"Oh, my, Mr. McCoy. You've kissed a girl or two before, I'd guess." She stood. "Come," she said.

They went to the other door and through it and were in her bedroom. It was done in soft pink— the wallpaper, the bedspread, the pillows, even some painted furniture. She sat down on the edge of the bed, urged him to sit beside her, and then caught him around the neck and pulled him over on top of her as she lay back on the bed.

Francine smiled, nibbled at his lips a moment, then nodded. "Now, Mr. McCoy, you may try to continue to convince me that I should let you lift my skirts."

He curved one hand around her flattened breast and bent and kissed the other through the thin fabric of her dress. Then he blew hot breath through the cloth onto her breast.

She moaned. "Well, now, that's an interesting method."

He unbuttoned the three large fasteners down the front of her dress and spread the cloth away. Her chemise covered her breasts, and he lifted it around her neck to reveal her twin treasures.

McCoy kissed each on the ruby-red nipple, then showered each with kisses around the lighter-colored areola until she moaned again and wiggled on the bed. He helped her sit up and bunched the skirt around her waist, then lifted the dress over her head. He removed her chemise as well, and found hand-sized breasts with nipples already hardening and lifting to do battle. He kissed each, sucked them into his mouth one at a time, and chewed gently on them until she moaned again and reached for his crotch.

Gently she undid the buttons on his fly, then found his belt and opened it to spread back his trousers. Her hands wormed under his short underwear until she came to his already hard erection.

"My, my, but you are quick," she said. He kissed her again and she surged toward him kissing his neck, his face, his ears, then falling onto the bed and surging on top of him pounding her hips against his.

She stopped and panted.

"Oh, God, I think I'm going to die If you don't do it soon. Right now, please, Spur McCoy, make love to me right now!"

He pulled down her bloomers and ripped them off one leg, then kicked out of his boots and pulled his pants and short underwear off in one move. He tore off his jacket and his shirt.

She had turned over on her back and spread her legs, lifting her knees, watching him from slitted eyes, her breath coming in ragged gasps and gulps. Her arms went out for him and he slid between them, his knees between her legs, his crotch aiming at hers.

"Do it! Do it! Do it! I can't stand it another minute with you not deep inside my little hole."

McCoy lowered toward her treasure, found the right spot, and eased inward. Her hand grabbed his hips and jammed him forward so he slid into her with one deft stroke.

"Eaaaa!" she moaned. "Just right, darling. Perfect! Don't ever move it. I want your big cock inside me that way every minute of every day. We won't even eat. I want you a dozen times tonight. Don't tell me you can't do it, we'll try!"

Her hips began a little wiggle and then a round-and-round move. McCoy knew that would set him off too quickly, and he held her hips with his hands, then stroked all the way out and when she whimpered, he lanced back into her vagina slowly, making her beg for every inch.

Four times he played that slowdown game; then she reached up and nibbled on his man nipple and he moaned in response. Francine grinned and reached behind him, her finger working to find his rectum.

He moved her hand and stroked a half dozen times. Now when her hips responded he let them, and she ground right and then left, then in a circle. She gripped his thrusts into her with her inside muscles, milking him each time.

He pushed her legs upward until they rested on his shoulders, then worked higher at the new angle and pounded into her a dozen times.

Francine whimpered, then wailed as her whole body shook with a shattering climax and her eyes went wild and her hips thundered at him as the vibrations and the spasms rattled her time and time again, until she whimpered one last time and sighed long and low and he thought she had either died or gone to sleep.

A moment later she was watching him; her legs came around his head and she humped at him.

"Your turn," she said, and her inner muscles grabbed him and before he could stop it the floodgates opened and the rush to the final curtain had begun. He poked at her as hard as he could, pushing her higher and higher on the bed, until at last he brayed with a sound he had seldom heard before as his last six strokes drove deeper into her and he planted the seeds into her canal.

McCoy fell on top of her and she strapped her arms and legs around his body so he couldn't get away.

He rested.

Ten minutes later she let him go and he rolled away from her and sat up.

"Fantastic," McCoy said. "Have you been waiting for a spell?"

"Until I found the right man. I've had dozens of chances. I can't go to the store without getting ten or twelve offers. They seem to think I'll do anything for enough money. That isn't what I look for."

She reached over and kissed his cheek. "Damn, but you are good. You're a natural. I bet the first girl you ever fucked you were this good, a born natural."

McCoy chuckled. "My first time I lost it twice in my pants before I could get it out. Then when I finally was ready, she wasn't and it took me another half hour to get her in the mood again. When we finally made it, she wasn't impressed. It was my first but must have been her hundredth."

"Wager it didn't take you long to learn all the tricks." She sat up and stood naked in front of him. "Now would you like some brandy? I think I remember where I hid it. My cook nips a little."

She found it.

They sampled it, then again.

Another go-round in bed led to their decision that he didn't have to go up to his room tonight. They alternated making love and sampling the brandy. After the fourth bedding they settled on the brandy, but both drifted off to sleep before they could find the bottle. It was empty anyway.

Chapter Seven

Bryce Jeferies viewed the raw, rowdy town with a cool eye. He had struggled so hard to get here that it was almost an anticlimax to have at last set his feet on the solid ground of Dawson City. The mood passed quickly. He appraised the town, mostly tents and a few slapdash shacks made from available saw lumber and a few bigger buildings.

Bryce had been warned to trust no one in Dawson City. He looked at his two companions.

"Preacher Tom, you hold down the boat here and I'll go look for a place we can stay the night and store our goods. We don't want some sourdough stealing everything we've hauled in here."

It took Bryce a half hour to find a spot. It was a tent a man sold cheap since he was heading to the outside world on the next steamer to make the run downriver that same afternoon.

Bryce bought it for $20, and quickly rented a wheelbarrow to start hauling their goods into the tent. By the time he and Preacher Tom and Percival had their boxes stowed in the eight-foot-square wall tent, there was barely room to sit down. They restacked the food and supplies, making space for three bedrolls, and then collapsed for the night.

Percival asked what would happen to the boat.

"Somebody will probably tear it apart for the lumber," Bryce said. "Might as well be you. I donate my part of the craft into your hands."

Preacher Tom grinned. "I'll give my blessing to that and give you my part as well. Come morning I'll be searching for a likely spot of creek to stake out a claim."

Bryce and the other two had talked it over. They would watch their belongings for each other. One of them would be in the tent at all times, or close by.

When the other two awoke the next morning, Bryce was gone. They saw that some of his goods were missing as well.

"His cigars!" Preacher Tom said. "He must be out selling them. That young man will do well here in Dawson."

Bryce was on the street with his stogies. He carried a carton and smoked one long brown cigar as an advertisement. He had talked to a man who had left Dawson and who'd bewailed the fact that there was no pipe tobacco and no good cigars in the whole city.

The wafting cigar smoke did wonders in that cigar-starved town. Bryce soon discovered that there still were no cigars of any sort in Dawson besides his. It was a steamy, muddy town of

30,000, mostly men, all without cigars.

Bryce set up on a corner under a store's over-hang and began selling. He began offering them at a dollar each, but when men bought four or five at a time, he raised the price to two dollars each on the second case.

Then he went back to the tent and waited two hours. When he went back to the same corner with three cases of cigars, there were 20 men milling around his small sign announcing the cigar sale. He then sold the cigars for five dollars each. He had few complaints as the men lined up to give him their money and gold dust.

It was his first introduction to accepting gold dust. The first man to use the dust told him that it was usually worth $20.67 an ounce. Since most gold dust in the Yukon was mixed with extremely fine black sand that couldn't be removed, the dust was sold for $16 an ounce.

He soon devised ways of judging the amount of dust in a leather pouch, often selling enough cigars to use up the ounce of gold.

In three days, Bryce sold his 5,000 cigars and had in hand a little over $21,000. He had opened a bank account at the Canadian Bank of Commerce the first day. He deposited his gold dust and the Canadian and American paper money and gold coins. The bank had been hauled in overland a year before and was now well established.

The fourth day, Bryce looked around for a business of some kind to buy. Several owners were selling out and moving back to the Outside as they called it.

"I figure that Dawson City has about run its course," a man selling boots, overcoats, and placer mining equipment told Bryce that fourth day.

Bryce couldn't afford the $35,000 the man wanted for his big inventory and the frame building. He moved on down the muddy street he found out was called Front.

Preacher Tom talked to Bryce the next day.

"I'm heading into the brush. Want to leave most of my food and gear here until I tie down a claim, if that's all right with you two."

"We'll watch it like it was our own," Bryce said. He shook hands with the bearded Baptist preacher, who still had a serious case of the gold fever, and watched him head toward the gold creeks. Bryce didn't hear from Preacher Tom for three months.

Percival, the carpenter, went to work the next day after he arrived, building a new store. He told Bryce that he was hired at the first place he'd asked for work at.

"I'm getting paid as much an hour here as I was making for a day's work back in Vancouver." He scratched his head. "Course, flour is thirty-five dollars a hundredweight here and it was a dollar-twenty back home." He shrugged. "Still and all . . ."

In his spare time, Percival had torn the boat apart and stacked the lumber near the tent.

"I'll put it to good use one of these days," he told Bryce.

After two days of diligent searching, Bryce had not found a business he wanted. Instead he spent $700 for a log cabin half a block back from Front Street and moved in his supply of food and the rest of his belongings. He gave the tent to Percival, who promptly began to build a wooden frame over it and then close it in with saw boards from the boat.

The first day in his new home, Bryce watched a woman carrying water from a small creek 100 yards from her house. She had to set the pail down four times before she got it to her home. Bryce ambled over, and when she set down the bucket again, he picked it up and carried it for her.

"Ma'am, how much would you pay a strong man to carry water to you, say, twice a day?"

The woman, a solid-looking matron of about 40, looked at him and scowled. "Now why would I want somebody to do that?"

"So you wouldn't have to. I'd imagine that you could afford the luxury of two buckets of good sweet water a day sitting in your kitchen."

She smiled and nodded. "Now I sure can afford it." She frowned at him and cocked one fist on her hip. "I'd offer that man a quarter a day for water."

Bryce nodded. "Too bad. I'm starting a new service here in Dawson. Your bucket of water delivered twice a day for fifty cents a bucket."

"That's a dollar a day!" the woman roared.

"Quite right. Shall we start tomorrow morning?"

The woman laughed and nodded. "I'd say you better. The clean bucket will be outside the door at 8 A.M. I'll pay you the dollar when you bring the second bucket in the evening."

Bryce held out his hand and the woman shook it.

The rest of the morning Bryce canvassed the area near where he lived. He lined up 20 cabins to take his water service. That afternoon he found two out-of-work miners who would carry water for him for three dollars a day.

He had just made a business deal to clear $14 a day. By the end of the week he had signed up more than 80 customers for his Port-A-Bucket water service. That was a profit of $56 a day! That night he went to a cafe for a grilled steak dinner to celebrate.

A week earlier, Liza Cromwell had stood at the rail of the *Belle* as she eased up to the one dock along the two-mile shoreline that fronted Dawson City. She had never seen such a ramshackle, hodge-podge bunch of tents and slapdash buildings in her life.

A gentle rain had just stopped falling as she carried her two leather cases down the gangplank. There was no one there to help her, no porters or hacks or anyone for hire.

This place was ten times muddier, more misshapen, and more woebegone than the little town of St. Michael back on the coast. She took one deep breath, then followed half a hundred other passengers who struggled through the mud toward the street of buildings just ahead.

The hotels were much like those at St. Michael, a row of tents extending back from a larger tent on the street front. None advertised that they were for women only. As she looked around, she saw almost no women on the street. Hundreds of men, maybe thousands of men, walked up and down the muddy space between the buildings and tents. She wondered where all of the miners were.

The first tent-hotel she walked into was not the right one. Two men guffawed when she asked for a room and told her this wasn't Seattle. The men leered at her and she glared at them and left.

The next place she saw was the New York
Saloon and Theatre. It was a real building, one
of the largest she had seen so far, and advertised
that a song-and-dance team from Vancouver was
now playing twice nightly.

She pushed open the door and walked in. The
floor was dirt and sawdust, and tables for drinkers and gamblers lined the walls and the center of
the room. At the far side was the bar. The place
was crowded although it was only ten o'clock in
the morning. She pushed her way through the
crush of men to the bar and waved at the bar-
tender.

"I'd like to see the manager, please," she said.

The man behind the counter looked up and
grinned. "Hey, you must be our new songbird.
The other one flew the coop on the first steamer
downriver a week ago. Come over this way and
I'll take you upstairs."

A few minutes later, she sat in an office on the
second floor. It was small and had a window
where the owner could view the saloon below
and what she now realized was a curtained-off
stage at the far side.

From behind a cluttered desk, a man stared at
her. He was about 40, she guessed, balding, and
wore eyeglasses. The barkeep had introduced him
as Josh Pointer.

The man stood and she saw he was only a few
inches taller than her own five feet two. He had
a potbelly covered by a suit, white shirt, and tie.

"You are not Jean Marie Trudeau. I've seen her
picture. Who are you and what do you want?"

"I'm Liza Cromwell from Toronto and I've
come to sing and dance for you here in your
theater."

He nodded, came around the desk, and walked past her, then circled her.

"Yes, yes, even if you can't sing and dance, you might do. Can you sing?"

"Of course, I worked for six months at the Variety Hall—"

"In Vancouver," he said, cutting her off. "How is Old Brassie anyway? Still chasing the dancers?"

She lifted her brow and he raised one hand. "I'm sorry, I shouldn't have said that. If you worked for Brassie, I'm sure you can both sing and dance. You're prettier than anyone I have working here now. The Klondike is not a magnet for pretty women. Why did you come up here?"

She told him.

"Well, I hope you find him. First, you'll need a place to stay. Within a week there'll be another five thousand people in town. Most of them men, and about half of them trying to find gold. It might take you a week to locate your man. In the meantime you can stay in one of the rooms in back.

"I take care of my ladies. None of them sleep with the customers from downstairs. I don't allow that. You'll have a place to work and to live. We have a community kitchen where we take turns cooking. It's a lot better food and cheaper than eating out."

"What are you paying the other dancers?" Liza asked, aware by now that she'd have to speak up if she wanted to be paid well.

Josh stared at her with a slight smile. "You're not bashful about money, are you, Liza?"

"Not a bit. How much do you pay?"

"All of my girls get twenty dollars a week and free board and room."

Liza laughed. He looked up and frowned. "I was getting thirty a week from Old Brassie, and filling his place every night," she said.

"Thirty . . . I don't know."

"Josh, you watch my first two shows, then we'll talk about my wages. If we can't get together, I'll go make some other saloon owner rich."

Josh chuckled. "You just might at that. You get settled and then I'll tell you how to find your intended. At least you can see if he ever arrived. I've heard of dozens of men who started here and never made it, for one reason or another."

Liza looked up, surprise, then fear touching her pretty face. "You don't mean that—"

He raised his hand and stopped her. "Just want you to be ready in case he turned back for some reason. He come on a steamer or did he go over the pass?"

"He told me in a letter that he'd go up the Yukon."

"Takes time, but it's easier. I'll help you tomorrow. Now, bring your bags and I'll show you a room. You'll have two roommates, but they're good girls. You'll get along."

The small room on the second floor had one bed on one side and bunk beds on the other. There was a dresser and a rod to hang costumes and clothes on.

"This is your dressing room as well as sleeping quarters."

Two girls were already there. They smiled as he introduced them. She remembered their names, Jerri and Phoebe. She was good with names. When Josh left, the girls came over and shook

her hand and asked where she was from and
where she had worked.

Within five minutes they were good friends.

"You want an upper or lower bunk?" Jerri
asked.

"I like the upper," Liza said, and they all
laughed. The other two had already claimed
the lower bunk and bed. By the time their
early supper was ready, Liza was starved. The
two girls who had cooked the meal met Liza.
There were seven of them for supper, including Josh and the head cashier at the saloon.
He was a tall, thin man who seldom spoke and
kept to himself. He came in, sat down, ate, and
left.

Liza looked around and smiled. She was going
to like it here in Dawson City, and at the New
York Saloon and Theatre.

Arthur Walling Hallifax stepped off the steamer
at Dawson City. He was a dozen people behind
Liza. It was June 10 and he wasted no time finding the biggest poker game he could. He had
played some on the boat, but the captain had
warned him that if anyone was caught cheating
at poker, he would be tossed into shallow water
and left to wade ashore in the wilderness.

Not a man on board the boat had cheated at
cards.

Hallifax was confident he had changed his
appearance and his name enough so no one
could recognize him. If by some chance a photo
of him arrived in Dawson, it would bear little resemblance to the clean-shaven, hard-eyed,
short-haired gambler he had become. He had tak-
en to wearing a fancy vest with a watch, and gold

chain and fob, a derby hat, and the best suit that he'd found in Vancouver.

The first day he made $30 at poker, but was shocked to find that a fine steak dinner with all the trimmings and a good brandy cost him $15.

It was a high-priced town. He would not deign to stay in a tent, and looked around until he found a room for let in a cabin not far from Front Street. He paid $40 a month for the room, which had a bed, a chair, a dresser with a cracked mirror, a pot of water and a washbasin, but no way to heat the room. He was expected to furnish his own bedding. There were no cooking facilities.

He bought bedding, including three heavy comforters for the cold winter ahead, made up his bed, and then went back to the big saloon and settled in at a game of cards. The poker they played here was different from the popular games in Vancouver. There was also 21, the roulette wheel, and half a dozen other gambling games including faro, but he concentrated on poker. Within two days he had all the angles figured and knew the best way to play the game.

Next he worked on ways to cheat that could not be detected by the simple, hard-working miners. He learned to judge the amount of gold dust in a poke, and always had any argument settled by calling the cashier with his scales. The cashier almost always found Hallifax to be correct. At the end of each day, Hallifax made certain that the cashier received a good tip.

The first few days, he realized that maybe 20 percent of the men there were Canadian, and many of them had strong English accents they hadn't lost. It meant he didn't stand out, but according to his plan, he began to lighten his accent as much as he could, to blend in better with the broad American twang and the more clipped Canadian accents.

He had been wary for a week or more, worried about each new face he saw, checking doorways, watching for law officers. The Royal Canadian Mounted Police were in charge. He had never seen such a strictly controlled society.

No handguns of any kind were permitted in Dawson. Inspections were made of those coming over the pass and in from the steamers. Hallifax had been told of the ban, and had taken special care while still in Vancouver to buy a .45-caliber two-shot derringer. He'd hidden it and a box of ammunition in some of his supplies, and it had come through the inspection unfound.

There were small knives permitted, but no fighting knives. Axes were necessary, and hatchets. He heard that more than one miner had gone to an early grave with his head split in half by an ax-wielding killer.

The second week Hallifax was in Dawson, he chanced into a game of poker in the New York Saloon, and was there when Liza came out to sing. He recognized her at once as the Vancouver Blue Bird, and sent a note backstage, but she didn't answer it or invite him back. He shrugged. There were several other pretty girds in this raw, rough-and-tumble town.

That second week, Hallifax was stopped dead in his boot prints in the mud by the head policeman, Superintendent Irons of the RCMP.

"You there, just a moment," the big policeman called sharply.

The officer bent and picked up a two-dollar bill which had fallen from Hallifax's pocket.

"Sir, I think you dropped this when your hand came from your pocket," the Mountie explained.

Hallifax had been stunned by the order to stop. He was ready to turn and run, or even to fight. The sudden reversal of what he'd expected as a threat came as a shocking surprise.

For a moment Hallifax couldn't speak, then he chuckled.

"Yes, of course, Superintendent. I thought I felt something drop. Thank you for your thoughtfulness and your honesty."

"Only doing my duty, sir," the policeman said. He handed the bill to Hallifax and went on his way.

Hallifax shivered slightly, took a deep breath, and watched the policeman walk away with his measured stride.

Chapter Eight

Spur McCoy had a big breakfast at Francine's. She smiled secretly at him at the table. There were only four men up for the morning meal and when the other three left, she came over to McCoy and stood close to him.

"Last night . . . the best night of my life. I want you to know that. No sham or pretend, no feminine wiles. I was so totally satisfied that I cried. I still feel close to you, warm and safe and fulfilled."

McCoy smiled and kissed her cheek. "It was a fine night. I won't forget it for a long time."

She caught one of his hands and put it over one of her breasts. "We could taper off with a quick one right now." Her face turned up to his. She was so lost in the moment, so vulnerable that he wanted to hold her and protect her. McCoy had seen that look before and knew he had to move delicately.

"Francine, nothing I would like more, but I have to get to work and find a business venture I can buy before the good ones are all taken. Not sure I'll be here for dinner, but I'll be back for supper. Maybe we can play cards or something tonight." He bent and kissed her lips lightly. She clutched at him a moment, then smiled and let him go. Her brows went up and she sighed.

"You men are always running off. It was so good. Just promise me that we'll have more of the same."

"We will, you can count on it. I know you had a long wait, and I'm flattered. I'll be back, no doubt about it."

He slipped out of the dining room and through the front door. He would have to tread softly around Francine. She was amazing in bed but she might be one of those possessive women who didn't want to let go. Just so she didn't become obsessive about it and demand all of his time.

McCoy knew he had barely scratched the surface in searching the available gambling halls. Now he made a systematic search starting with the Pioneer, a respectable-looking place with a false front and a large gaming room. Before he was done he would check out the Dominion, the Opera House Saloon, the New York Saloon & Theatre, the Monte Carlo, the Bank Saloon, the Combination, the Pavilion, and the Mascot. These were only the larger of the gambling halls, but the kind he figured Walling would frequent. He wished he knew what name Walling was using now. That would make it a lot easier.

His usual method of search followed a pattern. He walked into the place, bought a drink, and toyed with it as he wandered around from table to table eyeballing every gambler. When he saw a possible match for the description he had on Walling, he'd stop beside that table and pretend to be interested in the game.

He quickly discovered that the hard-line gamblers weren't there yet. Time and again he saw a miner keep betting on a hand that was obviously losing. On a jacks or better opening for draw poker, he watched one miner bet 20 dollars even after he drew two cards and had only a pair of tens in his hand.

That man definitely wasn't Arthur Walling.

McCoy spent an hour in the first saloon. By that time his drink was nearly gone. He had nursed it well. He had checked out every possible player and dealer. None was Walling. He made a note to be sure to watch the dealers as well. Walling could take a job dealing instead of playing.

He left the first saloon and marveled at the mass of humanity on the muddy street. It had rained again and he saw a team of horses struggling through knee-deep mud trying to pull a wagon. The driver gave up, unharnessed the team, and rode them away from the wagon trying to find more solid ground.

There was little around. There were the sand and rocks on the beachfront along the river, and the frozen and unfreezing ground.

McCoy leaned against a rough lumber building advertising mining outfits. He watched hundreds of men wandering the streets. Most of them had nowhere to go, nothing to do. He kept hearing that almost every good claim along the dozen or so creeks had been staked. There were some shelves and benches where claims were available, but those took massive amounts of hand work before any chance at hitting paydirt was possible. Most of the men didn't know how to work up there, and didn't have the capital or the inclination to try. They wanted to pick up nuggets out of a stream and load them into a wheelbarrow.

Many of the men simply wandered, waiting for mealtime so they could go back to their tent or shack and cook their own meal from the 1,000 pounds of food they had brought in.

Every ship that came up the Yukon with eager faces lining the rails soon turned around and went back down the Yukon with half a load of exhausted and disgruntled stampeders who had given up the great adventure and were heading back to the Outside where they could find jobs and get on with their lives. For them the wild, thrilling, never-to-be-forgotten experience of a lifetime had ended. They were heading home.

McCoy hoped that Arthur Walling didn't have the same idea. No, for him there were plenty of chances. Miners still came in every day with pokes filled with gold dust. Few of them took it to the bank. Most were bent on spending everything they had dug out of the rivers and streams and gopher holes just as fast as they could on gambling, food, whiskey, and a wild, wild woman or two before they headed back to the grubbing, backbreaking job of washing sand and gravel and the thawed-out frozen soil from deep in some gopher hole.

McCoy headed into the next saloon, the Dominion. This one was different from the first. It had a huge Canadian flag covering one wall. In here he heard many more English accents. There was a chance that more of the English and Canadians patronized this saloon and gambling emporium than some of the others.

Irons had told him that about 30 percent of the men in town were from Canada and England. The rest were Americans. The whole town had a decidedly American slant.

He paused inside the door, went to the bar for his usual drink, and then circulated again. There were more men in this place, but the tone of the place was quieter. He spotted three sandy-haired gamblers almost at once, and checked each one out. One of the men was far too short; the second had a full beard as well as sandy hair, but when he spoke the words came out with a Southern drawl to them.

The third man turned out to be a poor poker player and lost his poke before McCoy could get a close-up look at him.

McCoy had worked the saloon thoroughly, and was about to leave when a new player came in. He was tall enough, had sandy to blond hair and no beard or mustache. He sat down at a table, dropped a poke of gold dust on it, and asked for some chips.

The U.S. Secret Service agent worked closer. The man's English accent came through on some words, but not on others, as if he were trying to conceal it. McCoy took more interest. Age? The man looked to be in his late twenties, which would be in the right range.

McCoy moved to the table, spotted an empty chair, and sat down.

"Mind if I join you?" McCoy asked.

Five men looked at him. Most simply nodded. One gave him a friendly "Sure," and the suspect watched him a moment.

"If'n you're bringing in new money, we won't mind at all." The words had the lilt of England about them, and McCoy took out a roll of U.S. and Canadian bills and put them in front of him.

It was not a big-stakes game. A quarter bet was usual, and McCoy played three hands before he won one. He figured he was about a dollar short.

Then the Englishman won two hands in a row. One man grumbled and the Englishman eyed him coldly.

"You've something to say to me flat out?" the sandy-haired man asked the grumbler.

"You're winning too much. I don't like it."

"That wasn't so hard to say, was it?"

Tension around the table relaxed.

On the next hand the Englishman dealt. McCoy sat beside him. He spotted the bottom deal when the man dealt himself three draw cards in draw poker.

McCoy's hand darted out and nailed the dealer's hand to the table showing a card halfway off the bottom of the deck.

"Well, now, I'd say we have a bottom dealer here, what do you other men think?" McCoy asked.

"If we was back in Texas, we'd string up the son of a bitch," a lean man of about 40 said.

"Let him chop wood for Irons for a week," another one said.

McCoy lifted the cheater's hands and pushed his stack of coins and bills into the middle of the table.

"I'd say you gents just take what money he cheated you out of and we'll call it square."

"I lost nearly ten dollars," another man said.

"Sure, but you're a piss-poor poker player," the Englishman said. Everyone laughed. The tension had broken.

The Englishman stood. His hands hung at his side for a moment. Then he drew an imaginary six-gun and blasted McCoy three times.

"Just wish I had the Colts I wore in Montana," the cheater said. "Then this wouldn't turn out the same."

"Hell no," the Texan said. "By this time any one of us would have shot you dead. Now get out of here and call yourself lucky you ain't in Montana."

McCoy watched the man go. He wasn't Arthur Walling. He was a street Englishman, living by his wits in a new land. He had no polish or style, and did not use the vocabulary of an English gentleman. Certainly not the son of a duke.

McCoy bowed out of the game a dollar short and looked over the rest of the men in the room. Some fine accents, but they didn't go with the right kind of hair or a tall enough man.

He went back to the boardwalk. In this year of 1898 there weren't a lot of boardwalks in the wild gold rush city of Dawson. Most businesses of any note had built plank boardwalks four to six feet wide in front of their own establishments.

When you came to a vacant lot or several vacant ones on Front Street, there was no boardwalk, leaving either mud or dirt depending on the time of year and state of the weather. He passed one building with a simple sign on the outside in three-foot-high black letters on a white board. It read "Store." On past a wooden frame with a tent over the top for the roof and a sign that said a highly skilled watchmaker worked inside.

The next building was the two-story New York Saloon and Theatre. McCoy walked inside. It was a little larger than some of the others, with a small stage to the rear, sawdust on the floor, and lots of tables for poker and all forms of gambling.

McCoy knew he couldn't limit his search to the poker tables. This Englisher might fancy faro or the wheel, or even dice. He'd have to be more watchful.

It was slightly after noon, but he wasn't hungry. He surveyed the poker players, then the 21 tables and the two men at the roulette wheel. It wasn't operating yet. The two men sat and waited. They probably had nothing else to do.

Here as at most of the saloons, there were bar girls to drink with you. A girl came up to him as he bought his drink and watched him.

"You drinking alone?" she asked.

McCoy looked down. She was short, with a round, fat little body and a pretty face. Her gray green eyes sparkled as he watched her.

"You just standing there or are you gonna buy me a drink?"

McCoy chuckled. "Be glad to buy you a tea you call whiskey if we can talk for a few minutes."

The girl signaled a waiter, who promptly went

behind the bar and brought her a shot of whiskey McCoy knew was cold tea. He paid for it and they sat at a table against the wall.

"You been around long?" he asked her.

"I wintered over, not a pleasant memory. Least-wise I didn't starve or go to cannibalism, but I had my moments."

"So you're one of the old-timers around. This revue any good, the new one they're talking about?"

"Damn well better be. That's what drags in the big crowds. Got a new girl singer. She was great last night."

"Sings well?"

"Damn good and she's a looker. Don't try, she's got men hanging all over her by the dozen after only a few days. She's looking for her intended. He came up here instead of marrying her. The sod must be daft in the head, or the crotch, and probably both places."

"I hope she finds him. Now, what about you?"

"Me? I'm a bar girl. We don't got no upstairs here, so I don't have to frig the customers, but I can if'n I want. Sometimes I do for a few extra dollars. Does that make me a whore?"

"Not a chance. Have another tea."

"Thanks." She signaled the waiter. "My name's Lottie, what's yours?"

"I'm Spur McCoy."

"I'm from Seattle. Figured this'd be a good place to make a lot of money. So far I'm half right. Where you from?"

"Anywhere from St. Louis on west to the coast. I'm here looking for a man, but don't tell any-one."

"You a lawman?"

"Sort of. Gent I'm gandering for is an Englisher, sandy hair, nearly six feet tall, maybe twenty-five or twenty-six."

Lottie drank the tea and looked at him. Then she scratched one of her breasts.

"So, watch me. If my tit itches, I scratch it. I'm not asking you to scratch it. This Englisher, he got a name?"

"Two or three of them by now. Killed a gent in London and ran away. They want him badly over there."

"Why is a U.S. lawman hunting him?"

"He probably came through Alaska, so we have part of the task. Oh, this one likes to gamble. Not sure what his favorite game is, but he's probably a professional by now."

"Haven't noticed him, but I'll be watching." She looked up at McCoy and grinned. "Yeah, you'd be right for her sure as rain. You seen our girl singer, our Liza Cromwell?"

"Afraid I haven't."

"You be here for the eight o'clock show tonight. She's a knockout, a wonderful person. I want you to meet her. I know people, believe me, I do. Want you to talk to her tonight after her first show. I'll set it up. You be here for the show. Come early 'cause the place will be packed after it starts. Always is."

Lottie stopped, pushed away the shot glass, and shook her head.

"Damn, I'm doing it again. I see this mountain of a great-looking man and right away I make arrangements to introduce him to a cute friend. Am I crazy?" She looked at McCoy. Then she laughed. "Hell, yes, I'm crazy. Why else would I be up here in this frigid, goddamn fucking place anyway."

She snorted, shook her head, and stood.

"Look, you just be here at eight tonight and I won't be taking any of your horse turds for excuses. You be careful, McCoy. Don't get yourself beat up before tonight."

Lottie turned and walked away. She let all of the pounds shake and roll as she walked. McCoy had seen fatter women from behind but he couldn't remember just where.

He began examining the clients in the saloon. Most were gambling. Some sat and drank, but the majority played some kind of game of chance. He worked through each one, checked out every table and player. None of those present could in any way fit the description of Arthur Walling.

He headed for the door, watching Lottie until she turned and saw him. He waved. She mouthed the time of eight o'clock, and he nodded and walked out into the perpetual Klondike sunshine.

McCoy stared at the mass of men who wandered the streets. The muddy street was crowded already. What would it be like in another month when all of the new cheechakos arrived with visions of gold dust in their heads?

Even in San Francisco with ten times this many people he had found his man. At least there life had been organized. Here a man could drop out of sight and not be seen for a month.

McCoy walked down the planks toward the next saloon. Another wave of stampeders was arriving every day. He looked out at the Yukon and saw 20 more small boats surge up to the shore. There was no shoreline left. Now boats tied up to boats until the mostly abandoned craft extended six deep out into the shallows of the river.

Just one man, that was all he had to find, capture one man. But with hundreds more men arriving every day, his job became harder and harder.

Chapter Nine

The first night she spent in Dawson City, Liza performed with the other girls in the show. It wasn't much of a routine, and Liza caught on to the simple steps after one quick run-through. Jerri turned out to be a good teacher and Liza liked her. She was a tiny blond with long hair she usually braided, a perky face, a turned-up nose, and sparkling blue eyes.

Liza flashed her stage smile when she went on. The platform they danced on was only ten feet deep and 20 feet long. She'd been used to a stage three times that big in Vancouver. It would have to do.

The audience here was much different from Vancouver as well. Nobody stopped gambling or drinking for the show. The talk and laughter in the saloon was nearly as great when they danced and sang as when they didn't.

Their only accompaniment was an out-of-tune piano.

When the last number was over, Liza grinned at Jerri. "Tomorrow I'm going to get together with the piano player and work out three numbers. Does he play by ear?"

"Honey, that's the only way that Parnell can play," Jerri said.

That night was Liza's first in Dawson City. She was tired from the dancing and slept quickly and soundly in the room in back of the saloon.

After a breakfast the next morning at ten, Josh Pointer took Liza across the muddy street and down a block to the Royal Canadian Mounted Police office.

Inside a corporal nodded at her and shook hands with Josh.

"Good to see you Mr. Pointer. Any problems at the saloon?"

"Not a one, Sykes. One of my new dancers here, Liza Cromwell, has some questions for you."

"My intended came to Dawson last year and I'm trying to locate him."

"We keep a record of everyone coming and leaving, miss. What might his name be?"

"Walter Livingston."

The corporal looked in one book, then in another large record volume, and finally nodded.

"Yes, here it is. He arrived downriver from the pass in June 1897." He looked up. "So he got here and there's no note that he left. Which means he should still be here."

Josh thanked the corporal and they went outside and back toward the saloon. Just across the street was the Dawson City Royal Recorder's office.

"Every claim has to be recorded in there," Josh said. "No claim is legal until it's staked properly and then recorded at this office. They should be able to tell us the number and location of your young man's claim."

A line of men in work clothes extended two hundred feet down the boardwalk and into the street. These men were waiting to file a claim or make some adjustments. Josh looked at the line a moment, then took a five-dollar greenback from his purse and went to the side door of the office and knocked. Somebody looked out. Josh gave the man the five dollars and the door opened and they stepped inside.

They were in a separate room that had access to the front office. The clerk peered at them over his half-glasses and nodded at Josh's question.

"Yep, if it's still his, I can tell you where it is." He checked one record book, then another. Josh looked at him sharply and he lifted his brows.

"Sometimes a claim is under two names and it has to be double-filed. Takes me longer to find it that way."

He checked a fourth book and at last smiled. "Yep. Here it is. Walter Livingston and Frank Davis. But a note on it shows that Frank Davis has sold his half to Walter Livingston. It's on the El Dorado plot, number Thirty-Seven Above."

Josh cleared his throat. "Could you tell us about where that is?"

"Map right over there on the wall. The El Dorado claims are about five miles upstream on the Klondike and to the right up a creek. Some good claims up in there. Thirty-Seven Above means it's the thirty-seventh claim upstream from the original staking in the El Dorado section. That's rough country. Might be best for a lady not to go up there by herself."

Liza wrote down the number of the claim and the partner's name in a small notebook she carried in her black reticule. They left the office and once outside, she turned to Josh.

"Will you help me go up there? I want to go today and tell Walter that I'm here and fine and then we can find a house to rent here in town when he comes down from the mine."

Josh took her arm and guided her across the inch-deep sea of mud that passed for Dawson City's Front Street.

"Young lady. I never go into the back country. It's murderous for a town man. I'd strongly suggest that you not go out there either. Your man will come into town sooner or later. Many miners come in every week. Put up a notice on the message tree and chances are he'll see it."

"No!" Liza shouted. Her face clouded. "I've come six thousand miles to find him. I'm not going to let five more miles stop me."

Josh nodded. "Liza, I know how you feel, but now is no time to do something stupid like trying to find him alone. Wait until you have made friends here in Dawson. Then one of your men friends who's reliable and trustworthy will lead you to El Dorado. I simply can't do it."

They stepped out of the mud to a rough walk plank in front of the New York Saloon and Theatre.

"Let's get inside and see if the piano player has arrived. You said you wanted to work on some songs with him for tonight's show. Tonight is when we decide how much I'm going to pay you."

Reluctantly Liza went inside. She knew Josh was right. She couldn't go by herself, but who would help her? She'd be watching for some kind, reasonable, honest, and trustworthy man to help her. In Dawson City that kind of a man might be a tall order to fill.

Parnell, the piano player, was there trying to tune the instrument. He gave up and grinned at Liza.

"I hear you sing."

"I hear you play."

They both laughed. An hour later they had worked out three numbers. Terri was right. Parnell could not read music, but Liza couldn't either, so they were even.

Josh Pointer had not watched the rehearsal. Liza decided he wanted to be surprised that evening.

There had been no real place to practice except right there in the saloon. It had been open and doing business all day. As she sang softly to the accompaniment of Parnell's playing, a cluster of miners, drinkers, and gamblers gathered around. They cheered when she stopped and she smiled and bowed to them.

After the last run through of "Charlie" the men clapped and hooted and cheered and begged for more.

"I'll be singing tonight at both shows," she called to them. "Come then and hear me." She smiled, waved, and hurried up to her room.

Jerri watched her a moment, then smiled. "Hey, you really can sing, girl. I was listening. You're good, better than anybody who ever sang in this town."

Liza smiled. "Thank you, Jerri. I appreciate that.

I still feel like the new girl here."

"Not for long. I saw the way Josh watches you. He's never even taken a second look at any of us girls before. He's got eyes for you, young lady. I'm sure of that."

Liza felt a sudden warm glow. Maybe this was going to work out. Now she had to find Walter. Jerri had no suggestions for a reliable man to lead her up to Johnson Creek.

"I don't know any good men in this town," Jerri said. "Know a couple who ain't so good, but they won't do for this."

That night Liza had time to watch the audience. She quickly learned that the claims in this area were all placer mines. She found out that meant gold could be panned out of the gravel and sand in many creek bottoms. Then there might also be gold where the creek bed had flooded or changed course in the narrow little valleys.

She watched the men who came into the saloon. Most were dead set on spending all the gold dust they brought with them. The girls said many of the men went out and worked their claims for a week, sometimes two weeks, then came to town to drink and gamble away all that had struggled to dig out of the ground.

"We might as well get our share," Jerri said. "The waiters and the bartenders cheat the men. The miners must know it, but they never make a fuss."

Jerry pointed to a waiter bringing three whiskeys to a small table with three miners around it. One of the men gave the waiter a leather pouch with gold dust in it. The waiter took the poke back to the bar where the cashier weighed out as much gold as was needed to pay for the drinks.

On the way back to the table with the pouch, the waiter deftly took out a pinch of the gold dust and put it in a pouch of his own.

"Not only that," Jerri said. "When the cashier weighs the gold dust out he 'accidentally' spills a little onto a wet bar towel. After his shift ends, the cashier washes out the bar towel and catches the gold dust in a pan. He might have an ounce or two of gold there."

That night at the eight o'clock show, the girls danced two numbers to the banging of Parnell's piano; then he did a little musical fanfare introduction they had planned and stood.

"Gentlemen of the New York Saloon and Theatre. The management is proud to present to you, direct from the boards of Vancouver, the amazing songstress . . . Liza!"

Liza stepped forward. She wore a dress with puffy sleeves and square-cut bodice and a skirt that was a scandalous three inches off the floor so she could also dance in it. It nipped in tightly at her waist accenting her slender figure and big breasts.

She sang the first number. As she began the noise level was high, as usual, but as she continued to sing, more and more men quieted and turned their chairs to watch and listen.

By the end of her first song, it was totally quiet in the big hall. Then someone shouted and clapped and the crowd erupted with a thundering applause. She held up her hands to quiet them and nodded at Parnell, who banged out the second number. She closed with "Charlie," a favorite of many of the men.

They stomped on the floor and shouted and clapped and all stood up and clapped more until she sang "Charlie" again. Once more they burst into applause and she waved them quiet.

"Thank you, my new friends. I thank you from the bottom of my heart. Tell your buddies to come to the ten o'clock show and hear me sing, then come back for two shows tomorrow night. I'll be grateful." She smiled coyly and bowed, then faded back into the rest of the line of girls, and Parnell swung into the next dance tune.

Two hours later, when the girls came out for the ten o'clock show, the crowd had built until there was barely room to walk through the place. The barkeeps were going crazy trying to keep up with orders for drinks and the gambling tables overflowed with players.

Josh Pointer stood at the side grinning and watching the show. He looked like a happy man. Tonight Liza would talk to him about her wages. She wouldn't come cheap.

She danced and sang and danced again. She had to sing the three songs a second time, then the clapping and chanting miners and drinkers demanded that she do the set again. When she at last begged off and headed for the stairs, a waiter came up to her with a note. She was used to getting notes in Vancouver. This was the first one in Dawson City. She went upstairs to her rooms before she read it.

"Pretty Lady. Thank you for coming to Dawson and raising the level of entertainment here. You sing like an angel. Could I meet you? I'd be delighted if you could find time to say hello." It was signed "Bryce Jeferies, Dawson merchant."

She smiled. A merchant. Now he just might have time to help her find her intended. Liza hurried out to the main hall and down the steps. She found the waiter who had given her the note, and he led her to a man sitting at a small poker table against the wall. He had a drink in front of him but he wasn't playing cards. He stood at once.

Liza saw a young man not much older than herself. He was about five-ten and had broad shoulders and a slender body. He wore a jacket, white shirt, and a tie. At first glance he seemed more a gambler than a merchant. His brown eyes widened when he saw her coming and he stumbled as he tried to get up too quickly. He had brown hair and a wide-open, honest face. She liked him at once.

Liza held out her hand. "Mr. Jeferies? Bryce Jeferies? Are you the one who sent the nice note backstage?"

Bryce at last found his voice. He nodded and stammered as he held a chair for her. He could only nod again. She sat down.

"Y-yes, Miss Liza. That's me. I'm overwhelmed that you're here. Thanks for coming. I loved your singing."

He sat down. "Would you like something to drink? Water, sarsaparilla, milk? No, no we don't have any milk in Dawson. That was crazy."

He looked up at her and she laughed softly. "Mr. Jeferies, I don't think I've ever seen such a nervous young man. Just relax, I won't bite you."

He grinned and took a deep breath. "I'm so surprised I don't know what to say. I've only been in Dawson for a week. You're the best thing that's happened to me since I came."

She thanked him, asked the waiter to bring her a sarsaparilla, and settled back in the chair watching him.

"What work do you do in town?" she asked.

"I sell things. I brought five thousand cigars in over the pass and sold them in two days. Now I'm doing a lot of things. I have a water service to bring fresh water to households twice a day. I'm trying to buy a store but haven't found one that I like yet."

She made up her mind about him at once. Liza knew she could trust this young man. "Mr. Jeferies, do you know where the El Dorado claims are

He frowned. "I believe they're north a ways. Not far. Some good strikes up in there."

"I need to go up there and look for El Dorado Thirty-Seven Above."

He frowned. "That's not easy country. Tough brush, hard going. Could I ask why you want to go in there?"

"Yes, of course. You see my husband-to-be has a mine—no, a claim—up there and I need to let him know I'm here."

Bryce's features turned from pleasure to disappointment. "Oh, I see."

"Mr. Jeferies, I won't deceive you. I'm promised and I want to find Walter Livingston, my fiancé."

"I'm crushed, I admit it. You just blew me off my feet when you sang. I instantly fell in love with you. Now to find out that you're promised . . . it's a real shock."

"Mr. Jeferies. I'm willing to pay you to be my guide and bodyguard to the claim and back if needed."

"You would be need to come back. No woman could stay out on a claim." He took another deep breath, stood, and walked around the table, then sat down.

"Yes, I'll take you in. You need someone to help you, and I won't trust most men up here to do the job. Damn. You're promised to someone else. My luck. Well, I guess I can be your guide and bodyguard."

"Oh, good!" Liza squealed. Her face was a glow of delight. "Let's go tomorrow. How early shall we start? These long days are still confusing to me."

"Tomorrow?" Bryce shook his head for a minute, then shrugged. "What the . . ." He stopped. "Make it the day after tomorrow. You have some rough clothes? Some pants, riding breeches, heavy shirts, and a sweater?"

"I'll buy some pants. I have boots."

"Can you ride a horse?"

"Well enough if it doesn't want to buck."

"Good. I'll pick you up here at eight A.M. the day after tomorrow. Eat a big breakfast, you'll need it. I'll bring along some food for our midday meal."

Liza sipped her soft drink and for a moment felt woozy. Her head spun at the thought that Walter was so close! That she would see him in two days! She took a deep breath to get her emotions under control and then looked at this young man.

"Mr. Bryce Jeferies, I'll be counting on you to help me find my intended and to protect me from any and all dangers."

"Miss Liza. I'll surely do my best. Oh, do you have a last name?"

"Certainly, it's Cromwell. That is until I change it by marriage. Which won't be long after we find Walter." She stood and he jumped up.

"I better get some sleep. It's nice to meet you, Bryce Jeferies. Good night."

He watched her as she walked away. Soon she

was lost in the crush of men and slipped to the upstairs door and vanished.

Her work day was over. In two days she would find her true love! It was almost more than she could stand. For a moment she leaned against the staircase wall and took three big breaths. Then, smiling, she went on to the top of the steps.

Josh Pointer met her in the hallway above. He'd been waiting for her.

"Oh, Josh. Do you know anything about Bryce Jeferies? He's a merchant here in town and is going to take me to find Walter."

Josh shook his head. "Never heard of him." His frown changed to a smile. "I watched your show tonight as you suggested.

"Liza, you're going to be the queen of the Yukon before you're through in this town. I want to help you. I've never seen any act in my place quiet the gamblers before. You did it in a trice. I'm amazed. I'll offer you forty dollars a week to sing and dance two shows a night, with Sunday off."

Liza heard it and inwardly gloried, but she frowned at her employer. "What's the name of that big variety hall down the street? Is that the Klondike Variety? I hear they have a stage much bigger than yours."

Josh scowled and walked around her and planted hands on both his hips. "All right, all right, I can make it fifty dollars a week, but that's absolutely the top."

"Fifty for me and only twenty for the other girls? I think you should give them each a five-dollar raise, and I won't tell them what you're paying me."

"Five more for each one?" He walked around her again, then shook his head slowly. "You're a tough bargainer, Liza. But I guess you're worth it. The place was packed tonight, wall to wall gold dust in there. Let's get them all to your room. I'll tell the girls tonight about their raise. Should help them sleep better."

When Josh assembled the five other girls in Liza's room and told them about the five-dollar raise, they screamed in delight. Josh left quickly and Jerri pinned Liza to the wall.

"You made him give us a raise, didn't you?"

"I only suggested it."

Jerri grinned. "I bet. I don't even want to know what you got for yourself. Whatever it is, it isn't enough." She kissed Liza on the cheek. "Thanks, Liza. All of us appreciate it, and we understand that you're the star of our small show."

Chapter Ten

Spur McCoy awoke in his own bed in Francine's boardinghouse. He groaned and turned over. It couldn't be six A.M. yet. It was.

He got up and sat on the edge of the bed wearing his short underwear and nothing else. The room was chilly enough at night to pull up the sheet and a blanket.

Somebody rattled the doorknob. He frowned for a moment. His six-gun was too far away. But nobody else in town had one either. He started to rise when a key turned in the lock and someone came in and closed the door so quickly that it took him a moment to figure out who it was. Then he saw a generous flash of bare breast and he knew.

"Francine. You're up early this morning."

She still wore the filmy nightgown he had pulled up around her neck last night. Now she lifted it over her head and stood there naked and pretty, her hand-sized breasts lifted when she sucked in her breath. She had glossed her nipples and areolas with some kind of paint or fruit juice because they were a brighter red than usual.

She walked toward him with a calculated wiggle, letting her breasts bounce and roll all they could, her crotch with its small forest of blond curls swishing one way and then the other as she came toward him. She walked up until her belly touched his face.

"How about a bite or two or twenty of appetizer before breakfast?"

Spur growled and grabbed her and lowered her to the bed gently, then rolled on top of her and slammed his hips into her crotch three times.

"That's the general idea, but it'll work a lot easier if you get rid of that damn underwear and poke it inside me. How quickly you have forgotten."

Spur did what she suggested. He was rock-hard, pulsating, and his holding power at a minimum. He drove into her without worrying about how it felt to her. Her juices came quickly and he powered half a dozen times more, then lifted one of her legs and bent her knee and placed the leg against his chest. He drove at her a dozen times, then felt the wave of satisfaction roaring down his tubes.

Spur grunted and panted and brayed like a jackass as he gunned the last four times hard against her, planting his seed deep and sure. He bent and kissed her mouth, then came out of her and lay there panting.

She rolled on her side and propped her head on one hand and watched him.

"That certainly was a quick one, an appetizer before breakfast like I said. Next time I'll be a little more specific about just how the hell I want to get fucked."

Spur grinned. "Hell, you said an appetizer. I've got three days' work to get done today. No chance I can play fuck-the-landlady with you all morning."

"Beast, you could at least try."

"Three times last night wasn't enough for you?"

"Three hundred and I'll be looking for more. You angry with me?"

"Not at all. What's for breakfast."

"He's mad, I know he's mad as hell."

"Not mad, not angry, not upset, not anything, except fucked out for a day or two. What's for breakfast?"

Francine pulled on her thin nightgown. "Hell, maybe the big stud *is* fucked out. Maybe his balls are sore this morning. Yeah, that must be it. Sore balls. So why didn't you say so." She smiled. "I don't know why I'm so easy with you, McCoy. Today we're having eggs to order. Now that you mention it, I'm getting hungry myself."

That morning, McCoy worked the rest of the saloons, big and little. He surveyed the customers, talked with the cashiers, and the managers if possible. Nobody had noticed a new Englishman who had enough money and was a good-to-expert poker player.

"Be on the watch for you if'n you want me to," the cashier at the Opera House saloon said. McCoy showed him a ten-dollar bill and the man grabbed it quickly.

McCoy worked the rest of the biggest saloons: the Monte Carlo, the Bank Saloon, the Aurora, the Combination, the Pavilion, and the Mascot. He came up empty. He even tried the smaller saloons, but many of them didn't have gambling.

For two hours he went into the retail establishments along Front Street asking about the Englishman. No one had remembered seeing him or having talked with him. The description was a little broad, and without his new name it was a task worthy of the best detective in the world to run down Arthur Walling.

McCoy turned in at the Yukon Steamship Company and asked when the next boat would head downstream.

"We have two due in today, sir, and they will be here overnight to give the crew a little rest. Then they head back at dawn day after tomorrow."

McCoy thanked the man and wrote a letter to General Halleck in Washington, D.C., urging him to ask the British to utilize their source inside the Walling Estate to find out the name that Walling was using in Dawson. With the name they could track him down. Without the alias Walling hid under, there was damn little chance of ever finding him among the 30,000 nameless miners, merchants, loafers, and carpenters. McCoy didn't expect any results. The letter would take two weeks at least to get down the Yukon on the steamer, then another two weeks to get to Washington. Another three or four weeks by boat to London. When he thought it through he decided it was a waste of time, but sent off the letter anyway.

The steamship line would post it in St. Michael and it would be on the way. The trip down the Yukon was much faster than the one coming against the current.

McCoy left the steamship company's office feeling angry and frustrated. He didn't have a single lead. Nothing to go on. Not even the Mounties had anything. How in hell could he find one man out of 30,000 with nothing to work with?

McCoy wandered past a tent that had a sign that boasted the best waffles in town. Two waffles and a cup of coffee were a quarter. He bought them, had syrup, and stood at a counter to eat. The waffles were good. Half a dozen other men ate along the plank counter, which was nearly chest high.

Just before he finished a tall man with long hair walked by. It was sandy-blond, and McCoy left the last two bits of waffle and hurried after the man. He seemed to know where he was going, and turned into a general merchandise store that was housed in a frame building that had cracks a half-inch wide in the siding where the green lumber had shrunk after being nailed in place.

The store was narrow and not deep, and McCoy examined a pair of shovels as the long-haired man talked to the owner. Spur McCoy moved closer so he could hear.

"I don't care, I won't pay any more," the store owner said.

"Best claim in the creek. Up to you. I'm heading out on the next steamer day after tomorrow. Make up your mind by then or the other gent gets the claim." The long-haired man turned sharply, and bumped into McCoy in his haste to get out of the store.

McCoy waved at the owner and went outside. The long-haired man had a decided American accent with a bit of a twang from Texas. Not Walling by any stretch.

McCoy saw that he was near the New York Saloon and Theatre, so he went in for a drink. A shot of whiskey might perk up his spirits. He spotted Lottie at a back table sitting with another girl. When Lottie saw McCoy, she got up and went up to him.

"Somebody I want you to meet, cowboy. She's becoming a celebrity in our town. Remember I told you about her? Her name is Liza Cromwell and she's the star of the New York Saloon's gala revue. You look like you could use a friend about now."

"It shows that much, does it? I should take some acting lessons."

He let her lead him to the table, and he took off his hat and smiled.

Lottie introduced them. Liza smiled and showed a dimple and McCoy sat down. She was the prettiest woman he had seen in Dawson.

"Lottie's been telling me about you," Liza said. "You're a real live lawman?"

"Something like that. I don't want it to get noised about too much, but yes, I am a United States Government Secret Service agent. That means a federal lawman. Something like the Mounties."

"How exciting. You're chasing somebody really bad?" Liza grinned, and he had the idea she was teasing him just a little.

"He's just terribly bad. Lottie tells me you do some singing and dancing?"

"True. I'm really here looking for my fiancé. But it's hard to find one man in twenty or thirty thousand."

McCoy laughed. "Liza, on that point we have something in common."

Lottie stood. "I need to go on a short errand. Be right back." She hurried toward one of the doors that led to the back of the saloon.

"Are you making progress finding your man?" Liza said. "I didn't mean to tease you before."

"No offense. The problem is I am not making any progress, and only now am I admitting it. I'm in a blind alley in the middle of a dark night and I have both hands tied behind my back. It's a helpless feeling."

"I'm having trouble finding Walter too." She told him about how Bryce was helping her and they would go up to the claim the next morning.

"I wish I could help, but I don't know what I could do. The Mounties will do what they can, I'm sure."

"I wish he was closer so I could be there at the claim and then we could come back here at night to a cabin. That would be just so fine. Now I'll have to wait for tomorrow.

"I just pray that Walter is there, and that it isn't too far away. There's a chance that the claim didn't work out and that he sold it and moved to another one, or that he's working for somebody in another mine somewhere. Then how would I find him? I'll be so relieved after tomorrow."

Lottie came back just then and her smile was an ax-handle wide.

"Come on, you two, I have a surprise for you. Now that Liza and I have a lawman for protection, we're going on a picnic. I know of a little stream that comes into the river about a half mile away that's surrounded by trees and some real grass and wildflowers.

"I've whipped up a picnic lunch and all we have to do is walk out there."

McCoy chuckled. "Been a time since I've been on a picnic. Do we have a blanket and everything?"

Lottie's brows went up and her hands flew to her face.

"Goodness! I forgot the blanket. I'll be right back."

She ran to the door that led to the steps and rushed out of sight. When she came back about a minute later she was flushed and panting.

"Now we're ready," Lottie said, and the three went out a back door and through the small kitchen. McCoy picked up the picnic basket and the blanket and they went out the side door.

It was almost a mile to the creek. But it was a pleasant walk, no one bothered them, and they saw few men after they left the immediate area of the river.

The small stream hadn't been prospected and there were no sluice boxes or unsightly piles of gravel. It was a pristine little stream five feet wide that chattered down across rocks and branches and a few old tree trunks.

They settled down under a grove of birch trees. A robin flew out of a birch, sat on a branch near some blue lupine, and cocked his head at them. When he decided there was no danger, the bird flew back to the top of the birch, where they suspected there was a nest.

"Look at the flowers!" Liza whispered. There were tears in her eyes. "I haven't seen flowers like these since I left Toronto. What are they?"

Lottie began to point them out. "Over there near the lupine are arctic poppies. They seem to sprout just everywhere. Then there are yellow daisies, arnicas, and out there closer to the bank a whole field of crimson fireweed. All of these are wild and they seem to shoot up overnight. Actually it takes them about a week, maybe two, to grow after the sun gets warm enough in the spring.

"This time of year they have twenty to twenty-two hours of bright sunlight," McCoy said. "That must make them grow and mature and blossom twice as fast as flowers would in Toronto or Seattle."

"Probably three times as fast," Lottie said. "They have such a short growing season they have to rush to get the job done before they freeze."

Liza sprang up and went from one group of blooms to another until she had picked a bouquet and brought them back. She arranged them on the blanket, then looked up. "Where's the food? I'm starved."

Lottie had fixed sandwiches for them, ham and cheese and a dozen pieces of cold chicken left over from the night before, along with some iced tea and rice pudding they had been going to have for supper, which Lottie had snitched off the shelf.

After they ate, they gathered up the leftovers and stowed everything in the basket.

McCoy had been watching Liza. She was a compact five-two, slender, with long dark hair and large dark eyes that were wide-set. She turned and smiled at him.

"Mr. McCoy, you haven't told us anything about your work. How do you track down some wild killer? Do you work on the plains with the cowboys? Have you ever had to fight with any of the terrible Indians down there in the States?"

McCoy grinned. "You sure you don't have any questions, Miss Cromwell?" They all laughed.

"My work. It's just what I do. There's a problem somewhere involving some government official or something the local people can't handle, the general—he's my boss—sends me in to see what I can do to help."

"One good guy taking on all the bad guys in town?" Liza asked.

"Usually not. Quite often there are a lot of good folks in a town and they need help to stop one or two bad men who are taking advantage of the public. I almost always have help in catching those bad guys you talked about."

"What about the Indians?" Lottie asked. "You ever been in a real Indian camp?"

"More than I want to talk about. I get along with most of the tribes, but some of them trust no white man at all. With them the only convincer is to have more men and horses and more rifles and maybe a cannon or two. They understand and respect force, especially when it is greater than what they can muster."

"Do you wear a gun usually?" Lottie asked. "You ever killed anybody?"

"Lottie, what an undiplomatic thing to ask," Liza said. "It's none of our business if Mr. McCoy has had to use a gun in the line of duty. We shouldn't pry."

"I don't mind answering. Yes, I usually carry a gun. I like it this way, though, where nobody can have a handgun. In a similar gold strike in the States it would be much different. In the little town of Bisby, California, they had about twelve thousand people there, a third of the size of Dawson. At the height of the gold strike there they averaged one murder a day. As I understand it, so far there hasn't been a single murder in

Dawson or the surrounding area. In Bisby in a year and a half, they would have killed five hundred people."

"That's just awful," Liza said. "I think the Mounties did the right thing about the handguns here. I wish they would outlaw guns entirely."

"There has been some talk about that," McCoy said. "Some people say then the only people who would have handguns would be the police and the criminals. That might not be such a bad idea."

They talked about other things then, about how to make the dance numbers better. Liza suggested doing some skits instead of just dances. She said they had done that in Vancouver and it worked well.

The sun came down hot. McCoy guessed it was more than 80 degrees. Liza slipped off her shoes and stockings and ran to the creek and held up her skirts and splashed. Her skirts lifted above her knees and McCoy saw shapely, beautiful legs. She wasn't the least bit embarrassed about showing a little, but neither did she mention it.

Lottie played in the water with her hand and skipped rocks across the surface. McCoy took off his boots, rolled up his pants legs, and splashed a little with Liza. Once she slipped and he caught her, one hand around her waist, the other directly on one breast, but he kept her from falling. She stood up slowly and he released his hand from her breast.

"I'm sorry, I didn't mean to touch you . . ."

She waved aside his apology. "Mr. McCoy. You were gallant. You saved me from soaking myself in the stream. I'm grateful." She reached up and pecked a kiss on his cheek.

McCoy grinned and thanked her and they went back to the shore. He found himself staring at the girl. She had a tiny waist and large breasts. He wondered what they . . . Quickly he looked away. He was thinking things about this young lady that he shouldn't. She was enticing, alluring, beautiful, and so sexy it made his crotch throb. But she was also a lady and promised. Hands off.

Lottie grinned at him. She hadn't missed a beat. They dried off in the sun.

There were no shadows to hint at the time. McCoy looked at the position of the big star but had no idea what time it was. He checked his Waterbury and discovered to his surprise that it was after five.

"We better be starting back," he said.

"Yeah, we don't want to be caught in the dark out here!" Lottie laughed. "Course it won't be dark until October or November."

They gathered up their things and walked back toward Dawson.

"Wouldn't it be nice to have a cabin out here away from all the noise and all the people?" Liza asked.

"Sure would be," Lottie said. "I know a gent who'll build you a nice cabin for only three hundred dollars. You furnish the land and he'll bring the logs."

It was nearly six when they got back to the New York Saloon. They said good-bye at the side door, and Liza hurried inside. Lottie hesitated.

She watched McCoy. "Spur, new friend. I don't want you getting any crotch kind of ideas about young Miss Liza. I saw that look in your eye. She's a lady, and you keep your mitts off her young, delicate body." Lottie grinned. "Course now, if'n the urge is too much, you can come around to my place right now for a quick tension reliever. Or to put it another way, a fast fuck."

She watched him.

McCoy chuckled. "You read me like a book. Half the men in Dawson must get a hard-on just watching her sing. She's special, but I wouldn't touch one strand of her beautiful black hair. I know when a claim has been staked.

"But I don't see any claim stakes around you." He reached out and stroked her breast and Lottie whimpered.

"Don't get my hopes up, cowboy." She put her hand over his pinning it to her breast. "Maybe sometime?"

"We might work something out. Right now I got to scramble for my supper." He reached in and kissed her cheek, then hurried down the block toward Francine's boardinghouse. He should be able to make it in time for supper. Tonight he had some hard drinking to get taken care of and then some low-stakes poker. Maybe he could forget what a tough damn assignment this was.

Chapter Eleven

The next morning, Bryce met Liza in front of the New York Saloon at five minutes to eight. Liza stood waiting. She wore stiff, new men's jeans she had cut down to fit, boots, and two heavy shirts over her blouse. She had a hat that tied under her chin and she looked like a teenage boy ready for a lark.

Bryce had to look twice to be sure who she was. She laughed.

"Two men tried to hire me this morning to work in their gopher hole tunnels," she said. "What's a gopher hole?"

Bryce explained it to her. "When the creek is panned out, they dig holes down through the frozen ground hoping to find more pay dirt, or maybe even an old streambed loaded with gold. The shaft is a gopher hole.

"Lots of time they use small boys in the holes

so they don't have to take out so much worthless soil to get to the pay dirt."

Liza shivered. "Glad I didn't hire on."

Bryce helped her mount the smaller of the two horses. He'd had to look for two hours this morning to find the nags. There weren't more than 20 horses in all of Dawson City, and they were treasured for summer transportation. There were a few wagons in town, but with the muddy streets they weren't much use.

He mounted and they walked the animals down Front Street north along the side of the Yukon River.

There was a semblance of a trail where miners had walked for a year to the El Dorado fields. In places it crossed small creeks and skirted upthrusts. It took two hours of steady walking by the horses to find the right creek. Someone had erected a crude wooden sign that pointed to the right saying: "El Dorado." Almost at once they came to staked-out claims. About half of them were being worked.

Men had dug out and sluiced the gravel in the stream that crossed their claim. Bryce told her that each claim was 500 feet long along the river. The valley here was no more than 50 yards wide, then rose sharply on both sides. Each claim ran across the creek and up the slope to the top of the ridges on both sides.

Some of the best bearing sand had been found by digging gopher holes straight down near the stream where the streambed might have been. Sometimes these holes were only two or three feet deep, sometimes they went ten feet down. If good gold-bearing sand was found, a tunnel would then be dug to follow the old streambed.

The dug-out material was put through a washing sluice box on the stream to pick up any bits of gold dust or flakes that might have washed out of the stream during high-water flooding.

Now and then a hole would strike the old streambed and produce rich sand with a pan of material yielding up to two dollars' worth of gold.

The horses picked their way through the gopher holes and Bryce waved at the miners.

"What number claim are you?" he asked one redhead who shoveled sand into his sluice box.

"Twenty-One Below," the youth called back, never missing a shovelful.

They worked higher. At last they came to the original claim and then One Above.

"We need to go to Thirty-Seven Above," Liza said.

Bryce nodded. It was nearing noontime. They found an open spot where the sun shone through the trees and tangled brush and they dismounted and had their lunch.

He had made sandwiches of cheese and some expensive ham. There were apples, and cold water from a nearby spring.

"You came to Dawson to get married?" Bryce asked.

"Absolutely. I'll get married today if I can talk Walter into coming back to town with us. Oh, is there a preacher here, any kind of a preacher who might marry us?"

Bryce chuckled. "I think we can find one or two for you when the need arises."

They mounted and worked on up the small stream. Bryce wasn't sure how such a stream, barely six feet across at this point and nowhere more than a foot deep, could be the source of all the excitement and wealth. But it certainly was.

An old man with a shack of sorts built on the far bank of the stream told them that his claim was Thirty Above.

Both looked hopefully upstream, but found only a tangle of undergrowth and brambles. They detoured around them going up the side of the ravine, then back down.

Now Bryce checked the claim stakes and found Thirty-Five Above. No one was there but it had been worked recently.

He found no stakes on Thirty-Six Above, but then found the next claim, and the stakes showed it was the one they hunted.

It looked abandoned. There was no 20-foot-long sluice box in the stream. No rocker box. One shovel lay against the bank. There was only one gopher hole started in a low spot next to the stream.

"This is it," Bryce said. "Doesn't look like there's anybody around."

Liza dropped off her horse and stared at the empty diggings. Tears crept down her cheeks.

"I don't believe it!" she cried. "Where is Walter? I've come six thousand miles to find him. Where is he?"

Bryce shook his head. He didn't know what to say. He looked around some more. He found the remains of a tent. It looked as if a bear had ripped it into tatters to get at what was left of the food in it. There were three blankets, some cooking gear, and a small pile of wood chopped into fire length. He found where there had been a fire, but it too had been pawed and ripped by powerful claws.

Bryce feared for the worst, but there were no

remains of a human form as he kept searching.

"He must be here, Bryce. He simply must be. If he isn't here, whatever in the world will I do?"

Bryce stared at her a moment. She was so beautiful he wanted to hug her right there. To take her in his arms and comfort her and tell her that he'd take care of her forever and ever—her long dark hair to her waist, her round face and high cheekbones, and that delicate little nose. He had fallen in love with her the day he saw her.

He cleared his throat. "Miss Liza, seemed to me that you did just fine for yourself last night with the singing. You can set your own price in this town. So you can sing and support yourself as we continue to look for Walter."

"The singing. That's just until I find Walter. Then I'll be his wife, go with him, do what he wants to do." She paused. "I see what you mean. I can support myself until we find where Walter is. He must have moved to a new claim or gone in partnership with somebody."

"Miss Liza, it's plain to see that Walter isn't here. We'll talk to the claims close by and see what the men there can tell us."

A rustle in the brush to the north brought Bryce around to face what could be a threat. He had visions of a 12-foot-high grizzly bear charging through the woods at them. He lifted the hatchet he had brought along for their protection.

A miner came tromping down the trail along the creek. He had a packsack and led a mongrel dog. He saw them, stopped, and scratched his head.

"Well, you be the gent what owns the claim, I guess. You finally come back."

The man came on to where they stood. He was

in his forties with a full beard and long hair, clothes that showed patches on patches, and a sweater over a shirt even though it was a warm day.

"Hello," Bryce said. "I'm Bryce Jeferies and this is Miss Liza Cromwell. We're here looking for the gent who owns this claim. Have you seen him?"

"Nope, can't say that I have. Well, I saw him oncet, long time ago. Him and his partner were finishing up panning out the last of the sand they had dug up during the winter. Then he was gone and so was his partner. Figured maybe they be back anytime."

"How long ago was that when you saw Walter Livingston?" Liza asked.

The miner dropped his pack and scratched his jaw, then took off his hat and rubbed his head.

"Well now, don't know the name, but he was signed on this claim. Been, what, about three trips to town. Could be one, two months or so ago. Just after the last little bit of snow we had."

"You haven't seen him since then?" Bryce asked.

"Not hide nor claw of him. No, siree. Oh, I borrowed his long box if'n you want it back. It's a good one and I figured somebody'd just steal it, him not being here and all."

"Your name, sir?" Liza asked.

"Begging your pardon, miss. I got no manners. Just that I ain't never seen a lady up in here before. Name's Lefty Green. I'm on Forty-Above."

"Pleased to meet you, Mr. Green. As Bryce said, I'm Liza Cromwell and this gentleman is Bryce Jeferies. If you think of anything more about my Walter, you let me know. I'm singing at the New York Saloon. Just give a message for me to one of the waiters and he'll deliver it."

"Singing? Wheeeeeeee. A regular celebrity. Gosh darn. I'll shore come and listen. Now, I best be moving on, I want to get a supper tonight."

He waved and walked on down the trail.

"So, your Walter was here and worked the claim. All that's good news for you, Miss Liza. He's probably taken to town life. We'll put a notice on the bulletin board and you can ask about him one night when you sing."

"You're saying there's nothing more we can do here?"

"I'm afraid not, Miss Liza. We best be getting back as well."

They were less than half a mile down the trail along the Klondike heading for town when two men appeared in front of them. One had a black-snake whip and the other a club.

"Time to stand and deliver," the smaller of the two, the man with the blacksnake, yelled. "Get down off those animals. We'll be taking your mounts and your purses. You too, boy."

Bryce and Liza got off the horses slowly, Bryce was closest to them. He held his hatchet behind his leg as he faced the two. The larger one with the club lumbered forward to take the horses' reins. Just as he reached for them, Bryce swing the flat side of the hatched forward sharply.

It struck the big man on the side of the head and he went down in a heap like a head-shot antelope.

"What in blazes?" the whip man shouted.

"Drop the whip or this hatchet sinks into your chest!" Bryce bellowed. The smaller man snarled, thrust the blacksnake behind him, and was about to whip it forward when Bryce threw the hatchet. It spun one and a half times. The broad, blunt back of the hatchet hit the man's chest and they heard a bone snap.

He screamed in pain, dropped the whip, and sank to the ground bellowing and whimpering.

"You broke my collarbone!" the small man shrilled. Bryce sprang forward and grabbed the blacksnake whip and the hatchet.

"What's your name?" Bryce demanded.

"Elliot, Jay Elliot. You got to give me a ride into town to the doc."

"Don't know if there's one in town or not. I ain't seen one. You better take care of yourself. You're lucky to be alive. Half a turn more with that hatchet and you'd be a corpse right now."

Bryce and Liza remounted and rode away. Bryce coiled the whip neatly and tied it. He'd turn it in to Superintendent Irons of the Mounties when he got to town. It was classified as a deadly weapon and illegal.

Liza looked at Bryce. "You're a handy man to have around, Bryce Jeferies. Does this sort of strong-arm robbery take place often up here?"

"Now and then, I've heard. Superintendent Irons is rough on any of the men he catches. I'll report this and give him Elliot's name. He shouldn't be hard to find with a broken collarbone."

"Was it chance the hatchet hit him with the head instead of the blade?" Liza asked.

Bryce chuckled. "No, Miss Liza. I had three months with nothing to do while building our boat and waiting for the ice to break up. I knew the hatchet would be my only weapon, so I practiced two hours a day with it. I can stick my hatchet in a tree twenty-five times in a row at twenty feet. I didn't want to kill the man."

They rode up to the New York Saloon a half hour before suppertime. Liza thanked Bryce for helping her.

"I'm in your debt, Bryce Jeferies. I always pay my debts. If you hear anything about Walter, you be sure and let me know."

She touched his shoulder, saw the quick way he looked at her hand, and then was gone into the saloon.

Bryce stared after her a moment, shook his head in wonder and frustration, and hurried back to the small store a half block down that he had bought the day before from an Englishman who was heading back to Toronto. The store held a fair stock of mining tools, shovels, hammers and nails for making sluice boxes, flat pans for panning gold, and a variety of other tools and gear to help men working on the surface and down in the gopher holes.

There were buckets and pulleys and rope of three kinds as well as diagrams for braces and square sets and star drills, which would never sell in this place.

The soil they dug through, even in summer, was frozen solid. They had to build a small fire in the gopher hole, and let the wood burn out so it would melt the soil enough so it could be shoveled out into a bucket and carried to the surface. When all of the melted frost was dug out, another fire was built. The rock-hard sides of the gopher hole were left frozen and would never collapse, so there was no need for shoring and no need in the low tunnels for any square-set bracing.

Bryce had bought the store to have a location where he could run his other activities. Now he had four men hauling water for him. He had started a bakery, and had two men on regular routes delivering fresh-baked bread to men in their tents and cabins where they didn't have ovens or to men who didn't know how to bake. He had pondered the price for a loaf of bread and at last settled on fifty cents. Most men bought two loaves at a time so it eased the problem of making change.

He had been watching for a good claim to buy, or at least part of a claim. Placer mining was hard, wet, dirty work, and some men with good claims didn't have the stomach or the back for the work. Claims were being sold daily, often ones that could produce thousands of dollars worth of gold dust.

He agreed to hire men to work a 100-foot strip of a claim for a man who wanted to maintain it without working it himself. It was one fifth the size of a full claim.

"If I don't work my claim for six months, it's deemed abandoned under law, and then can be claimed by someone else," the owner told Bryce. "So with you working part of my claim, I won't lose it."

They had a 60-40 agreement. Bryce would do the work or hire it done and pay that cost. Any improvements would be paid for equally. They would split the gold dust with 60 percent going to Bryce and 40 percent going to the claim owner.

Bryce hired two men at four dollars a day to begin working the strip. First they made a 20-foot sluice box and set it in the stream where they could start or stop the flow of water through it. The trough was a foot and a half wide and had foot-high sides. Across the bottom along the length, half-inch high cleats were nailed to create baffles. Behind these the heavier gold would settle, while the light sand and gravel washed to the end and back into the stream.

He had the men working for a week before he thought about El Dorado Thirty-Seven Above again. If Liza's intended didn't show up soon, the claim would be deemed abandoned. He talked to Liza that night between the shows at the New York Saloon.

"What I suggest is that we go to the registrar and tell him you are Mrs. Walter Livingston and request that the claim be reestablished in both of your names. That way you can then work the claim so it isn't lost, and it'll be waiting when Walter returns."

"Yes, yes. Dear Bryce, you are so kind and thoughtful. I never would have known about doing this."

"So it isn't abandoned, I'll hire two men to stay at the claim and work it, and we'll pay them from the return from the gold dust they produce."

Liza frowned a moment. "Bryce, you're a good businessman. You have a claim that you're working on shares, you told me. Why don't we do the same here? You keep track of all expenses, and we'll work the claim. All the gold we get will be recorded. Use that to pay expenses, and then if any is left over, any profit, then we'll divide it equally."

"Extremely fair, Mrs. Livingston. Liza Cromwell is now your stage name. That's what we'll tell the registrar if he questions it. Unfortunately, your marriage certificate is somewhere back in Toronto. I'm sure he won't question you about this matter."

The next day they went to the registrar and he quickly made the needed changes.

"Mrs. Livingston, we'll change that claim so it reads, Walter Livingston, or Mrs. Liza Livingston. That way either of you or both can take total claim to it."

That same afternoon, Bryce led two men up to the claim with a packhorse loaded with supplies so they could begin work on the placer at El Dorado Thirty-Seven Above.

He had selected the man in charge with simple expediency. In one of the saloons he raised his voice.

"Men, I'm looking for two honest workers to help me on a claim I control. The pay is four dollars a day, and a bonus if we hit it big. I'll be right outside for anyone interested."

Ten men lined up outside. He went through four before he found one he wanted, a strong young man from Minnesota who spoke English with a strange accent.

The second man he found with the eighth interview.

"You say you're a preacher's son?"

"That's right, a Methodist minister's son, a P.K."

"Preacher's Kid. Right. Do you believe in the Church?"

"Oh, yes, sir. I'm a devoted Christian and have my own service every Sunday."

"Hired."

He explained what he wanted them to work first. Some of the gravel and sand along the 500 feet of the claim had not been worked through the sluice. They would do the stream gravel and sand first and the streambed, before they tried gopher holes.

The three of them worked upstream, found their loaned-out sluice box, and carried it down to Thirty-Seven Above.

There was a small tent on the supply packhorse and Bryce left them to set it up. There was also a leather pouch filled with smaller pouches that would hold a half pound of gold dust each.

"Fill them up, lads," Bryce said. "I'll be out in a week to bring more supplies and food and check your progress. I'd hope by then you'll have enough gold dust to set us even with the greengrocer."

Bryce rode the packhorse back to Dawson, and that night reported to Liza that their claim was up and running.

"Any day now you'll be rich," Bryce said.

"I'd rather find Walter. Isn't there anything else we can do to hunt for him?"

Bryce had posted notices on the big bulletin board, but no one came forward. Twice now she had made pleas from the stage for anyone who knew anything about Walter Livingston and El Dorado Thirty-Seven Above to come forward and talk to her. Only two men sent her notes. Both had seen Walter just after the freeze broke when he and his partner were working their sluice box.

"He was working hard, finding good color, and seemed happy," the second man said. Liza gave him a five-dollar gold piece and thanked him. That night Liza cried herself to sleep.

Arthur Hallifax won just over $50 his first week of gambling in Dawson. He was not entirely confident with the men he played against, not sure of their moods or if they were bluffing or not.

He took a job dealing 21 at one of the smaller gambling houses and began a week of learning how to read the sourdoughs. Many were bearded, which made his task harder. At last he concentrated on the men's eyes—a twitch, a slightly hooded look, the darting glances, the closed eyes, a slight crease of an eye barely moving. He became an expert in reading a gambler's eyes as they related to what cards he was holding.

Twice more he had encountered members of the Royal Canadian Mounted Police. They had nothing but a courteous word for him. He learned not to twitch when they were near. It was plain they had no warrant for his arrest. But he never let down his guard.

Two weeks after taking the dealer's job, he quit to gamble on his own. One night he found a man who wanted to bet on his hand but had no more money.

"What do you have of value?" Hallifax asked.

The man frowned thinking, then he grinned. "I've got me rent receipt for another three weeks at the New Portsmouth Hotel. Best hotel in town. It's even got its own kitchen."

Hallifax won the hand, and the hotel room and kept it for the full three weeks. It was comfortable, and even had a heating stove for the winter.

The room gave him a convenient place to entertain a lady friend when he wanted one. Three more times he sent notes back to the Vancouver Blue Bird, using that name and asking to meet her, but Liza never replied. He turned to more available companionship.

Slowly Account Number 152 in the Hallifax name in the Canadian Bank of Commerce grew. It was his intention to work here the summer, shear the lambs for every cent he could, and be out on the next-to-last boat leaving before the Yukon froze solid. It would take careful timing, but he could do it.

More and more he used the simple ways to cheat, and moved from game to game so the miners wouldn't remember him. He began to dress in various ways to further confuse those he played against.

Once a man challenged him and threatened him with a knife. Hallifax jumped up and reached for his own knife, but remembered it was only a legal three-inch folding penknife that would be useless in a fight.

Before he could reach for his hide-out derringer, one of the Mounties grabbed the offending blade man from behind and hustled him off to the jail. He would chop wood for the Mounties for a week at least. It was one of two punishments the Mounties used. Chop wood for the Mounties' office and barracks for the long winter ahead, or be banished from the city and sent down the river on the next stern-wheeler.

Arthur Hallifax had been in town for over a month when he had the scare of his life. He had adapted to his new style of living. Gone were his superior airs and his condescending treatment of servants and the common workingman. He had become much more democratic and found that it paid off for him in the long run. Now he realized that he could cheat a workingman just as easily as a lord, a duke, or an earl.

He had been playing poker all morning and

won more than $200, mostly in gold dust. He was standing in line at the bank to deposit it when he overheard the man just ahead of him talking to the bank manager, who had been called to the teller's window.

"So that's about the story. I'd appreciate it if you would watch for any drafts from England coming through written to this Arthur Walling. I've shown you the arrest warrant. Superintendent Irons has a copy of it and I'll post one on the bulletin board. It's been some time now and his appearance may have changed, but I've been following his trail ever since he left the boat in Halifax, and I'm almost sure he's here in Dawson."

Arthur Hallifax reached out to steady himself by holding to the bank teller's wide counter. His head felt light, and for a moment he was afraid he might faint. He concentrated hard and held the counter a moment more, and the dizziness left him. He looked up as the speaker turned away from the window.

Hallifax rubbed his forehead with his hand, effectively blocking his face from view, and watched the form of James White-Smith, the Vicar's older son from his hometown in England, walk away from the window. He was the brother to the stupid one who'd gotten himself killed defending his sister's honor. The man was the very same one who had threatened to track him down and see justice done. How could he have found him all the way up here in the Yukon?

For one horrendous moment James White-Smith had looked at Arthur Hallifax, but with his face half covered there was no way he could recognize his enemy. White-Smith had walked away. The hunter had not recognized his prey.

The teller cleared his throat.

"Sir, you're next. Mr. Hallifax, are you ill? You look like you had a bit of rancid pork for your supper last night. Mr. Hallifax?"

"Yes, yes, Lester. Sorry. Just a touch of dizziness. I think it's the pork, you're right. I do have a deposit for you. Dust off your scales and give me a high figure."

Hallifax left the bank with the new total in his account book and walked straight to his room at the hotel. He didn't come out for the rest of the day. Perhaps James White-Smith would grow tired of the rough conditions of Dawson and leave on the next steamer. Perhaps, but he guessed the man would stay on his trail like an English bulldog.

Chapter Twelve

Spur McCoy finished supper and whispered to Francine that he had some contacts to make before he would be done with his business for the day. He promised that he'd knock on her door when he came in.

He went straight to the Royal Canadian Mounted Police office when he got to Front Street. He was constantly surprised at how much daylight there still was. It was past seven and the sun loitered so high in the sky that in Montana it would be noon on a summer day.

Superintendent Irons looked up grimly when McCoy came in.

"You hear something or do you have little feelers out that sense when something is about to happen?"

"Feelers, instinct, the breeding in the blood. What are you about to do?"

Superintendent Irons stood and took a deep breath. Then he nodded. "Yes, I guess you should come along. Your government has cooperated with everyone on this nicely. Fact is, we have a lead on this Walling killer, and we're closing our trap on him tonight, in about an hour. Can't count on using any darkness to help us, so another man would come in handy. You're not armed."

"Oh, but I am," McCoy said. He stood. The Mountie stared at him. With caution, McCoy reached inside his jacket and under his left arm and brought out the derringer.

Irons grunted. "You have a fine tailor. If I tried that I'd have a lump the size of a baseball in there."

"What's the operation?"

"An English gambler has a private game set for tonight. High stakes, which is all legal. It's in the back room at the New York Saloon. Supposed to start the game at eight o'clock. We'll be there at eight-thirty. Two doors out of the room they'll be using.

"We'll cover both doors, then move in with six men rushing into the room. We don't expect any trouble. Nobody is supposed to be armed, but my bet is that some of the professional gamblers have hide-outs such as yours. My men will be issued handguns for the strike."

"Sounds like it should work. You sure this is the man?"

"We've had some leads. He asked twice at the bank if he could cash an English bank draft. He paid a postal clerk twenty dollars to go through the M names looking for a letter for him from England.

"He's also a gambler. Keeps to himself. He's almost six feet tall and has light hair and no beard. We won't know for sure until we bring him in for questioning, but I'd say the chances are good. He fits the facts we know about Walling."

McCoy grunted. He was about to ask about the show of force. Why not arrest the man at home in his room where no one else could get hurt? He didn't ask. Maybe the superintendent needed a little show of force with the Klondikers now and then to remind them that the long arm of the law had reached even Dawson here deep in the Yukon.

"Yes, I'd like to tag along. You won't need me, but never hurts to have more men around. Is this man a fighter? Will he try to get away?"

"We don't know. He's never been in any trouble here in town. I'd play it soft too, if I was in his place."

McCoy nodded. It wasn't his operation; he'd stay on the fringes. It this was Walling, his job in Dawson was over and he could be on the next boat down the Yukon. It sounded too good to be true, so it probably was.

At eight-fifteen they went into the New York Saloon by the side door that McCoy had been through with Liza and Lottie. One of the doors in the high-stakes poker game room opened into the far end of the gambling hall. The other opened into the small kitchen and storage area, where McCoy and the Mounties were.

Irons looked at his troops. All were in uniform except himself and McCoy. "We don't want too many uniforms out front. McCoy, you and I and Officer Emerson will take the front door. I have the word that the game is in progress. The three of us will go in the front door almost as soon as we get there.

"I'll yell out a *now*, loud and clear, and you other men come storming in the back door. Everything clear? No gunplay unless it's absolutely necessary. That applies especially to you, McCoy."

The agent nodded, and they walked into the main gambling room and around to the door at the far edge of the hall. They stood watching the games a minute. Then Irons moved to the door, turned the knob, and thrust it open.

The three men charged into the room. McCoy saw a flash of a poker table under two lamps, with six or seven men around the table and cards and money in evidence.

"Now!" Irons bellowed, and the back door burst open.

After that it was one mass of confusion. All of the men except one sat as if nailed to their chairs. But that one man stood so fast that he tipped over his chair. His hand whipped to his left side and drew a derringer.

He had it placed against Superintendent Irons's side before the big man could bring his six-gun into play. His eyes were wild as he pushed Irons toward the gambling hall door. McCoy was six feet away; he drew his own derringer and took two steps, then dove at the tall man pushing Irons. McCoy's right hand held his derringer, and he brought it down on the tall man's gunhand wrist like a sledgehammer.

The steel of McCoy's weapon smashed against the skin and bones of the man's wrist. He let out a wild roar of pain and anger.

McCoy heard wrist bones crack and saw the derringer loosened from the gambler's spasming fingers and falling to the floor. It bounced off the boards and went off with a roar, but the slug only nicked a gambler's boot and buried itself in the side wall.

McCoy continued his dive, forced the gambler away from the superintendent, and rode him to the floor. McCoy spread his legs as he lay on top of the man so he couldn't be thrown off. Then he caught the man's right arm, bent it behind him, and twisted it upward until the man below him bellowed in pain.

Slowly the echo and the roar of the derringer shot faded in the room. Irons had the other poker players lined up against the far wall. He picked up the derringer, took out the second cartridge, and slid the weapon in his jacket pocket.

He knelt next to the man on the floor.

"Are you Arthur Walling?"

"What? Hell no, I'm not Walling," the man said with an English accent. "My name is Thatcher, Amos Thatcher. What right do you have bursting into our game this way?"

"I knew you were armed. That's against the law in Dawson as you know. Now you've added assault and battery of a RCMP officer, and the use of a deadly weapon. That's a serious offense."

"I'm not Walling. You've got no warrants for me."

"I do now. Let him up, McCoy, we've pulled his fangs."

McCoy frisked him before he let him rise, and took a four-inch stiletto from the Englishman's boot and gave it to Superintendent Irons.

"More illegal weapons. I'm afraid you're in for more than just a ticket down the river, Mr. Thatcher. Much more. Get up now and come along out the back door. Don't add any more crimes to your current string. First, let's see any identification you might have."

The man showed him papers from a wallet. He indeed did have items showing that he was Amos Thatcher, from Liverpool. There was a steamship ticket with his name on it for the third boat that had come up the Yukon.

Irons turned to McCoy while two of his men marched Thatcher out of the room. He waved at the poker players. "You're free to continue or to do as you please," Irons said.

"It looked good for a couple of minutes there," McCoy said. "He could have been Walling. But the way he talked didn't sound like the son of a duke to me."

"Right, he probably is who he says he is. It was a good chance; we just had the wrong man." Irons paused, looked away, then back at McCoy. "Thanks for getting me out of a nasty spot. He would have been away and free by now if it wasn't for you. I still don't see how you got there so fast and slapped away that derringer before he could pull the trigger."

"Mostly luck, Superintendent. That and the fact that most men are reluctant to shoot another human being, especially if they've never done it before. I had all the advantages on my side."

"Well, my side appreciates it. I'll be sending a commendation to your superiors in Washington. I'm in your debt."

They left then. McCoy was sure that Thatcher wasn't Walling. The man had reacted like a man familiar with the lower life of the streets of London or other big towns, rather than a nobleman's son. So Arthur Walling was still out there in Dawson hiding, probably gambling right under their noses, and hoping nobody knew he was here.

McCoy left the Mounties and wandered back into the gambling hall. He hadn't been inside the far door two minutes before Lottie rushed up to him. She had on a revealing dress that showed three inches of cleavage. It held in her bulk but made you wonder what she would look like naked. Her smile was curious and a little frightened.

"Were you back there where we heard the shot?" she asked him.

"Nearby. Nobody got shot. Maybe a broken wrist. The excitement's all over."

"Don't just stand there grinning and handsome. Tell me what happened."

She led him to a table near the back and they sat down. He told her briefly about the try to get the Englishman, who turned out to be the wrong one.

"Wow, I wonder how many of the real gamblers have hide-outs on them. More than we know. Irons might take to frisking these gamblers just to be on the safe side."

"Might."

"Hey, if he wasn't the Englisher you want, I might have a suspect for you. Interested?"

"Always interested. That was a great picnic."

"And you got to see most of Liza's bare legs."

"Yours too."

"Not all that much." She moved closer to him. "Hell, you can see all of me anytime you want, you know that. How about tonight?"

"Maybe. You said you have an Englisher. Is he a gambler?"

"I've seen him at the tables, but that's all you get out of me until you get into me. Fair enough?"

"When do you get off work?"

"Now, anytime I want. I've been here since Eve."

"Where's your place?"

"About a block away. I board and room and I have an outside entrance. I insisted. The landlady used to be a whore in Seattle until her body caved in. She understands. I'll meet you outside the side door in five minutes. See, I can't waltz you out of here bragging like I'd like to do. Company policy. See you soon."

McCoy watched her leave and grinned. There was a lot of girl inside that dress and he was going to see what it all looked like.

He had a shot of whiskey and went out the side door. Lottie tapped her foot on the hard-packed dirt as she waited for him.

Five minutes later she opened the door to her room and let him go in first.

"Nice thing about a twenty-two-hour day, we don't have to fool with any lamp, just keep the shades drawn."

He went in behind her and saw that the room was ten feet square, with a bed in one corner with a flowered spread, a small dresser, two chairs, a window which Lottie promptly covered with a blind, and a washstand, pitcher, and bowl.

"Home sweet home is where the bed is," Lottie said. She started to unbutton the front of her dress. "You want to talk a little or get right to it?"

"Your party, however you want to play it."

She grinned, unbuttoned the dress to her waist, and pulled it off over her head. Then she removed three petticoats and her chemise, which had been cut low so it would show off her breasts. She was down to her knickers. She turned so he could see her breasts. They swung out like a pair of melons, pink-tipped with areolas three inches wide.

"My God, Lottie, that's a lot of tits."

"Figured you was a tit man. Help yourself. Nibble a little, chew away. I got enough tits to last you until morning."

McCoy sat down on the bed and she dropped beside him. He chewed on one breast, then the other until he heard her start to breathe faster.

"Like that?"

"Does a fish like water? Chew me all day." She grinned. "Course there is another fancy little spot that would love to be chewed on a little. Trade you even up."

She caught at his fly and pulled the buttons open, then undid his belt and pulled his town trousers down. His short underwear bulged.

"Lord love a duck, look what I found under all the clothes. Got me a right nice stiff cock here. Hope to hell that it works."

She looked at him.

"I don't remember any complaints."

She chuckled and stripped down his underwear and dropped her mouth over his erection. McCoy felt the old urges pounding through his veins. His hips began an automatic little dance that he swore he had nothing to do with.

In a minute the dance turned into a steady pumping. She caught his waist and held him as she lay back on the bed and rolled over on her back. He was over her. She nodded.

"Do it right now all the way, McCoy. Been me a long time since I ate me a cock right down to the jism."

He straddled her and pumped with caution. She nodded and held him so he wouldn't go all the way down her throat. His hips humped and he knew it was coming. She held him tighter to increase the friction but her mouth serviced his hot poker.

"Yes, yes!" she gurgled around his shaft. He picked up the speed, and then the sky exploded and the building vaporized and the whole world imploded turning his life into a single cell no larger than a grain of sand.

He soared past the stars and their moons and planets, circled a globe that was deep blue showing much surface water and a moderate climate, then fired from orbit in a slingshot and sailed around the known galaxies as his hips drove six, seven, then eight more times and he came back to earth with a long wail of delight and satisfaction.

She rolled him off to his back, where he lay panting.

Lottic sat up, a big grin spread across her face.

"Oh, yes, yes, yes. I'll tell the girls about that one. So damned fine. So pure, so wonderful. Feels like the start of a great night."

McCoy knew Francine would be waiting for him. But he couldn't walk out on Lottie. Besides, she might have a suspect for him to track down. Bar girls heard a lot working around the card games all the time.

He lifted up, propping his head with his hand so he could see her. One of her hands rubbed with gentle pressure across her crotch still covered with the bloomers.

He moved her hand and did the honors himself. He quickly found a moist spot and concentrated there.

"Now, you were saying something about an Englishman, a gambler who was a blonde, and who might be my man."

"Might be is the word. Can't tell for sure. He's been around long enough to have come up on the first or second boat this year, a newcomer, a real cheechako.

"His hair isn't blond, more half-blond, half-brown. No face hair and he talks with what I'd guess was an upper-crust kind of British lingo. He sure talked fancy. He was in every night for a time.

"Then I didn't see him for a week. Last night he was in again. Said he won a half claim from a gent in a poker game. He went out to look at it. Should pay off big. He's back out there now, helping to work the claim."

"An upper-crust Englishman stooping to manual labor? That's all there is to do on these claims, from what I hear."

"I'd guess he doesn't do much but supervise and order the hired help around. I don't know, you'll have to ask him."

His hand had turned the damp spot into a soaked piece of fabric. Lottie squealed and sat up so she could slide the bloomers down and kick them off the bed.

Lottie was fat. He'd never realized just how fat before, but now he found fold after fold and rolls of flesh and skin everywhere. Her upper thighs were huge, and when she spread them as wide as she could, he still couldn't see any pinkness.

"Damn, she's got to be in there somewhere," McCoy said.

"I could pee a little and give you a direction," Lottie said and giggled.

He pushed his hand in and saw her jump, and then felt again for the familiar formation of skin and crotch and the soft petal lips of her treasure.

"I think I've found it."

"McCoy, don't waste time. You ready yet? You must be, it's been ten minutes." She caught his crotch tool and pumped him and fondled and coaxed and soon he was hard again.

She pulled him between her massive thighs.

McCoy could never remember doing a fatter woman than Lottie. For a bit he wondered if they would ever connect. Then he turned her over on her stomach, and had her lift to her knees but keep her head and shoulders on the bed.

When he spread her bottom he found what he searched for and in one swift, rapierlike move, he jolted hard into her glory hole.

"Oh, damn! Christ, you'rc in! Had one gent search for a half hour one night and I had to do him by hand. He never found me." She lay there panting. She looked over her shoulder. "Damn but you're good, McCoy. You should move to San Francisco and rent your cock out by the hour to those fancy dames who live on Knob Hill. They'd pay you fifty bucks a pop."

"Please, Lottie. I'm not that kind of a man."

She looked at him and they both broke up laughing. Then Lottie began a little dance with her entire south forty, and her muscles inside did their seize-and-release game, and before he could figure out how he could make it so quickly again, McCoy exploded in one of the truly finest orgasms he'd had in weeks.

He shouted and pumped harder. He bellowed in delight and spurted again and again. When he slammed into her the final time, she collapsed back on the bed and he came from her and fell on the mattress beside her.

It was ten minutes before he could breathe, let alone talk. She sat up watching him.

"When you make it work, you really do a job, don't you? I still think San Francisco matrons would go crazy over you."

When he could talk, he turned to her. "Hey, that's two for me and none for you."

"I almost never climax. I've done it twice that I remember. Once when I was thirteen and a virgin when my uncle showed me the wonders of sex. I wasn't altogether against the idea, and we reached an agreement he wouldn't enter me, but then he got so excited he held me and fucked me proper. I climaxed that day and figured I would every time.

"Didn't work out that way. I hit it big about two years ago in Seattle. Didn't plan it. My roommate just broke up with her gentleman friend and she was crying and I comforted her and held her, and things just kind of progressed and before I knew it we were loving each other like I'd never done before.

"That night before things were over, she'd used her tongue on me and made me come for so long I hurt for a week."

McCoy looked her in the eyes. "Do you like men or women better?"

"Don't know. Never did anything like that with a woman again. It was just a happenstance."

"But it sparked your sexuality. It made you climax. Maybe you would like women best. Worth a try sometime."

She snuggled against him. "Yeah, I suppose, but I love the way a man smells, love to have him jamming his pecker inside me, love it when he shoots me full of jism."

"Maybe a tongue is the secret. You tried that since that first time?"

She lifted her brows. "No, not really. Once almost, but he came all over my legs and he was done for the night."

McCoy put his arm around her and she buried her face against his chest.

"Oh, damn but I love the smell of a man. Whatever it is, I love it."

He tilted her face up and kissed her lips.

"Lottie, I need to know the name and location of that Englisher's claim. Can you do that for me?"

"Yeah, sure. He's Quincy Rumbert . . . bit of an odd name, but he's all right. I mean he's a handsome chap and I'd dearly love to get the chance to take down his pants."

"Where's his claim?"

"That I remember. He's on Bonanza Eleven and One Half Below. He said it was easy to find."

Spur reached over and kissed both of her large flattened breasts. "Tell the girls good night for me, Lottie. I'm on my way out to the claim. I want to be sure he's still there. By this time the crew will be dog tired and sleeping. Best time for me to pay them a visit."

"But I thought you'd be staying all night."

"Not tonight, little sweetheart."

"No tongue job?"

"Soon, but not this time. It's my job to find this Englisher. Anything else is just playtime for me. Right now I'm doing too much playing and not enough hunting."

She sat up and watched him as he dressed.

"Lord suck a goose but I love to watch a man get into his clothes. So easy, so practiced. No wasted motions. Settle the crotch down and move on."

"Habit of the species," McCoy said. He slipped into his jacket and then pulled on his boots. His high Western boots had served him well in the ruts and mud holes of the Dawson streets.

"Take care, Lottie, and I'll see you soon and let you know what happened out at the claim."

He walked through the door, waved to her, and closed it softly. Now all he had to do was find out where the Bonanza claims were and how to get there.

Chapter Thirteen

Josh Pointer, who owned the New York Saloon, watched Liza do her last number and then met her at the head of the stairs.

"Liza, could I talk to you for a few minutes?"

It was between shows. They had an hour to rest and get a drink of cold water before they went back on. Liza nodded.

"Let me get that sarsaparilla and I'll be right down to your office." In her room she blotted her forehead, then changed out of her costume into a loose-fitting dress and took her bottle of the cold soft drink and went down the hall to the owner's office.

She stood a moment watching the gamblers below. Liza saw Bryce at what had become "his" table. He sat there almost every night playing nickel-and-dime poker with whoever wanted to play.

He always sent a note backstage and after the last show, Liza always came to his table and they talked. Mostly it was about the claim and what was happening. So far it had been in operation only two weeks, but they had realized a profit of over two hundred dollars. She had been delighted. When Walter came back it would be developed enough for him to complete the streambed dredging and then work the gopher holes on the rest of the claim.

"Liza," Josh said.

She turned and sat down, watching him. In the time she had been here, she had grown to trust Josh Pointer. He was honest and fair and ran a decent saloon.

"Liza, you've been doing well for us here at the theatre. Our income is way up, we're doing better than any other saloon or variety hall in Dawson." He lit a cigar and nodded. "Still, you have to think of your future. There are some moves, some techniques I can teach you that will make your act even better. Now, this is just if you want me to.

"You know, I was in Chicago for years running one of the largest song-and-dance variety halls there. I had the biggest acts in the States back then. You might have heard of some of them. They were professional all the way. They would rather perform than eat. Do you want me to do some polishing?"

When he began, Liza had resented what he said, but as he continued, she reconsidered quickly. He was thinking of her, not of how he could make more money. She listened closely.

"But, Josh, you know I'm only doing this for a short time. As soon as we find Walter, I'll quit here and be his wife."

"You'll scrub floors and wash his underwear and freeze up here in the winter and grow old before your time? Is that what you want, Liza?"

"Josh, it doesn't really matter, does it? When I'm married that all will be up to my husband. I'll do what he says, go where he goes, do what he wants me to do. That's my duty as a good wife."

Josh went to the window and looked out below, turning his back on her. When he spoke it was softly and Liza had to strain to hear him.

"Liza, have you ever considered the fact that Walter Livingston might not be here in Dawson anymore?" Josh turned and took a deep breath. "Liza, everyone else has been talking about it. You're known by everyone in the Klondike by now. If your Walter was here, he would have come forward . . . if he could."

Liza's eyes blazed. She was instantly furious. Then she bit her lip a moment and controlled her temper. When she spoke it was softly and well controlled.

"Josh, I've thought about that since the first day when we found his claim torn up and scattered. It could have been a big bear or some wild Indians. Right now he might be lying cold and dead in some unmarked grave somewhere." Tears streamed down her cheeks.

"I know he might be dead, but until somebody proves it to me, I'm going right on hoping and looking and asking and searching for Walter Livingston."

She turned sharply and marched to the door. Then she stopped. Her shoulders sagged and she looked back. "Josh, I'm sorry I was cross with you. I'm worried sick about Walter." She wiped the tears from her cheeks and blew her nose daintily, then looked up at him.

"Josh, I'd be pleased to take lessons and instructions and suggestions from you about our acts and my singing. Anything you can do to help make the shows better will be appreciated by me and the rest of the girls. Now, I want to lie down a few minutes before the next show."

"I understand."

Josh told the other girls about his plans, and the next morning in the largest of the store rooms behind the saloon, they began what turned out to be a small song and dance class that Josh taught.

He showed them some new moves and formations for the dances. He confessed that he had been a song and dance man once himself. For an hour he told them about proper breathing for a singer and how to get more volume and project their voices to the farthest corner of the hall.

Liza was fascinated. She'd always just done what worked, and built on that. Now she learned why some moves and sounds worked with an audience and why others did not. She picked up quickly on the lessons and put them to use the same night.

Even Bryce could tell a difference in the productions.

"Liza, tonight the shows had a little more polish, more class. They weren't just girls showing their legs like they used to be."

"Why, Bryce, you mean you don't like to see our legs?"

Bryce laughed and shook his head. "Hey, no, no. I love to see all those pretty legs, but now the show is a lot more."

She touched his arm and saw the way he looked at her. Poor Bryce. He was getting serious about her and she liked him only as a friend. How could she tell him? No, he understood that she had to find Walter. It would work out. Walter would come back from being upstream on some fantastic new strike and . . .

She turned to Bryce and caught his hand. "Bryce Jeferies, are you my good friend?"

"I like to think that I am."

"Good friends can see each other cry. You've seen me cry when we went to find Walter that first time. I might cry again tonight. Josh says there's a good chance that Walter won't be coming back to Dawson. He says every day that passes the chances are greater and greater that Walter is gone for good—or that he is still right here and . . . and dead." Tears seeped down her cheeks. "Dear Bryce, what do you think?"

He caught both her hands and wanted desperately to put his arms around her, but he knew he shouldn't. She looked up at him and her large dark brown eyes held him demanding an answer.

"Liza, you must know there is nothing in this world that I would do to harm you, even to make you unhappy." He looked away, and she caught his chin with her hand and turned him back to face her.

"But the facts as I've found them, and the logic of this violent and uncivilized and sometimes lawless place, demand that we look at the chance, just the chance, that Walter has met with foul play. Through no fault of his own, he may have been harmed, or robbed, or who knows what?"

Liza sobbed softly for a moment. She took his arm and put it around her shoulder and slid her chair close to his, and he held her tightly against his side. Slowly her sobbing slowed and then stopped.

All around them men were shouting and calling for a waiter and making bets and laughing and singing bawdy songs. Their little world stayed an island of anguish as the result of the reality of logic and reason facing despair.

Liza wiped the tears from her cheeks and eased away from him. She stared at him, her face passive; then a smallest hint of a smile edged onto her face and she leaned inward and kissed his cheek.

"Dear Bryce, what would I ever have done without you? You rescued me and took me to the claim. Ever since I've been leaning on you for support, and not once have you asked for a thing in return. I really don't deserve a loyal friend like you."

"Beggars never make demands on the queen," Bryce said. He watched her and she began to stand. "Please, could you stay a while longer? We have a little business to talk about."

He quickly told her that they had almost finished working the streambed and that they would start with new gopher holes the next day.

"That will mean slower profits for a while. Maybe none at all, we don't know. Or it could mean we hit an old streambed where the gold is so heavy it will take two men to lift one pan of sand."

She smiled, but the tear stains still showed.

"What I want to ask you is if you want to invest in any more claims. The official government survey team is in town, arrived today from Vancouver, and they will survey and mark out precisely the hundreds of claims, maybe over a thousand, that have been paced off by men of different heights and strides."

She frowned. "I don't understand."

"With a steel measuring tape, five hundred feet is five hundred feet. No argument. But if I pace off my five-hundred-foot claim, and you then pace off your five-hundred-foot claim, the two distances might differ widely.

"So the surveyors will start with the original claim on each stream and chain off the five hundred feet for each one. Often there will be a wide discrepancy between some claims. Some will overlap, and those will be divided down the middle of the disputed ground. Some will be long and leave gaps between claims. These bits and pieces are called 'splinters' and will be open to be staked and claimed by someone without a claim on that area."

"Are you going to look for a splinter?"

"That I will. I'll be along with the surveyors, as will dozens of other men, watching for a good splinter on a high-yielding stream."

Liza frowned a moment, then her brows went up and she shook her head. "I don't think so. I have one claim now and a song and dance show to do. That's enough. You claim three or four and have fun."

"Or get rich, which is my purpose." He watched her closely. "After this is all over, when the gold is gone at Dawson, what will you do, Liza?"

"Afterwards? I haven't thought that far. How long will the strike last here?"

"Some say another year. Some say that by winter of '99 there won't be two hundred souls left in Dawson City."

"Oh, dear. I don't know. If . . . if I don't find Walter, then I'll have to make some decision. I can always go back to Toronto."

She had told him about leaving Toronto to find her true love. Her mother hadn't been enthusiastic about the idea.

"Will your mother welcome you?"

Liza laughed. "I'm afraid not. By now I'm sure she thinks I'm a fallen woman."

"Parents can be ridiculously unfair at times. I've made plans. I came here to make my fortune. So far, I've done fairly well, but I want much more. I'm working on buying another claim or two. I think I can work them on shares and do right well. We'll see. Then there is another business I want to buy. But the secret will be knowing when to get out while prices are still high and values are up. Get out just before the bust."

She touched his arm. "Dear Bryan, I have so much to thank you for. Now you're trying to save me from a dying Dawson City. Let's put off talking about that for a while. I haven't even started making my fortune yet."

She stood and he popped up beside her. They worked their way through the tables and drinkers to the door that led upstairs.

Liza brushed her lips across his cheek and then hurried through the door.

The next morning, Bryce was out on the closest creek where the survey team began its work. The first dozen claims proved to provide little in the way of splinters. Then on the Above section a gap of 40 feet developed. Bryce looked at it with two other men. Not much had been coming from this section so they all passed on it. A man new to

Dawson rushed in and staked it.

That afternoon on the Below section a splinter of 85 feet developed. Three men vied for the right to claim it. Bryce was one. The survey team flipped coins until one man won.

A chicken farmer from Oregon staked the claim, and Bryce went away mumbling about a double-headed nickel.

Later Bryce claimed a 40-foot-wide piece of land that turned out to be pie-shaped. It would cover the creek and go all the way to the ridge on one side but not on the other side. Bryce staked it and went back to the registrar to sign for it officially. There he found the man from Oregon. He sat in a wheelbarrow while a man who claimed he wasn't a doctor but had done some healing worked trying to set the man's broken leg.

The Oregon man screamed as the bones meshed back in place, and the would-be doctor smiled and applied a thin board to each side of the leg and bound it tightly with stout string. Soon he mixed up a bucket of patching plaster and lathered the man's leg and the boards with the sticky white substance.

Bryce stopped by an hour later and the man still sat in the wheelbarrow. He was trying to sell his new claim, which he had signed for.

"Only asking a thousand dollars for it," the chicken farmer said. "I've got to be ready to make the six o'clock steamer for St. Michael."

"Give you four hundred, cash in hand," Bryce said.

The man shook his head. "I might come down to eight hundred."

"Four-fifty is about the best I can do."

Say six hundred."

"Five hundred and it's my last offer," Bryce said. When the man didn't respond he turned away.

"Sold!" the chicken farmer said. He signed his just-registered claim giving Bryce control of it, and Bryce went to the bank for the money in Canadian bank notes.

By noon the next day, Bryce had two men hard at work on the new splinter claim. They built a sluice box and a rocker and got down to the serious business of working the sand and gravel in the 85 feet of river channel.

Before Bryce left on his horse, they had produced the first pan of dust.

"At least a dollar a pan right here," one of the sourdoughs said. Bryce felt better as he headed back for Dawson City.

The dancers at the New York Saloon had Sundays off. This Sunday Liza insisted on a ride out to the claim Walter and she owned. She wanted to see if she could talk to any other miners around Thirty-Seven Above.

They took a picnic lunch and got there before noon. The men were working, and Bryce put on gum boots and pitched in shoveling sand and gravel and dirt from the gopher hole into a rocker and into the sluice.

He came over and showed Liza the gold dust in the bottom of a pan. He put in a little more water and made a swirl of the heavy black sand and the gold dust and she squealed in delight.

"That's real gold dust?" she asked.

"You bet it is. It takes a lot of panning like this to get enough for an ounce. That's why we use the sluice. It works like forty or fifty pans all at once."

They had their lunch and Bryce left the men some supplies. He picked up two pouches of gold dust and hid them in his clothes.

Then Liza asked if they could try to find someone who might have seen Walter. Workers at the first four claims they visited upstream had not seen anyone on Thirty-Seven except the two men there now. They tried downstream on their way back to Dawson.

Five claims down they found an older man sitting beside the stream. They rode up to him and he waved. Bryce stepped down and saw that the man had twisted his leg. He helped the man to stand and hobble across the creek to his small tent.

Liza came over and they talked about claims.

"Did you ever meet the first two men who worked Thirty-Seven Above?" Liza asked him.

He'd said his name was Larson. He looked up and nodded. "You and this gent was up here a time ago. I didn't let you see me that day. Now I figure I owe you.

"Yep I seed him. Right nice young feller. Walter was his given. Said he was from Toronto. Always making sketches of things in a kind of notebook without no lines on it.

"Anyway, he was there and he and his partner worked the gravel. Soon as the thaw they worked dawn to nighttime. Took out some good color from what I heard. He'd stop by of a night a time or two and share some fruit with me, or just to talk. Nice kid."

"What happened. Why isn't he here now?"

The old man looked at Liza and then glanced away. "Don't rightly know. They was working it hard, and then there was news that the ice was breaking up in the Klondike. The *Betsy Rose* was due to sail. She'd been frozen in here all last winter. Heard that both of them were planning on being on the steamer. Then Walter told me that he'd decided that he'd stay on.

"Next thing I know is that there ain't nobody at the place there at Thirty-Seven Above. Both of them just vanished. Don't know if they ever got the steamer or not, but neither one of them been back."

"So there's a chance that Walter went downstream on one of the early boats?" Liza said.

"Chance, miss, but not a good one. Walter told me he wasn't gonna leave Thirty-Seven there until he'd wrung every dollar out of the sand and the gopher holes all the way to the rim on both sides. Said his partner was selling out to him. I believed him."

The old man filled his pipe and lit it. Liza watched him, her frown deepened.

"So, where is Walter?"

"Dad blamed if I know. Got troubles enough of my own with this rheumatiz. Ain't been to town but once since the thaw."

They talked a while more and then Liza said good-bye, stood, and walked to her horse. She hardly said a word the rest of the way back to Dawson City.

At the side door of the New York Saloon, Liza stepped down from the horse and handed the reins to Bryce. She rubbed her chin and then looked at him.

"Bryce, do you think that someone has killed Walter?"

"It looks like that could be one answer to why he's missing. But we can't say that yet."

"You mean someone has to find his . . . his remains before I'll know for sure?"

"I'm afraid that's about it."

Liza turned and walked quickly into the saloon and up the stairs toward her room.

Bryce had planned on taking Liza to dinner that night at the best cafe in Dawson City. She later sent him a curt note stating that she wasn't feeling well and asking if they could have their dinner at another time.

Slowly, ever so slowly, Bryce saw that Liza was coming to understand what he had known since the first day when he discovered the ravaged claim. Walter Livingston was dead. But Liza was right. They needed a body before they could prove it.

Chapter Fourteen

It took Spur McCoy less than five minutes to find out where the Bonanza Creek strike was and an hour to walk out there. He hadn't seen a livery in town even though he'd seen a few horses. This time of night he had no idea where to get a horse. So he hiked along the Yukon to the right creek and soon found claim stakes.

By his Waterbury it was a little past nine P.M. when he came up to Twelve Below. The stakes were marked. A 20-foot box sat alongside the stream. It was 15 feet wide here but no more than a foot deep. He saw the remains of a fire and some lumps under blankets, where he figured the miners must have collapsed after doing a ten-hour day.

It must be tempting to work 20 hours up here in this daylight. With him it would depend on how rich the works were and how much of the claim he owned.

Five hundred feet up the stream he came to claim Eleven Below and a campfire that still blazed.

"Hello, the fire on Eleven Below," McCoy called out. "All right if I come in and talk a bit?"

McCoy waited on the trail until he saw somebody come out of one of three tents pitched on the rocky shore along the far side of the stream.

A short, chubby man jolted out of the tent rubbing his eyes. He checked and saw McCoy, and waved him on in.

"Just nigh onto stripping down to get some rest," the man said with a decided English accent.

McCoy groaned. Not a chance in the world that this could be Arthur Walling. McCoy went on in and held out his hand.

"Evening, I guess it is. I'm Spur McCoy and I'm out hunting a gent but I don't think you're him."

"I'm English but not the right Englisher, right?"

"True," McCoy said. "Somebody else talked to you?"

"Superintendent Irons himself, and another gent from London but I forget his name. You'll have your hands full tracking down every Brit in the Klondike."

"I'm finding that out."

"Care for a tip of a bottle? I have some sipping whiskey that isn't half bad, really."

McCoy nodded, offered his thanks, and sat down beside the fire. It must have been well after ten by that time, yet the sun refused to get lower than a quarter of the way down to the horizon.

The Englishman came back with his jug and offered McCoy the first drink. McCoy tipped it and swallowed and grinned. He tipped the bottle again and smacked his lips.

"Now there is some good Tennessee sipping whiskey, best I ever tasted."

"Well, a gentleman who knows his liquor. I like that. I've been known to tip the bottle now and then. As you can tell, I'm English. I plain admit that I'm here on a lark, one last great adventure before I go back to the estate and learn how to run my father's businesses and settle down with the wife who has been picked out for me."

"They still do that?"

"In my social group, unfortunately, a good marriage is made for the family fortune and alliances with other fortunes, rather than for the welfare or happiness of the couple involved. All sounds stuffy to you, I'm sure. Does to me now that I see how well you Yanks do the marriage thing here. I spent a year in Seattle before I came up here."

The man was educated, alert, friendly, and a good man to talk to, and he had a great bottle of booze. McCoy tipped it again and felt the cool burning as the liquor slid down his throat. He'd spend some time talking here before heading back. The night was wasted anyway.

McCoy stared at the stream a minute, then looked up. "Oh, my name is Spur McCoy and I work with the U.S. Government. A kind of State-side Mountie."

The short Englishman with the ruddy cheeks held out his hand. "Welcome to my half a claim. The name is Henry Thorndike. Unfortunately, I'm the first son and heir to the Earl of Thorndike, now in its fourteenth generation. That's why I'm bound and determined to have one last fling at freedom and the damn open road before duty calls me home to Mother England."

They shook.

"Sorry to hear about your upcoming wedding. The lady is selected, you say?"

"Oh, quite so, since we were ten years old. An old alliance of two great families. Unfortunately, the Beckworth line has nearly died out with no sons this generation and only Elizabeth as an offspring."

Henry Thorndike brightened. "But let's talk about more interesting things. For two months I plowed around this country looking for the mother lode. Where did all of this placer gold come from anyway? At long last, and with some help from a geology friend of mine, we figured it out."

"Mother lode?" McCoy said, his interest picking up. "Yes, like up in the mountains of California around Hangtree and Sutter's Mill. So where is the mother lode and why isn't there a mine started there?"

The Englishman took a pull on the bottle and passed it back to McCoy. "Figured it had to be here. But then I got set straight. All of this gold dust had to come from somewhere upstream, right? How far upstream?"

Thorndike let out a great burp, settled beside the fire, and put on some more sticks.

"Well, see, I had this friend who had some books about this part of the world. Geology books. Turns out that the Klondike runoff here in the Yukon isn't much different from hundreds, maybe even thousands of other watersheds on the plateau in the interior of the Yukon.

"See, there wasn't enough moisture in the Yukon to support an ice age when the rest of the northland got swept by those crunching, gouging-out glaciers eons ago.

"So what you see here today is simply the effect of millions and millions of years of erosion. A geologist could trace a million years down the walls of some of the canyons and sides of the valleys around here."

Thorndike looked up at McCoy. "Hope you don't mind me jabbering away. These blokes I have working my claim are grand fellows, but two don't read, and the other four or five certainly haven't read beyond the eighth-grade level." He tilted the bottle and passed it back to McCoy.

McCoy eyed the bottle a minute. About three more shots from that marvelous juice and he wouldn't want to walk back to his boardinghouse. He snorted, took a long pull, and grinned at Thorndike.

"Mr. Thorndike, sir. You do yourself proud knowing about this land in which we now are marooned. Carry on." McCoy listened to the sound of his words and was mildly surprised. He sounded half smashed. He wasn't drunk. Sure, he'd been hitting the straight whiskey, but drunk? Hell, maybe a little.

"Damn good, this Tennessee whiskey." Thorndike paused, blinked, and then frowned. "Now, sir, we were discussing the geological formations of this area. Mile-wide valleys dug out from the plateau from nothing but erosion. No glaciers in here. Lots of bench land that must have come from some volcanic action or just a buckling of the earth's crust from some deep-down movement of the gigantic plates of the earth.

"Before long, way down in the bottoms and the

pits of the erosion there developed blue-white creeks that worked their way through moss and willows and through the gravel that looked like chalk.

"So why no mother lode of hard rock that had thick veins of fabulously wealthy gold? The damn erosion.

"Now, most of the creeks with heavy placer gold come down from a point called King Solomon's Dome. That's probably where those thick veins of gold were concentrated. But the erosion of millions of years ground down the dome and shattered the hard rocks, and spewed their gold out into the creeks.

"By now there just isn't anything left of the rich veins of gold except where it lodged in the runoff from the creeks and streams and rivers that spawned here through the ages.

"No more wasting time hunting for the mother lode, kind sir, because there just isn't one."

McCoy put the bottle down and frowned. "You said gold on the benches, way up high. How did it get there?"

"In the early days when King Solomon's Dome might have been twenty-five thousand feet tall. The erosion began and when it hit a gold vein, it shattered it and spewed it out. Then there were no giant gorges or valleys, so the gold was deposited on the benches, long before the river ditches were carved. That's why some of the richest deposits around here are going to be on those benches. Going to take a lot more work to get at the free gold down there, but it's there."

"Then why don't you go get it?"

"Money. Take a million pounds to do the job right. I'm here on a lark, not trying to gamble

away the family treasury. I'll leave the benches
up to you, old friend."

The bottle kept passing between the men. Once
McCoy felt himself slipping into sleep, and he
shook his head and sat up straighter. Somehow
the fire had gone out. It wasn't cold, but a little less warm than during the morning daylight
hours. The sun still hovered on the horizon, just
over the last ridge.

McCoy didn't even know which way it was from
him, north or south. He asked the Englisher, but
got no response. McCoy looked over and saw the
short, chubby future earl curled up on his side
snoring softly.

Time to get back to the boardinghouse. McCoy
tried to stand up, got to one knee, and fell on his
side. He laughed, tried again, and this time got to
both knees but couldn't generate enough balance
to get any higher.

McCoy snorted, dropped down to the ground,
and stretched out. He could find the way back
to Dawson much better in the morning. He set
the whiskey bottle upright out of danger of being
tipped over, then closed his eyes and slept at
once.

Morning came for McCoy with a gentle nudge
of a boot against his shoulder.

"Mr. McCoy, sir? Are you dead and gone or
would you like a spot of breakfast?"

McCoy came out of the sleep with a throbbing
head. He sat up holding his skull. "Somebody get
that steam locomotive out of my brain," McCoy
whined. He touched his head tenderly. A miner near the fire laughed and McCoy thought his
head would explode.

"Easy lads," Thorndike said to the four men sitting around the fire. "This gent has a touch of the hangover this morn, so we should be gentle and soft-spoken."

Thorndike knelt beside McCoy. "Would some coffee ease your pain?"

Instead of nodding, which he figured would tear his head right off his shoulders, McCoy uttered a whisper of "Yes."

"How about some hot cakes and syrup and some bacon strips? My men eat as well as any in Dawson. My pledge to them. If you have a dollar or two, why not spend it?"

"Sounds good," McCoy said. He stood with considerable effort, went aside and relieved himself, and came back with a strong pledge building in his resolve never to touch whiskey again as long as he lived. Vaguely he remembered making the same pledge before.

The breakfast revived him somewhat. The sun was half a day into the sky already and he still didn't know one direction from the other. Downstream, that was the way he needed to go. Downstream was always good if you were lost in the woods. Down to the Yukon, then to Dawson. Simple.

Thorndike sat down beside McCoy and worked on a second cup of coffee.

"Some talk we had last night,"

"Most of it I don't remember. Been a while since I've put away that much of the corn."

"You did fine. Most I can put under the table quicker than me, but you outdid me last night. This Englishman you're hunting. Any description?"

McCoy told him what he knew.

"I played some poker with a countryman one

night. Saw him dealing off the bottom and winning hands, so I quietly got out of the game. He fit your description. He didn't use a name. I watched him. He won six hands in a row, then got out of the game before anybody had lost too much.

"I followed him out of curiosity. He did the same thing in another saloon, only in that game he got thrown out because he won four hands in a row. No real violence. One big miner threatened to tear his arm off and beat him with it if he didn't get out of the game. The gent left grinning."

"Sounds like my man," McCoy said. "If you spot him again, leave a note for me with the New York Saloon barkeep. I'd appreciate it. Some grieving mother in London will thank you as well."

McCoy was feeling well enough to travel. He said good-bye to the short Englisher and headed down the trail. At first each step hurt his head, but after a mile things eased off and the headache vanished as his blood started pumping faster. By the time he neared the Yukon he was feeling almost normal.

The rifle shot spoiled all of that. The round thundered in the quietness of the Klondike and at once sliced through his left arm up high, nipping a half inch of flesh and tearing out through his shirt.

McCoy went to the ground in a tenth of a second, rolled behind a downed birch log, and tried to get an idea where the round had come from. To the left somewhere. Nothing but a thick stand of birch, four- to five-inch trees. That meant a shooter would have to be near the edge of them to avoid hitting a trunk or birch tree branch. McCoy lifted over the trunk and scanned the area, then dropped down. He saw nothing out of the ordinary. No prone figure with a rifle up and aiming.

He pulled off his hat and lifted it over the log down two feet from where he lay. The rifle barked again and his hat flew off the stick. He lifted up and saw the white puff of powder smoke not 20 feet down the trail and behind a pair of birch logs that looked as if they had been stacked up to make a firing position.

McCoy groaned as if he were wounded. Nothing happened. He tried a faint call. "Somebody help me!" Again nothing happened. The bushwhacker might be waiting for him to die. How could a man with a rifle miss a man's body at 20 feet?

McCoy crawled along the birch log away from the shooter. The land dropped off a little as it slanted down to the stream. Another 30 yards upstream the water made a bend and beget a thick stand of birch and willow brush. If he could get there, he could get into the thicket and circle around the man and come up behind him.

He had moved 15 feet when another round slammed into the edge of the birch log he had just left. Good, the shooter figured he was hurt and still there.

McCoy moved to the brush, then crouched and worked his way through the birch and willow. He moved like an Indian making no noise whatsoever. He had learned how to do it from the Indians during his time on the plains. He never took a step until he was sure he would make no sound.

It was damp and wet in this area, almost like a bog where the stream had overflowed in the runoff and soaked the ground.

He paused and figured out where he was. Halfway there. The brush thinned a little, but he couldn't see anyone by the trail and the piled-up logs. Another 30 feet.

It took him ten minutes to make the distance. In that time the shooter below had fired once more. McCoy eased to a standing position behind a foot-thick birch and peered around it. There 40 feet below and slightly to the right lay a form behind the two birch trunks that had been piled up. The bushwhacker had a rifle and watched the place where he thought his target must be.

McCoy had ten feet of cover. Then little lay between him and the shooter but thin brush. He'd be in the open for the last 30 feet. No sense playing it safe. He'd get to the edge of his cover and then take the last 30 feet in a rush lasting a second and a half. Not time enough for the gunman to reverse the aim of the rifle.

McCoy worked downslope the ten feet, then pulled the derringer from his underarm holster, cocked it, and charged.

He took three steps before the man below heard him. A startled, bearded face turned and blood-shot eyes widened as he saw the victim blasting through the brush toward him.

The man had only time to swing the rifle halfway around before McCoy dove at him from six feet away and four feet up the slope. He crashed into the bushwhacker just as he started to sit up. The satisfying jolt as he hit the man drove the bushwhacker back to the ground and mashed him into the rocky old channel of the stream.

McCoy blasted his right fist into the shooter's jaw, then powered his left arm around his throat from behind in a choke hold and tightened the grip until the man bellowed.

"I should break your damn neck right here!" McCoy barked.

He eased off on the choke hold, and just as the man turned toward him, McCoy slammed the .45-caliber derringer down across the side of his head, blasting him into unconsciousness.

Spur McCoy sat back breathing hard. He examined his left arm and saw that the bleeding had stopped. It wasn't much of a gunshot wound, but was the kind that would leave a nasty scar unless it had some cleaning and care.

He examined the shooter's pockets and found six dollars U.S., a letter from home, eight more rounds for the .30-caliber rifle, and some spare change. McCoy stripped the laces out of one of the gunman's boots and tied his hands behind his back. Then he used the man's hat and brought a hat full of ice-cold water from the stream and sloshed it in the gunman's face.

By the time McCoy retrieved his black flat-crowned hat with the bullet hole in it, the gunman was conscious.

"Why the hell you tie me up?" he shouted.

McCoy grabbed him by the throat and pressed his thumbs on his windpipe. "Why the hell you try to kill me?"

"Why? Hell, Jordan, you stole my claim. Everybody knows it. Cheated me out of it."

McCoy slapped the man's face gently one way, then the other. "You asshole, look at me. I'm not Jordan. You almost killed the wrong man. How could you miss a man walking along the trail with a rifle at twenty feet?"

"Miss? I hit you."

"Clipped a half inch of skin on my arm."

The man began to sob. "Wanted to miss. I ain't never killed nobody before. I guess I wanted to miss. Jordan cheated me. I got no claim, no money, no job. I don't even have enough cash to buy a ticket back to the outside."

"You still got your half ton of food. Sell it. Maybe you won't have to. I'll turn you in to Superintendent Irons. You'll get a blue ticket down the river on the next boat. Come on, get on your feet. You and me have a date with the Mounties, and they won't be happy about you trying to kill me."

It took them two hours to hike back to Dawson. McCoy had put away his derringer and carried the rifle. The superintendent wasn't there, but a corporal took the complaint, impounded the rifle, and verified the bullet wound. McCoy signed the statement about the ambush, the place, the time, the day, and the extent of the wound.

The corporal read it over, nodded, and led the shooter to one of the jail's two cells. Two other men huddled there awaiting shipment back down the river. The boat was scheduled to leave that evening about six.

McCoy asked about a doctor.

"No real doctor has set up a practice. But old Doc Willoughby down about half a block can take care of that little nick. He's a barber but does a fine job on small wounds and he don't charge much."

McCoy had the barber do the work on his arm. The man applied some disinfectant to wash it out. The liquid made the wound hurt more than it had when he was shot. Then some salve and a stout bandage around the arm finished the job.

"Five dollars," the barber said. McCoy paid him,

made a note for his expense account, and headed for a good meal. He was starved and he had no idea what time it was. The crazy sun was at about 9:30 in the morning if he were in Wyoming. More likely it was well past noon. McCoy shook his head. He'd never get used to all of this daylight. Winter here must be miserable with only two hours of anything resembling daylight out of 24.

Chapter Fifteen

The second day after he started his workers on what he called Splinter Fourteen Above on the Willow Creek strike, Bryce walked out to the site. It was less than a mile from town and there was a good trail much used.

He found his two men on hands and knees washing out a pan of gravel beside the small stream. He came up to them and when they saw him they both screeched at once.

"Mr. Jeferies, you got to look at this!" one shouted.

"I ain't never seen nothing like it before!" the second one said.

Bryce looked in the pan they were washing and saw that they were almost done. In the bottom was not a trace, not an arc, but a *layer* of gold dust and small granules of pure gold.

"I'd say this here is at least a four-dollar pan of

gold, Mr. Jeferies. I think we got ourselves a good one here!"

They had just finished the 20-foot-long sluice box, and now they set it in Willow Creek where they could control the flow of water through it with a simple lift gate. Then Bryce shoveled in three scoops full of sand and light gravel and they let the water from the stream start the process of washing away the sand and gravel and leaving the gold and the inevitable heavy black sand.

It took nearly 15 minutes to wash down the first three shovelsful of sand. Then they looked at the baffles along the length of the box.

"Glory be!" the taller miner said. Bryce looked at the glittering gold dust and an occasional small nugget behind the baffles and shouted in wonder.

He figured there was more than an ounce there just waiting to be picked up and put in a poke. He checked the stream again. He had almost 85 feet of it, and a large wedge of the shoreline with a flat area a hundred feet wide that ran up to the ridge to the right when facing upstream.

"Take up the gold," Bryce ordered. "No sense the gate coming open and all that gold get washed down into the creek again." He'd seen it happen more than once.

As he stood there, his mind whirled with plans. He'd hire four more men this afternoon. There was room for two sluice boxes to work, and the second two men he'd put to digging gopher holes and hunting for an old streambed. There could be pay-gold all the way to the side of the ravine slope.

Two days later, Bryan hired four more men when they found two gopher holes with heavy gold dust in them. The pay dirt was only four feet down and they trenched rather than tunneled. He built another sluice box to work the gopher hole sand and gravel.

Within two weeks, Bryce had taken out more than $20,000 worth of gold from his splinter claim that he'd paid $500 for. He banked the money and bought his second store, one that specialized in men's working clothes. He learned a lot about clothes and boots in a hurry and ordered more from Vancouver.

That night he went to see Liza perform for the first time in nearly a week. She was on stage most of the time, and sang four numbers that they had built into a little skit. The show was sharper, funnier, more entertaining, more professional.

He sent a note back after the first performance and she came out at once to see him.

"I've missed you. I hear your splinter is a bonanza."

He had a cold sarsaparilla ready for her and she sipped at it and watched him.

"Yes, the claim is paying off handsomely. Thirty-Seven Above is doing well too. We just passed the four-thousand-dollar mark for profit. Your half is in the bank under your name as you suggested."

"Bryce, it's good to see you. I've missed our nightly talks."

"Me too, but I've been dead tired when I get home at night. I'm out at the claim every day now. Too much at stake to let someone else take responsibility. Oh, I saw your half-page ad in the *Klondike Nugget* asking for anyone who knew Walter. Did you get any response?"

Liza shook her head. "Nothing that amounted to anything. One man came and lied to me. I had Josh throw him out. Two men said they had talked to Walter at Thirty-Seven Above, but hadn't seen him since about a month after the first boat left downriver this spring."

"It's not looking good, Liza. You have to remember that."

She nodded, her lower lip quivering a moment; then she overcame the emotion and looked up at him. "Sounds like your goal of becoming filthy rich is fast coming true. I hear that you've bought six more claims from men who were sick of the life and heading home."

"Six isn't quite right. Actually, I have nine now that I'm working. Some on shares, some with hired men. It's keeping me hopping. I'm looking for one more like the splinter."

"How did you like the show?"

"A fine show. As good as many that I've seen in Seattle. It has that professional touch now, like the dancers really know what they're doing."

"Thank you. I'm never sure if anyone notices. We're working hard on the shows. Josh used to be a song and dance man in Chicago and he's teaching us in classes almost every day."

"One thing, at the end where you hold out your skirt and the men throw in coins and gold pokes. How did that happen?"

Liza laughed and covered her face with both hands. "Isn't that wicked of me? I started doing it in Toronto. Last week somebody tossed a coin at me and I tried to catch it and missed. When the next one came I held out my skirt and caught it.

"That brought a surge of cheers and clapping because when I do that I expose my legs to just over my knees. The miners liked that and showered me with coins and half-filled gold pokes. When I counted the coins and dust at the end of the night, I had over fifteen dollars! I figured that it was a fine finale and I've been doing it now for a week."

Bryce laughed. "Here I thought I was the sharp businessman. You've outdone me again." He sipped at his coffee and she finished the soft drink.

"Oh, did I mention that Josh proposed to me again? He wants to quit this town while prices are high and move to Chicago. He says he can make me a star there as well."

"Propose? Hey, I thought we had an agreement. The time when you start taking proposals seriously, I get to be the first one in line. That's what I've always thought whether I've said it or not."

Liza blinked back sudden tears of joy. "Bryce, that's so sweet! Of course I'm still promised to Walter and will be until we find him . . . one way or the other." She brushed away the wetness. "But I do promise not to accept any man's proposal until I talk with you. Fair enough?"

He caught one of her hands and kissed the back of it; then she looked at the big Seth Thomas clock and told him she had to go change her costume. He stood as she left, then slouched in his chair.

Josh Pointer? That old devil. He was old enough

to be her father. He must be well over 40! She wouldn't take Josh seriously, would she? He frowned. Maybe she would. He could make her into a big star in any town on the continent. He would have to watch that Josh Pointer.

Liza sat on her bed between the second and third shows that night and took stock. She had checked with the bank, and indeed there was a balance of over $2,200 in her gold mine account. She had been given a raise to $15 a day at the New York Theatre. That was a scandalous $90 a week. Back in Toronto she knew that half of the workingmen would slave for three months to take home $90 in cash.

Her private bank account had almost a thousand dollars in it. She spent little of her pay. These last few days she had been making another eight to $15 a night in tips thrown into her skirt. Now she did pay more attention to what she wore under her skirt. Sometimes only long stockings and small tight bloomers up high. Sometimes shocking pink bloomers that came almost to her ankles, which always drew a roar of approval from the miners.

She was doing well, but how long would it last? There seemed to be no letup of the stream of men coming into town. Most of them were far too late to find any claims worth working. Many of the men walked the streets for a month, never even tried to find a claim, and wound up taking the next steamer out for St. Michael on their homeward journey. They had "done" the Klondike; they had been in on the thrill of a gold strike without ever having panned an ounce of gold.

The town still had about 30,000 people, with

nearly the same numbers coming in as left each week.

Still, it couldn't go on forever. Bryce figured it would be all over in another year. It was true that a lasting city here would need to be based on what the men called deep-tunnel mines. Hard-rock mines that bored into the heart of a mountain somewhere following seams of gold quartz.

Everyone said that there was no mother lode here. So was Bryce right? Would it all be over quickly? Should she stay the winter? Winters were brutal here, everyone said. There was little money to be made since the streams were frozen solid and there was no way to wash out the gold dust.

Josh came around just before the show was to start and introduced a new girl. One of the regular dancers had had to rush home to Portland to tend to her sick mother. The new girl had been in a revue in the other variety hall in town and Josh had talked her into working for him with better wages.

"Hi, I'm Millie. You're Liza. I've caught your act from time to time. You're good and you sing like a happy little robin."

"Thanks, Millie. Welcome to the zoo; we perform regularly. Tomorrow we'll work you into the numbers. It might take you a couple of days to catch on to the steps and the moves."

Millie was short and chunky, but she had a large bosom and the men liked that. She had worked as a dancer and part-time waitress. That was one step up from working in "Lousetown" just across the river. Over there the whores grouped in houses and worked the miners in shifts. At the other saloon, Millie had also been a waitress and was expected to drink with the customers and take them upstairs to bed if they wanted to. She welcomed this step up in her life.

Millie had bright red hair, which she kept short because it was in such tight rings and curls that it was nearly impossible to comb out. She chattered like a talking machine, but now she was quiet, learning the girls' names and probably wondering if she could fit into the group.

That night a note came from downstairs. It was much the same as before. It said: "Hi, Vancouver Blue Bird. Glad you're still singing. I'd like to meet you if you have a minute between shows."

There was still time. She took the note and followed the waiter down the steps.

"Did he pay you to bring me the note?" Liza asked.

"Sure, a dollar. I think this one has lots of money."

"That would be a switch," Liza said.

The waiter led her to a table for two near the edge of the stage. These tables were reserved for big spenders. She saw a man sitting there in his late twenties. He wore a red and black checkered vest, a fine-cut black suit, and a heavy gold chain from vest pocket to pocket.

He saw her coming and stood. When she stopped near his table, he bowed. "Welcome, Miss Liza. Let me introduce myself. I'm Arthur Hallifax, gentleman about town. I'm one of your biggest fans. It's a great honor for me to meet you."

His slight English accent came through and she wasn't surprised. She had heard about "Lord

Hallifax" as some of the men called him. He was a gambler, and a good one. She'd heard he was not above cheating when he could get away with it. He had two ice-cold sarsaparillas waiting for her.

Liza looked at the clock. She still had 15 minutes.

"How do you do, Lord Hallifax. It's good to see who's been so persistent with the notes. I've heard a lot about your gambling exploits. Are the cards running against you and you're taking off the night to change your luck?"

"Not at all, Miss Liza. The fact is I'm on a run of good luck. I thought meeting you might encourage Lady Luck herself to stay with me. Your show is a lot different from the ones I saw in Vancouver. You've developed your talent as a singer and dancer nicely."

"Well, sir, I thank you. You probably know I'm up here looking for my husband, Walter Livingston."

He nodded. "I've heard. I thought perhaps I could gain favor with you by finding the young man, but he doesn't seem to be anywhere around."

Liza frowned. "That's not the answer I want to hear. How long have you been in town?"

"Since the middle of June, actually. I was on the first boat out of St. Michael. In fact, I saw you on that boat."

She sipped her soft drink and he sipped a whiskey. They looked at each other. There didn't seem to be much else to say.

"Well, I have to get back and change. We're on again soon. I thank you for being so persistent.

I'm glad I finally met you, and may Lady Luck sit on your shoulder for the rest of your stay in Dawson."

Liza stood, and Hallifax lifted off the chair smoothly and smiled.

"Thank you, Miss Liza. I'll enjoy your singing and dancing even more now. Perhaps one of these evenings I could escort you to the best restaurant in town."

Liza grinned. "You mean the Sourdough Hash-house, or the Klondike Hotel dining room. About the only two places that come anywhere near to being restaurants. We'll see. I do keep busy."

"Perhaps this Sunday evening, when you're off work?"

"I can't say for sure right now, Mr. Hallifax. Thanks for the drink." She turned and hurried to the upstairs door and vanished from his sight.

Hallifax sat down and thought about her. She would be a handful, but he could control her. She was probably making as much with her dancing as he was with cards. The gambling had taken a turn for the worse. Not even some mild cheating had kept him even. Some men wouldn't play with him anymore.

He was in the middle of a streak of bad luck with the cards, but he wasn't going to try the dice games that were flourishing. With cards there was at least a chance.

How could he contrive to meet her again, to wine and dine her? He needed contact with her so she could learn about his charms, his smooth way with a lady. Yes, she needed to know because Arthur Hallifax had decided. It would be a good move to marry the songbird; then he could help

shape her career. Take her back to Vancouver,
then to Toronto and Quebec, where some real
money might be made.

He could even book her in Chicago, perhaps
New York. His fantasy soared as he had another
whiskey. Then he fell into a small-change poker
game just to keep his hand in. His luck hadn't
changed. He lost eight hands in a row, but dropped only three dollars. It was enough for the night.
As he walked back toward his boardinghouse, he
couldn't get the sweet young songbird out of his
thoughts. There must be some way he could use
her to his own advantage. But just what was it?

As soon as Arthur Hallifax closed the door at
his boardinghouse, a man who had been following him turned and headed back to the nearest
saloon for a drink and some thoughts. His name
was James White-Smith and he had come this far
tracking the devious murderer Arthur Walling,
who had killed his brother.

White-Smith had turned in a warrant for the
man's arrest to Superintendent Irons, but so far
he'd had little luck in finding him. Then this
week he had tracked down another man with
an English accent and found him to be jokingly
called Lord Hallifax.

The man called himself Arthur Hallifax. The
Arthur was the same. White-Smith had come to
realize that Arthur Walling had left his passenger
ship at Halifax instead of his stated destination. It
had taken White-Smith a week to figure that out;
then he'd tracked him at last to Vancouver. He'd
missed him there by a month, and then got the
next boat heading north the way the man now
known as Arthur Hallifax had.

The man he had been following had no beard,

and his hair was much shorter than it had been in England, but he was certain this was the same man. Only how could he prove it?

Trick Walling into identifying himself? How? Perhaps with a letter containing a check for him from England. No, he probably already received regular stipends from his father, the duke. A poker game? No, he would never slip and answer to Walling.

A confrontation? Somehow it seemed the only way. He would simply walk up to Walling in a public place with many men and an RCMP or two around and accuse him of being Arthur Walling. He saw little he could lose.

White-Smith eased out of the saloon and went back to watch Walling/Hallifax's room in the boardinghouse. The man had one all to himself. The light was still on. Reading? Perhaps sharpening his tricks at cheating with cards?

Tomorrow, it would have to come tomorrow. Hallifax had been playing poker in a small place called the Klondike Gold Rush Saloon. White-Smith would take an RCMP man with him and confront the killer there. He would swear under oath that this man was Walling, and the Mounties would be honor-bound to arrest him. Then with Walling in irons, he would return to England for a speedy trial and a glorious hanging.

Only then could the White-Smith family be at peace. His sister had grown pregnant with no chance of a husband, and had been shipped off to a distant cousin in Ireland to have the bastard child. It had been put up with a poor family, which had been compensated for the child's care. Now his sister was home, acting like an old woman, with absolutely no prospects for a respectable marriage.

Tomorrow Arthur Walling/Hallifax would come to terms with his dastardly crimes. Tomorrow he would start the trip back to England and to his own hanging!

Chapter Sixteen

Spur McCoy decided he would survey the smaller gambling houses. There were more than a dozen. Four new ones had sprouted in the past week. He went into the Klondike Strike Saloon and looked around.

It had about 20 tables, most set up for poker. The only way you could play here was with chips. You bought the chips from the cashier, who took ten percent off the top. You got nine dollars worth of chips for a ten-dollar bill.

McCoy invested a 20-dollar gold piece and held his chips as he watched one game, then another. He heard a broad English accent and moved toward that table.

Although it wasn't ten o'clock in the morning yet, the Englishman was half drunk. He might have still been drunk from the night before. Most of these gaming houses were open 24 hours a day.

The game was no limit, but most of the bets were a dollar or less. McCoy watched the Englishman a moment. He was big enough, but had dark hair, though any smart criminal would dye his hair. He could be Arthur Walling. Only one way to find out. McCoy saw an empty chair and hefted it.

"Room for new money?" he asked as one man shuffled the cards.

"Damn right!" the Englishman said. The others nodded, so McCoy sat down and put his chips in front of him.

"Any special rules?" McCoy asked.

"Damn right!" The Englishman said. "No limit, table stakes, no dumb wild cards."

McCoy nodded and put a 50-cent chip into the pot. The dealer included him on the deal.

It was fair poker. McCoy had learned how to play money/gambling poker from a master of the craft on a Mississippi riverboat. He'd also learned how to cheat and how to spot cheaters. This dealer didn't use the bottom of the deck. It looked like a straight game.

McCoy won the first pot with a pair of aces on five-card draw, then lost four hands in a row. The men around the table relaxed. McCoy played his poker automatically, mostly watching the Englishman. He could be the one.

"You're from England?" he asked the tall man with the dark hair and no beard.

"'Tis a fact, sir," he said. "Outside of London a ways. I like it here better. More money in poker." He laughed, and McCoy couldn't read him.

The Secret Service agent forgot the chase for a while and concentrated on his cards. He didn't have a good hand but it looked good for what showed on the table. It was five-card stud and he showed a pair of kings. He was high man. McCoy bet two dollars and three men dropped out. The Englishman scowled, stared at McCoy's poker face, and met the bet and raised him a dollar. McCoy saw the dollar and raised five.

The Englishman scowled, mumbled something to himself, and threw in his hand. So the Englisher could be bluffed. McCoy figured the odds were that the other man must have had three of a kind, probably lower than the kings. He'd caved in.

McCoy lost the next hand, won the next two, and three men dropped out of the game. Now there were only three men sitting at the table.

The Englishman stared at McCoy.

"You think you're hot shit, don't you?"

"I play the cards I'm dealt. Are you in this pot or out?"

The other two anted in their chips.

"Seven-card stud," McCoy called, and dealt two cards down and one up for each man, then paused for the high man to bet. The redheaded miner threw in a dollar for his ten of spades and both the others met the bet.

On the next card the miner pulled a four of diamonds, the Englishman drew a king of hearts to go with his eight of clubs, and McCoy caught an ace of diamonds to go with his seven of hearts showing.

McCoy's ace was high. Nothing showed on the table. But McCoy had two pair, aces and sevens. The miner showed a ten and a four and the Englisher a king and an eight.

"Ace bets," the Englishman said. He scowled. "Hey, hot hand, you want to make a side bet on this game, say, fifty dollars cash?"

"A side bet?"

"Sure, nobody's showing anything on the up cards, no advantage. Luck of the cards. Only you lay the deck on the table and deal that way."

McCoy took two 20-dollar gold pieces from his pocket and a 10-dollar greenback from his purse and laid them on the table.

The Englisher put down five ten-dollar Canadian paper bills.

"Deal," the Englishman said.

McCoy developed a new interest in the game. He put the deck of cards flat on the table. This prevented any bottom-dealing and wasn't done often, but it happened.

McCoy laid out a ten of clubs to the miner.

"Pair of tens for the gent," McCoy said. He gave the Englishman an eight of spades. "Pair of eights for the visitor from England." His own card was a three of spades. "No help with the three. Pair of tens bets."

The miner grinned. He had another ten down, McCoy figured. He threw in a five-dollar bill. The Englishman stared at the miner, snorted, and met the bet. McCoy hesitated as if to throw in his hand, shrugged, and added a five-dollar chip to the pile.

McCoy stared at the hands again. Three tens would beat his hand. He turned up the next round of cards.

"Seven of diamonds, no help. Eight of hearts, three of a kind for our English friend. For me a three of clubs, no help. The eights bets."

The Englishman pushed $20 worth of chips into the pot. "Twenty," he said.

McCoy tried to figure the odds. He needed an

ace or a seven or a three to beat three of a kind. He figured the miner had three tens, so maybe the other hand had a full house, eights over something. His aces over sevens would beat kings over eights. Even another seven would give him a full house, or another three. So he had five chances to get a winning card on the next draw. Five out of 34 cards. Not the greatest odds. McCoy shrugged and added $20 of chips to the pot.

The miner squirmed. He must be trying to figure the Englisher for a bluff or a fourth eight or a full house. If it was a bluff he would win with three tens, but what about the dealer? The miner swore softly and folded his hand.

McCoy nodded at the cards face-down in the pot and dealt one card face-down to the three eights. He took one face-down and put it with the other two face-down cards and shuffled them before he peeked. He saw his ace of hearts. He took one off the bottom and put it on top of the three several times and looked again. He found an ace of clubs. He'd hit it! Full house aces over sevens.

"Now the real betting begins," the Englisher said.

McCoy decided to try dropping the name now and see if it had any reaction on the foreigner.

"Just make it easy on yourself, Walling."

The Englishman lifted his brows, then stared at McCoy. "You used some name. What name was that?"

"Walling. Thought somebody told me your name was Arthur Walling."

"Not me, son. I got a name, just don't use it much. It sure as hell ain't Walling. There's a Duke of Walling near my hometown out of London."

McCoy shrugged. "I must be mistaken. You betting?"

"Right you are, lad." He counted his chips, eyed McCoy's stack. "Twenty-five dollars. You can meet that."

McCoy stared at the hand. Three eights and a king showing. If the Englishman had three kings and two eights he still would lose. No way he could win unless he had another eight under. Not good odds.

McCoy counted out his 25 dollars and added them to the pot.

"Call, Englisher. What have you got?"

The other man turned over his cards one at a time. The last one was the counter, a king of spades. He had a full house, eights over his pair of kings.

The Englishman watched McCoy's face. It showed nothing. He reached for the pot.

"Just a minute," McCoy said. He turned over his seven of clubs, then tipped over the two aces.

"Full house, aces over sevens, beats your eights over kings."

"Be damned!"

McCoy pulled in the pot, then looked at the Englishman. "I believe this side bet of fifty dollars is mine as well." He pulled the money toward him.

"Be damned!" the Englishman said again. Then he stood and left the table.

The miner sat there shaking his head. "Yeah, at least I didn't waste that final twenty dollars. You both had me beat on the board. I kept hoping for another ten."

McCoy pocketed the real money, and took his chips over to the cashier to settle up. There was no fee for cashing in. The house made its money with its own dealers and with the ten-percent surcharge.

Outside the saloon, McCoy grinned. He hadn't found Walling, but he had eliminated another Englishman. That one had been a real possibility. He touched his wallet. He had also come out ahead by a little over a hundred dollars on the poker game.

McCoy walked up the street feeling the wild surging smell of the Yukon. It had an untamed, natural scent that spoke of trees and water, of frozen ground, of mud and rain and the open spaces.

Two men bumped into him as he stood in front of an outfitting store and he chuckled at himself. Lots of open spaces but not on the boardwalk on Front Street.

Francine. He had promised to come back to her last night. He should make amends or she might pitch him into the street. He was early for supper. His mood was light and he felt fine, even though he had missed Walling again. He would have to decide soon if this was a wasted effort. If he figured it was, then he would have to pack up his bag and board a steamer down the Yukon. The Secret Service would have to take its losses on the case and give up, turning it all over to the Mounties.

He was still smiling over the money he had won in the poker game when he walked into the entry way of the boardinghouse. The dining room door opened abruptly and Francine stood there waiting for him. She had one fist on her hip and a serious frown that should have warned him.

"A little late, aren't you, Mr. McCoy?"

He nodded. "That I am, kind lady. I've been on an all-night wild-goose chase up a creek hunting an Englishman who turned out to be pleasant, short and fat and not at all the one I'm looking for. In any case I apologize."

Her frown remained in place. She watched him and slowly her frown eased a little. She crooked a finger at him. He followed her into the dinning room, through it to the short hall, and then into her sitting room. Francine closed the door and stared at him.

"I was counting on being with you last night. I waited and waited."

"I'm sorry. I was in the middle of some creek-bottom chatting with this Englishman; then he brought out a bottle of some of the best Tennessee sipping whiskey that I've ever tasted . . ."

He stopped. Wrong tactic. He let both hands fall to his sides. "You're right, I should have told you before I charged off that way. But I am here now and there's another two hours before supper."

"Mr. McCoy, you do surprise me." Her frown eased a little more and her fist loosened and came off her hip. He took three steps toward her and Francine didn't move. McCoy bent in and kissed her lips gently, his mouth so soft on hers that she must have barely felt it.

"Mmmmmmmmm," she said.

He leaned closer, his arms around her and his lips hard on hers this time. Her eyes closed, and she let out a soft sigh and pressed hard against him. When the kiss ended, he held her a moment before her eyes opened.

"Oh, yes, Mr. McCoy, now that is more how a

lady likes to be apologized to. Can you say you're sorry again?"

He closed his hand around one of her breasts before he kissed her this time, massaging the orb, bringing a dozen soft biting kisses to her lips and cheeks and eyes as he petted her.

She watched him this time with hooded eyes and at last nodded.

"Yes, Mr. McCoy, I do believe that we have time for some serious considerations in my bedroom. Do you know the way?"

He did.

An hour later they lay on her bed resting. Her long brown hair flowed over her bare breasts creating a peek-a-boo situation with her firm hand-sized breasts and their bright pink nipples.

"Again," she said. "You know that once is never enough." She rolled over on top of him, her naked form pressing hard against him. "This time I want to do something different, something . . . you know, wild and strange and unusual."

McCoy feigned surprise. "What? I'm not that kind of a man. I don't do strange things."

She stared at him and they both laughed.

"Well, not really strange things. Any ideas?"

"From me? I'm all sweetness and innocence, I've never—"

He shushed her with a finger across her lips.

"If it's that wild, you'll have to seduce me."

Francine grinned. "I've had plenty of experience being seduced by experts." She laughed. "I even have an idea, that is, when I get you properly in the mood." She moved upward and slipped one breast over his mouth.

"Open up and have a few bites like a good boy," Francine said. As she fed a breast into his mouth, one hand found his crotch and worked on his flaccid member. It didn't take her long to bring him to life.

"Well now, that's better. Get a little life in the old prick yet, eh?"

McCoy lay there enjoying the situation. "You said you had an idea."

"True, but you need to get me sufficiently warmed up." She still lay over him, and now moved up until her muff of brown hair poised over his face. "Can you think of anything to lick a little to get me excited?"

Spur McCoy pulled her up more and spread her legs over him, then licked up the inner side of her thighs until she shivered. He licked both sides, then brushed across her moist, juicy outer lips and she jolted downward, almost climaxing. He licked her half a dozen times and she squealed. She moved off him and stayed on her hands and knees. She looked at him over her shoulder.

"Just pretend you're a big dog and take your pick of holes back there."

McCoy went to his knees behind her and parted her soft cheeks. Pink lips winked at him and he moved forward, positioned himself just right, and then edged into her channel.

Francine pushed back against him until he was firmly in place. She looked back at him again. "Now lean forward and grab my jugs up here and hang on. This should be a great ride."

McCoy leaned forward on her back, caught her hanging breasts, and began a slow stroke which she met with a backward thrust.

"Oh, damn! That angle sets me on fire, McCoy! I don't know how much of this I can take. Jeeeeeeeeeeeeeezzzzzz, but that is wild. Oh, damn, here I come already!" She wailed, and her whole body shook like a gopher caught by a dog. She bleated as series after series of spasms tore through her, bringing gasps and sobs and wails of delight from her.

"Oh, yes, oh, yes, oh, yes. Oh, God, so good! Don't ever stop. Keep poking me all afternoon and all night! Don't ever stop."

McCoy eased off on his rhythm, slowing it to control his own time and waiting until she had rattled and moaned and wailed for the last time. Then he let his hands come off her breasts, brought them back to her hips and grabbed at her waist, and pounded forward and pulled her back toward him at the same time.

"Jeeeeeeeeeezzzzzzzzzz, you're poking a hole right through my little cunnie. You're hitting something in there deep. Oh, damn!"

Another dozen strokes and McCoy climaxed in two powerful thrusts and was through. He lifted his brows. Each time had been different lately. Some more powerful and longer than others.

He pushed her forward so she lay on her stomach and he remained deep inside.

"Different," Francine said. "Different with you laying on top of me back there. Nice, but strange too. Not really strange, but a little . . . unusual."

She paused, tried to turn her head to see him. "McCoy, you all right? You didn't go and pass out on me, did you? McCoy, answer me, damn you."

McCoy grinned and moaned. "I'm almost alive. You're so damn sexy you damn near killed me. Hell, I'm not sixteen anymore. I need some recuperation time."

"At least you're alive. What the hell do we do now?"

McCoy rolled away from her and she turned and snuggled up against him.

"McCoy, why don't you just stay here and fuck me every night and play poker all day. Be a good life for you. I'll take care of all your little needs. Hell, I'm making a ton of money here. Salting away some in the bank. When this gold rush peters out we can go down to Vancouver or Seattle or Portland, hell, even San Francisco."

McCoy sat up and looked down at her. "Pretty lady, great lady between the sheets, I just can't do that. I have a job. I work for a living. I travel a lot. I told you I was looking for a business, but actually I'm a lawman. I work with the United States government. A kind of U.S. Mountie. Sorry, I just can't be tied down to one place."

"Oh, shit!"

McCoy grinned. "True, that's about the size of it. Now, how much time do we have before supper? Somehow I've worked up myself one giant hungry feeling."

Chapter Seventeen

James White-Smith arose early the next morning, went to the RCMP office, and talked with Superintendent Irons about his find.

"I'm dead sure he's the man. All we need is one admission that he is Arthur Walling, and you can serve him with the warrant."

"I know my business, Mr. White-Smith. I'll have a man following you without his uniform. When you confront this suspected killer, my Mountie will be within earshot. I've run down twenty suspects like this myself. Without finding this man. I hope you don't have any high expectations of success."

"I expect him to break down and confess on the spot. He's a sniveling coward and won't be able to stand the truth thrown in his face."

When White-Smith left the office, a man in civvies followed him. It took two hours for

White-Smith to find the man he knew had to be Walling/Hallifax. He was not at his usual gambling spot. He was at a new one and this time not dressed well, but looking a bit seedy to put off any player who thought he might be a professional gambler.

White-Smith let the poker hand end, then approached the man from the back. He tapped him on the shoulder, and when Walling/Hallifax turned, James White-Smith spoke.

"Arthur Walling-Hallifax, I'm here from England to arrest you for the murder of my brother."

Hallifax snorted and turned back to the game. White-Smith had figured on such a move, and jerked the back of the chair to the rear so forcefully that it slipped away from Hallifax and he tumbled to the floor.

Hallifax came up from the floor glowering. "What are you doing? Are you crazy? My name is Hallifax, Arthur Hallifax, and I come from Toronto. Get away from me or I'll call a Mountie and have you jailed."

"Arthur Walling, you're the one who will be jailed. You bedded my sister and ruined her, then you killed my brother when he challenged you. Then you ran from England hiding on a boat. Now I've found you and you're going back to England to stand trial."

Hallifax snorted and pointed his finger at his accuser. "One shred of proof. You don't have one picture, one witness, one tiny bit of proof. I could call you Lord Chamberlain just as easily and how would you prove that you are not he? Now get out of here you low-life rabble. I'm in the middle of a game with these gentlemen who have the good manners to work for a living instead of traipsing around the globe accusing men of crimes they haven't committed. Now be off!"

"You are Arthur Walling and I can prove it. You have a birthmark on your right hip." It was the one clinching bit of proof he had been treasuring for so long.

A crowd had gathered, and this brought a hum of comments from the men.

"Idiot!" Walling bellowed. "If I do, you could have seen it at the baths. No proof at all. Now away with you, I have important business with these gentlemen who don't like to be kept waiting."

"I can prove it's you because you get a check each month from London from the Earl of Walling."

"You have one of these checks?"

"Well, no . . ."

"Then you have no proof at all." He looked at the man who had edged up into the crowd. "There, Mountie Crandall, get this lying scoundrel away from me before I resort to violence. He's a fraud and a liar. I demand that you take him in hand."

Mountie Crandall shrugged. "Just talk is all I hear. Talk is legal. But I don't want to see any blows exchanged."

Hallifax waved at White-Smith as he would an unruly boy. "Now get away from me or the Mountie will arrest you." He turned his back on his accuser and sat down at the table.

"Let's see, gentlemen. Whose deal was it before that lout broke up our game?"

White-Smith scowled and marched out of the saloon. Walling had not cracked, had not come undone the way he'd hoped. Now White-Smith didn't know what to do. He would try for some firm evidence, but he had no idea what it might be. If he had a pistol he could take matters into his own hands some twilight night.

Only there was no darkness. It was summer now in the Klondike and the days had stretched out to give 22 hours of bright sunshine, and two hours of faded gloom that passed for night. You could still read a newspaper outside at midnight. There would be no darkness to cover a murder. He would have to plan it carefully. A club, that would be his best weapon. He strode down the street deep in thought.

Hallifax had quit the game as soon as White-Smith left the saloon. He hurried and caught sight of him, then followed his accuser to a tent where he evidently had rented a cot. Fixing the spot firmly in mind, Hallifax went into another saloon for a morning drink and pondered exactly how he would do it.

White-Smith had to die, there was no other way. Hallifax never questioned that decision. It had to be today before he caused any more trouble. He thought about it for an hour, then hurried to his room and wrote a note and sealed it in an envelope. On the outside he wrote White-Smith's last name and left the message at the big tent that was the office for the two dozen smaller ones that formed the "hotel." The clerk there said he'd be sure that it was delivered in hand.

Hallifax made a few preparations, then borrowed a hatchet from his boardinghouse woodpile, slid it inside his shirt, and walked out of Dawson along the Yukon to a shipwreck. The old steamer had gone aground some years before the gold strike, and now lay in the shallows rotting and sinking a little lower each year.

Near shore there was a fine stand of birch trees, and Hallifax found a spot where he could see the trail from town and settled down against a tree to wait. The hatchet was new and sharp with a 12-inch handle. It would do just fine. He had no way of knowing when White-Smith might go back to his tent and find the message.

Hallifax dozed in the warm weather. Some said it would hit nearly ninety degrees that day. The mud of the street had been long ago packed into a thousand dry, rutted boot prints, and the water at the edge of the river had even receded a little. There would be another two months of summer before fall came and then the sharp chill of an early winter. Hallifax would be gone down the river well before the first snowfall.

He came alert as two miners walked by on their way to town. Hallifax was 100 feet off the trail and well concealed. He checked down the track that extended a half mile into town and saw a figure approaching. He wasn't sure who it was, but the man didn't have a sack of supplies over his shoulder so it could be the vicar's son, James White-Smith.

Ten minutes later he was sure. James stopped on the trail and looked at the patch of birch trees. Then he consulted a paper he carried and turned into the woods.

There was no need for talk with his accuser. He had to make sure there was no chance for an attack by White-Smith. Just a quick blow to the back of the head and it would be over. He felt nothing, no excitement, no nervous energy, no satisfaction. Before in England he had killed a man in the heat of a fight. Now he was lying in wait and he felt no remorse, no fear, no anger, only the cold knowledge that this man must die.

Hallifax waited for the victim to approach. He hid behind a pair of foot-thick, sturdy birches and tossed his handkerchief onto the ground three feet in front of the tree.

White-Smith came in warily, he held a two-foot club two inches thick and looked ready for anything. When he saw the white handkerchief he stopped.

"Walling, you must be here. I won't let you kill me the way you did my brother. We don't have knives, but I'm armed so be ready."

White-Smith inched forward, lifting the club to the side ready to swing it forward. He reached the handkerchief and looked around. When he glanced away from the birch tree, Hallifax leaped out swinging the hatchet in a murderous arc. The heavy blade caught White-Smith on the side of the head just as he looked back. He went down in a spray of blood, and was dead before he hit the ground.

Hallifax stood over the body a moment, then flung the hatchet as far as he could into the swift-flowing Yukon River. He grabbed White-Smith by the feet and pulled him toward the water. The Yukon would claim him. He might not be found at all, or be 100 miles downstream when he was.

Hallifax pushed the body the final six feet into the edge of the Yukon River, and watched it sink and then slowly edge away from the bank in the current. He washed his hands, straightened his tie, and checked his suit for any blood splatters. He found a few, washed them out with his hand-kerchief and river water, then threw the white cloth into the river and watched it surge away with the strong current. Satisfied that he was presentable, Hallifax turned back to Dawson. He felt as if his luck had changed. Now he was in the mood to play some high-stakes poker!

Dawson's main thoroughfare, Front Street, had at last dried out, and now it was evident that a month had made a big difference in the look of the town. Dozens more buildings had gone up. The whine of the sawmills could be heard as the men worked 24 hours a day to turn out saw lumber for the ever-demanding market. There were more and more log houses rising on the hills just behind the mud flat where Dawson had been built.

New businesses had sprung up. "W. M. Gorman, Manufacturing Jeweler and Watchmaker," one sign proclaimed. "The Burlington, Liquor and Cigars." "Dr. J. L. Benson, Dentist."

"Shave 50 cents, Haircut 75 cents." "Mrs. McDonald, Fancy Dress Making and Ladies' Tailoring." "Mrs. G. I. Lowe's Laundry, Mending Free of Charge."

By now there were over 50 frame buildings along Front Street, covering both sides. Telephone poles marched up each side of the street with six wires on each pole.

On July Fourth there had been a celebration, even though this was in Canada. There was a lot of talk about where the correct boundary ran between Alaska and the Yukon. But most of the men in Dawson were Americans and they had their celebration and a parade with a makeshift band.

While the warm summer days lasted, the men worked at their sluices and gopher holes until they dropped. Gold dust continued to pour into the bank, and now and then someone found a good-sized nugget that had escaped the grinding action of the million years of erosion.

Thousands of young men who came to the Yukon to dig for gold found themselves doing just that—only they were working by the day on somebody else's claim. There were relatively few claims that proved rich enough for the owners to hire help. Most of the men had nothing to do but sit around, walk around, and eventually head back "outside" on a steamer.

Docks of a sort were soon built along the water's edge over from Front Street. They were set on six-foot-high pilings pounded into the hard ground so that when the river rose in the spring it wouldn't flood out the docks.

Stern-wheelers docked several times a week. Tons of freight piled up on the rickety platforms. Steam for the boat engines was generated from birch wood cut along the banks of the Yukon. Dozens of men earned their living cutting wood for the steam-powered riverboats.

By the second week in July, Millie had become a solid member of the dancing and singing team at the New York Saloon on Front Street.

Millie and Liza were by then fast friends. Millie told stories of how she almost starved to death during the winter of '97. There were simply too many people in Dawson at the time, and almost no food to feed them.

"I'm not sure I want to risk another winter here," Millie said, twisting some of her red curls around one finger. "It gets to be forty degrees below zero outside. Terrible. I've seen men freeze to death when they got drunk and went to sleep outside."

Liza encouraged her to talk. Millie was a wild one, and Liza learned a lot just listening to her. For several months now Millie had been keeping company with one Skagway Larson. Larson was a gambler who would do anything so he didn't have to work. He cheated at poker every chance he could and was often caught. More than once he had given the victim his money back rather than let the Mounties become involved.

"When I was a waitress at the other place, I'd try to see the cards some of the other players held and I'd signal it to Skag. Nobody caught on, and Skag usually won more when I was around."

Meanwhile, Bryce had been building his holdings. He had a knack for finding claims where the owners were discouraged and about ready to quit. He'd make them an offer for a lot less than the claim was worth, and usually they would go for it.

By the middle of July, Bryce had 13 claims working, mostly under the name of Jeferies Mining Company. On one 35-foot slice of a claim he hit a hot stretch of an old river channel four feet down, and in two weeks took out $25,000 worth of dust.

Nothing was seen of White-Smith for a week after he made his try at arresting Arthur Hallifax. Then a steamer came in with a body. It had been spotted floating in the Yukon about ten miles downstream. They grappled it and hauled it on board.

Superintendent Irons identified the body as that of White-Smith and gave him a burial. He duly noted the massive wound on the side of the head of the swollen and decaying flesh and listed the death as by foul play.

It was the first murder in Dawson City since the superintendent had arrived a year and a half ago. The Mountie remembered his talk with White-Smith about wanting to confront some Englishman with a murder warrant. Irons tried to remember the name of the man who White-Smith thought was the killer. He talked to his men, and found the Mountie who had been with White-Smith that morning two weeks ago.

The Mountie remembered the incident, but had no idea who the Englishman might have been. He was fairly tall, clean shaven, with a slight English accent. The trouble was that description fit any of 200 Englishmen in Dawson.

Spur McCoy heard about the tie-in with an Englishman and talked to Superintendent Irons.

"Yes, White-Smith was the Englishman who also was hunting Arthur Walling. I might not have given his accusation as much importance as I should. There are hundreds of Englishmen out there. I've confronted more than twenty myself with no luck."

"But now that this White-Smith is dead, it's looking more like he might have found the right man," McCoy said. "Could I talk with the Mountie who went with White-Smith that morning?"

A half hour later McCoy found Mountie Crandall guarding a shipment of gold heading to the bank. He listened to McCoy's question and shook his head.

"Mr. McCoy, I wrung out my poor brain a dozen times trying to remember who the chap was White-Smith confronted that morning. I've been on a dozen of these hunts for Walling and they all turn out the same. No way to prove that the Englishman is this Arthur Walling and that's the end of it. Same thing here.

"I do remember that this particular Englishman was abrupt with White-Smith. He was curt and annoyed and disgusted, but he showed absolutely no shame or anger or fear at the charges. I wrote him off as a suspect right then. Probably why I don't remember the name the man used. Gave it out right loud, he did. But I can't tell you what it was."

"In the Gold Nugget Saloon was where it took place?"

The Mountie nodded.

McCoy thanked the lawman and walked down the street toward the saloon he remembered as one of the smaller ones. Maybe the barkeep or some of the regulars remembered the confronted man's name.

During the last few weeks, Bryce Jeferies had found a man to help him manage his holdings, and now he came to the New York Saloon every night to watch the middle show and to talk to Liza.

Liza stared at Bryce this night and shook her head. "I'm wondering what I should do. From what Millie says there isn't much happening here in the winter. All of these men with nothing to do, but worse, not much money to spend. We haven't heard a word for weeks about anyone seeing Walter. What am I going to do, Bryce?"

"Young lady, you can do almost anything you want to do. You have a fat bank account. I've seen some of the nuggets the miners toss to you each night. I also happen to know that you have over

six thousand dollars now in your Thirty-Seven
Above account.

"You could even open a variety hall of your own
if you wanted to, run the whole thing."

Liza lifted her brows, then shook her head. "No,
that's too much business. I only like the performance end of the theater."

"You could always go with Josh to Chicago."
Bryce held his breath after he said it.

She shook her head. "No, he's good and kind,
but . . . I could never marry Josh. Walter, Oh,
Walter! Where are you!"

"You could always marry me and come back to
Portland and open a theater there."

She turned. "You're going to Portland? I
thought you said you lived in Seattle?"

"I did, but now I want to go live in Portland.
It's a lot like this country, young and new and
lots of opportunity." Bryce watched her. "Hey,
lady. I just made a kind of a proposal of marriage to you."

"Oh, Bryce, you weren't serious. You know I
have to find out about Walter before I can do
anything."

"What if we don't know anything more than
we do right now when the last steamer is getting ready to sail from the dock in the end of
September?"

Liza turned, her brown eyes somber, her face
troubled. "I just don't know, Bryce. I honestly
don't know."

The next day Bryce checked again with the Royal Canadian Mounted Police. A contingent of 12
soldiers had just arrived. They would be used to
safeguard gold dust moved from the creeks to the
bank.

Superintendent Irons nodded at Bryce.

"Sir, I'm still wondering about the missing man, Walter Livingston. I know you've found no trace of him. But what of bodies. Haven't there been one or two that were ruled dead by accident?"

"That there have—three, in fact. One last week on the Bonanza Creek diggings. But he was a little man, no more than five feet tall. This Livingston is said to be five-ten."

Bryce said that was right. He made one more try. "Perhaps the man who killed the Englishman White-Smith also did in Livingston?"

"A chance, but it would have been two or three months between the two. We'll keep a watch, believe me, Mr. Jeferies. I don't like to have a missing man on my hands. I'm near as interested in finding him as you are."

McCoy had taken to watching the singer at the New York Saloon where Lottie worked. He and Lottie had gone on the picnic with her weeks ago. He'd met Bryce Jeferies, and often now the two of them waited for Liza to come out between shows. Lottie showed up at the table half the time and the four of them had a lot of good laughs together between shows.

That was near the same time that Millie moved out of the dancers' dormitory upstairs at the New York Saloon and into a cabin that Skagway Larson had bought with some of his gambling winnings. She was happy as a bride for a week. Then she came in the next day ready to quit dancing.

"Millie, Millie, you've got to tell me what the trouble is," Liza said, stopping her before she could go see Josh. "Tell me what's troubling you, young lady."

Millie had let herself be led into Liza's room and they sat on the bed and talked. Soon Millie was crying.

"It's Skagway. Superintendent Irons caught him cheating in a big game, and sentenced him to a week on the woodpile and then a blue ticket on the next steamer to St. Michael. He's banishing him."

She broke down again, and it took Liza a half hour to get her quieted.

Liza wiped tears off her cheeks and hugged her, then offered a suggestion.

"Why don't you pack up and go with him?"

Millie looked up quickly. "Oh, my, no, I couldn't do that. We're not proper married and all. I don't know how he would act on the Outside. I've never seen him anywhere but here. Maybe I'm not ready to leave. Oh, I don't know what I think."

Millie danced that night, but the next day she didn't show up for the classes and rehearsal on a new number.

Liza told Josh about it and he was worried, but had a problem with one of the dealers he had to settle once and for all. The dealer had been skimming money off the top of the house money.

Liza went to Bryce's office, but he wasn't there. Spur McCoy sat in his office waiting for the gold-mining man.

"What's wrong?" McCoy asked.

Liza told him. "I know Millie must be sick or something. She wouldn't just walk away and not tell anybody."

"Maybe we should go to that cabin and see if she needs some help," McCoy said.

They walked through the hot summer day the six blocks to where Millie had said the cabin was. Liza said she expected to find both Millie and Skagway at home. When she knocked on the door, no one answered. McCoy pounded on it hard and still no one came. McCoy motioned her back and tried the knob.

"It's open," he said, and pushed the door inside the cabin.

They paused at the door. Neither one of them heard a sound. Liza looked in the small outer room that served as kitchen and living room. No one was there.

"Millie. Millie, it's Liza. I've come calling."

There was no response. McCoy held Liza back when she headed toward the other room, which must be the bedroom. He went to the door and knocked. There was no answer. McCoy pushed open the door. Inside he saw an unmade bed and some clothes hanging on a broom handle. To the far side sat Millie's pride and joy: a real steel bathtub you could lie right down in.

Millie's head showed over the top at the near end. McCoy waved Liza back, but she hurried forward and looked into the room. She saw the top of Millie's head over the end of the tub.

"Millie, this is a little late to be having your morning bath." Liza moved toward the tub and suddenly she stopped. The water in the tub was a dull red color. Both of Millie's wrists had been slashed in what had been warm water, and she must have layed in her tub and let all of her troubles wash away.

Liza turned and reached out for McCoy, who held her as she sobbed. "Millie, why did you do it? Why Millie, Why?"

McCoy took Liza back to the New York Saloon and told Josh what had happened. He notified Superintendent Irons and went back to the scene with the Mounties. They found a note and a will.

Liza didn't dance that night. Millie's note was direct. It also was a legal will, and left all of her worldly possessions to Liza. She said that Skagway had left on the steamer the day before he was supposed to start his week on the wood-pile. He wouldn't let the law push him around. He was headed for another gold strike somewhere.

McCoy helped Liza arrange for the burial, then helped her go through Millie's things. They found a dozen fruit jars filled with gold dust and gold nuggets. When they had it weighed at the bank, there was over $8,000 worth. She banked it and gave away Millie's clothes.

The next day she was back at the New York Saloon working on two new numbers for the show. She refused to let Josh hire anyone else to fill in Millie's spot in the chorus.

"No, don't you dare!" Liza said sharply. "Nobody takes Millie's place. No one ever can, nobody ever will."

Chapter Eighteen

The second day of prowling the Gold Nugget Saloon, Spur McCoy found a man who remembered the confrontation with the two Englishmen. The witness was a drinker, not a player, so McCoy wasn't sure how much of his story could be believed. He sat at a table just over from the poker games.

"Buster J. Prokosh," the man said, holding out his hand. Prokosh had a face like a mangy dog, with an uneven beard that looked as if it had been whacked off with a hunting knife or a pair of scissors without the aid of a barber or a mirror. His nose was softly red, puffy with large, open pores. His eyes sank deep into his skull and were shrouded by brows that tried to cover them. His hair was long and unkempt, and he still wore miner pants with mud stains on them and knee-high rubber boots as if he'd just come in from the creeks.

McCoy took Prokosh's hand and was surprised at the strong grip.

"Yes, sir, I saw the set-to, long about, what, two weeks or so ago. Whenever. This Englishman you said got himself kilt came up and accused this other limey of killing his kin and then pulled the chair out from under him, dumping him on the damn floor."

"Do you remember any names that were used?" McCoy pressed.

"Names. One was weird, a double name. White-Jones or something like that. He called this other Englisher some name and the guy swelled all up and said his name was Arthur something or other. Don't remember what."

"Then what happened?"

"Then the smaller Englishman kept yelling and screaming that this guy was Walling or something like that and that he ruined his sister and killed his brother."

"Was the poker player frightened by this?" McCoy asked.

"Hell, no. He waved it all aside like the Englisher was a pesky fly and called a Mountie out of the crowd to arrest the guy."

"This Arthur. Do you remember his last name?"

The man scowled. McCoy signaled a waiter, who brought two whiskeys to the table, and McCoy paid for them. The other man looked down at them and McCoy nodded.

"Have one. Soon as you remember Arthur's last name, you get the second one."

The drunk eyed the whiskey and caressed the glass, then lifted it and downed half the amber liquid.

"Arthur . . . Arthur . . . it was something Canadian, sounded Canadian. Toronto? No. Nova Scotia? Maybe. Halifax? I don't know. Something like that."

"Something like that doesn't help one hell of a lot, Mr. Prokosh. Sure you can't be positive on the last name?"

"Afraid not. I had a little to drink that day . . . well, you know."

Morgan pushed the other whiskey over to the man. "Remember any of the men who were in the poker game with the Englishman?"

"Nope, know that for damn sure. Poker players aren't free with their names. Then if they win, nobody can peg them. Usual they come to the same saloon to gamble, though." He looked around the room, then stood and made a circuit of the poker tables.

At one he stopped. Prokosh pointed at a man with a hat crammed down on his head almost to his ears. It shaded his face so it was hard to see. Then he came back to McCoy, who was still sitting with the whiskey.

"The crazy hat man was there. Don't know his name. He played in the game that morning."

McCoy walked over to the poker table, waited for the hand to end, then tapped the man with the hat on the shoulder and held out a ten-dollar gold piece.

"What . . ." The hat man turned and saw the gold and reached for it. McCoy pulled it back.

"Earn this ten by talking to me a bit. Sit out a couple of hands and talk to me."

"Hell, easy enough." He turned, and McCoy saw small dark eyes buried deep in folds of flesh. The rest of his body seemed normal enough, but his face was loose-skinned and fat.

"Understand you played some poker a week or so ago when one Englishman confronted another about being a killer. Remember that?"

"Damn right. Sure looked like a good fight brewing, but a Mountie was there and stopped it before it started. Figure the fancy gambler had a hide-out, but he never showed it. The other gent was English too. Said the one guy ruined his sister, killed his brother, and ran away on a ship."

"That's the one. Did he use a name?"

"Yeah. Unusual. Mostly we go by nicknames or no name at all in case we win a couple of dollars. Know what I'm talking about, young feller?"

"I do."

"Good. This gent just sang out his name. Said, 'I'm not Arthur Walling, my name is Arthur Hallifax and I'm from Toronto,' or some such place. He's the one, Hallifax. That damned gut-buster had been cheating and each time I almost caught him, he pulled back. Damn strange playing poker when you know there are at least six aces in the deck."

"This Arthur Hallifax, he keep playing after the incident?"

"Hell, no. He was ahead. I was pissed off at him. Said the charge upset him and he had to quit. Lost thirty dollars to the tall bastard."

McCoy gave the gold coin to the man, thanked him, and hurried out of the saloon. Where to check first? Arthur Hallifax was a gambler so he didn't own a claim. McCoy went to the Bank of Canada and talked to the president.

"Yes, Mr. Halifax does have an account with us. If Superintendent Irons authorizes it, I could give you his balance. I know you're a peace officer, but we do have our Canadian regulations."

"I understand. Could you say whether his account was small or medium-sized?"

The bank manager smiled. "If I could I would say it was medium-sized, but I can't tell you that, can I?"

McCoy chuckled. "Sir, if I had an account with you and it had five to ten thousand dollars in it, would that be a medium-sized account?"

"Mr. McCoy, if you did have an account here, those figures would describe a medium-sized account. I only wish you did have an account with us."

McCoy thanked the banker and left. He worked the gambling halls again. At each one he talked to the cashier and asked about Arthur Halifax.

He was known in the first three, but was not then in any of the establishments.

McCoy found him on the fourth try. He was in a high-stakes game at a table set on risers. There were six chairs around the table and all were filled. The chips and stacks of bills on the table set it apart from the other games. McCoy watched. The cashier at the New London Saloon had pointed Hallifax out. He wore a red checkered vest, white shirt, a 30-dollar black suit, and shiny black half boots. A gold chain connected his vest pockets and a large gold fob hung between them. The expensive suit fascinated McCoy. He'd paid five dollars for a fine suit with two pairs of pants and a vest. The fancy suit was an indication of vanity.

McCoy remembered seeing the man around the gambling halls. He had not known he was English. Now, did the dead Mr. White-Smith have some proof of the man's guilt, or had he been going by his memory? He hadn't showed any evidence at the confrontation from what McCoy had heard.

To McCoy that meant that White-Smith had had little more than his anger and outrage to use in charging the man with the kill. That didn't mean he'd been mistaken. McCoy knew the feeling of having the right man and not enough evidence.

McCoy would watch this man, talk to him, try to feel him out to see if he thought he was the killer. If he was, Walling might never get to London. Yukon and Canadian authorities could charge him with the death of White-Smith. *If he was the right man.*

The game rolled along. The Englishman didn't talk much, but he bid and asked for cards enough so McCoy could tie down that he was an Englishman. First test met. Now came the hard part. Was he Arthur Walling?

McCoy settled in at a different table where he had a side view of the player but would be out of his general view. The man played his cards. He seldom looked around. He sipped at a whiskey and made it last for two hours.

The Secret Service agent learned little more about the man in those two hours. He didn't yell and rant and rave. He kept his voice low. He bet well and never plunged. McCoy figured he was bluffing a little more than most poker players did, but you could do that when you were winning. Arthur was winning. Cheating?

McCoy wasn't sitting close enough to tell. That would have to wait for a later time.

The game broke up and half the men went to other tables. Arthur stretched, cashed in his chips, and walked outside. McCoy followed him well back. The Englishman went directly to the best cafe in town, the Sourdough Restaurant, and found a small table and ordered.

McCoy came in, made a show of searching the room, and when he spotted Arthur he went to the table.

"I beg your pardon, but someone told me you were English from near London. I wonder if I might ask you some questions about that area? I'm trying to decide if I should take a tour there."

Arthur Halifax looked up, annoyed, then lifted his brows. "I am about to dine. If you don't mind eating and talking, I think I could spare you the time. Have you eaten?"

Twenty minutes later their food came and they continued their discussion about the London area.

"What about this Shakespeare writer?" McCoy asked. "He's hailed as quite a genius by many. Have you read his plays?"

Hallifax scowled. "He was a complicated man who wrote complicated plays with outrageous themes that I still don't fully understand. A genius by all standards, but that doesn't mean I have to like all he wrote. I had to study him for two years in my schooling."

"That must have been interesting. Have you been to Stratford-on-Avon?"

"Yes, a tour. Dreadful, a lot of low-class people around. Dreadful, I'm afraid. But do take a tour of the place if you're in the area. In London there are many historic places you'll want to visit."

"I'd say you're sound a bit homesick."

"What? Me, homesick? Not in the least. Anyway, going back is out of the question. Oh, it all has to do with a woman who wants my body and my money. I brought most of the money with me but she has the rest of it.

"Well, it seems we have finished our desert. If you have no further questions, Mr. McCoy, I'll be getting back. I have a poker game arranged. Maybe you would like to play. We have a five-hundred-dollar buy-in with table stakes."

McCoy chuckled. "Afraid that's out of my price range. I never gamble more than I can afford to lose."

They stood and nodded and Arthur Walling, if it were he, went the other way out of the cafe.

McCoy walked down the street to the Royal Canadian Mounted Police office and marched in the front door. Superintendent Irons was busy. When he finished talking with a pair of sour-doughs, he came out and shook hands with McCoy.

"Doesn't look like you'll be around here much longer," Irons said.

"A gun or a club going to do me in?" McCoy asked.

"Neither one. I'd say it was probably your office in Washington, D.C. We have a letter for you. It started out as a telegram all the way to Seattle, then went into a letter and we got it this morning on the boat.

"The captains always keep any mail for the officers separate so they don't have to go to the post office. This one is rather large and sent to you in care of me." He motioned to a Mountie, who brought over an envelope.

Irons handed it to McCoy and grinned. "Either they want you to come home quick or they have a lot of special instructions for you. Oh, no extra charge for this postal service."

McCoy held the envelope and hefted it. More background on the villain, he expected. But the telegram would have taken two months to get here from Washington, D.C., on the two slow boats. He hated being two months behind on his orders.

"Oh, Superintendent, I don't think that the man who had that argument with White-Smith is our man on the Walling case. I found him, watched him play poker for two hours, then had a meal with him at a cafe. Either he's a damn good actor or I misread him from here to breakfast and back."

Irons scowled. "You can count him out, but to me every man with an English accent is still a suspect until I get convinced otherwise. At least now you have one less to chase down. I'll leave you to your mail." He paused. "Oh, if there is any new way we can be of help to you, let me hear."

McCoy nodded, sat in a chair in the rough-hewn waiting room, and opened the big envelope. He drew out a sheaf of papers held together with a pin. On the outside of them was a handwritten note. He read it.

"McCoy. This is all of the background we can get on the suspect Walling. London becoming impatient with no positive results. Family is evidently well placed in the English government.

"Also find enclosed details on a 'mad-dog killer' rampaging around Wyoming in the Jackson Hole area. Mr. Wood says to give you one more week there. If you can't track down this Britisher in seven days, you are ordered to return to Seattle by the fastest way. We realize this will take you some two months. Good luck and let us know by wire when you arrive in Seattle."

It was signed General Wilton D. Halleck, commanding.

McCoy pushed the papers back in the envelope. A week! How could he nail down the killer in a week? If he didn't, he'd have to walk away and leave the Brit in the superintendent's hands.

Only once before had he quit on a case before he solved it. It had been absolutely unsolvable. Two years later they'd discovered that the man he'd tracked through three states had killed himself by jumping down a thousand-foot mine shaft. They'd identified the body later by jewelry and by papers that were still on the clothes of the skeleton.

McCoy waved at the Mounties and walked out into the bright sunshine of the Yukon. It was hot, it was summer. At least he had over 20 hours of sunlight each day to work on the case. What first? He'd checked the gambling houses. What had he missed? The cafes and restaurants were never good sources of information. True, this Walling must be eating out three times a day. But waitresses don't know that much about their customers.

Who did?

McCoy snapped his fingers. He should have tried that route before. Who else but the fancy women, the whores of the Yukon. Many of them were Belgians brought in for their sturdy build to withstand long hours of work. Most of them didn't speak any English.

He'd have to concentrate on the English-speaking ladies of the evening and the sales ladies in the "cigar stores," where you could buy a good cigar and a friendly body at the same time.

McCoy stepped down the street with a new attitude. This was going to be the way he found the killer. He had a good feeling about this new tack.

Chapter Nineteen

For the next few days, Spur McCoy talked to half of the whorehouse madams in town and dozens of working girls. He found three who remembered Arthur Hallifax, but none could remember him saying anything incriminating, or talking about any killing in England.

Liza continued her dancing and singing but she was just going through the motions. Few of the customers noticed the difference, but Bryce did. Her sparkle was gone, she was mechanical. Bryce and often McCoy were back to their nightly visits to the New York Saloon.

The first two days after Millie died, Liza didn't come out in response to Bryce's note. The third night she came, and he could see that under her stage makeup she was pale and drawn.

Liza turned her still-red eyes on Bryce and frowned. "It really makes you stop and wonder what life is all about, doesn't it? I always thought I'd grow up and find a nice man I loved and get married and have six kids and raise them all to be doctors and lawyers and at least one elected to Parliament. Now that all seems so foolish. What chance did Millie ever have to be happy? Everything just piled up on her, smashed her down, tore her heart out, and what did she have left?"

Bryce sat there listening. He knew not to talk when Liza was pouring out her heart in one of her long talks.

"Poor Millie. She had gold, and she had a friend or two, but that was about it. So what do I have? A friend or two, a bank account and my work, my singing and dancing. *But singing and dancing are not important!* I used to know that. Now it seems sometimes to be the only thing left in my life. Oh, where, oh, where is Walter?"

She leaned against Bryce's shoulder. "Sometimes I get so sad I don't know what I'm going to do." She pushed away from him, her eyes wide. "Oh, I didn't mean . . . No, I would never do anything like Millie did. I don't mean that."

Bryce held her hand. "I know what you're going to do. You're going to come on a special picnic tomorrow, which is Sunday. We'll throw rocks in a creek and wade in it and splash water and cool off and have a wonderful picnic dinner."

A small smile crept onto Liza's pretty face and then burst into full flower. Her eyes sparkled. "Yes, oh, yes! It's been weeks since I've been on a proper picnic. You bring the blanket and I'll bring the picnic basket and the dinner and we'll find a place where nobody will bother us and we can talk and talk."

"I love the way your eyes light up when you get enthused about something. I'd like to kiss you right now, but I better not."

"Shame on you, Bryce. Don't be naughty. Now, when will we leave on our picnic? Where are we going? Can we walk there or will you have horses?"

"First I have to think of just the right spot that isn't all dug up by miners. Maybe along the river somewhere would be better. I'll decide."

Liza looked at the clock. "I better scoot. I'll see you at the side door in the morning. I'll fix our lunch. When will you be here?"

"Ten o'clock. Just be sure you bring plenty to eat. I'll find some nice wine."

"But I don't drink wine."

"You can just this once. It'll be a celebration."

Liza smiled, and hurried for the door that led backstage.

The next day Bryce decided this picnic was the best idea he'd had in months, as he watched Liza laughing and splashing water at him in the shallow place along the Klondike River's shore just down from a heavy stand of birch trees that hadn't fallen yet to the woodsman's ax.

She was relaxed and enjoying herself. This was the real Liza. How could he make her understand that they belonged together? First they had to know for sure about Walter. He had talked to the superintendent again. There was nothing more they could do.

"Some men vanish and are never found again," Superintendent Irons had said. "This may be one of those cases."

The picnic featured ham sandwiches and boiled eggs, potato salad, and even a cherry pie made from some canned cherries that Josh had brought in from Vancouver. There was also the wine. Liza sipped at her glass slowly, making a face as she did.

After they ate, they sat on the blanket and Bryce moved down so he could lay his head in her lap. He stared up at her.

"Now this is a new view of you, Liza. I don't think I ever realized just what a strong chin you have."

She punched him in the shoulder. "Be nice. I know my chin is too big."

"It is not, it's just right. You wouldn't be nearly so beautiful if you didn't have a chin."

She giggled and then laughed and bent and kissed his cheek. He caught her face and turned it and slowly pulled her lips to his. They pressed together for a few seconds and when he let her go, her eyes were wide and a tear crept out of one.

"Oh, my goodness. I'm not supposed to like that so much. My goodness!"

Slowly she bent and kissed him again, this time more demanding, and when she lifted away, she sighed and watched him with intent eyes.

"Oh, my!" She shook her head in disbelief. "I'll have you know, Bryce Jeferies, you are only the second man I've ever kissed. Walter and you. But I was engaged to Walter at the time. I . . . I guess I miss his kisses." She held his face in both hands.

"But I must admit, your kisses are just as sweet. Once more and that's the end of this."

She bent and kissed him again, her eyes closed, and she sighed as their lips touched and held the kiss the longest of any of the three. When it ended, Liza sighed again.

He sat up and his best smile radiated his pleasure. She frowned at him.

"Don't grin at me that way, Bryce Jeferies. You just better not tell anyone I kissed you. If you do, I'll deny it. I'll say to them—"

He put a finger across her lips.

"I'll never tell a soul. It will be our secret. But I can tell you that those were the sweetest, the best, the greatest kisses I've ever known. Believe it or not, young lady, I have kissed more than two girls in my lifetime."

"Well, thank you. It was sweet. I was carried away. Now, it's time to pack up and get home."

He touched her arm. "Planning time first. We talked about leaving while the gold is still flowing. I'm not looking forward to wintering here. There will be a boat leaving on September fifteen. I'm considering being on it. What do you think? I can escort you back to Vancouver or Toronto. I don't like the idea of you traveling alone."

"Oh, my." She looked at him and quick tears washed her eyes and fell away. "What if we don't know about Walter by then?"

"At sea they have a phrase that might apply. When a sailor is washed overboard in a storm, and they hunt for him and can't find him, they say he's 'missing and presumed dead.' Usually they're right. I think by the middle of September, if we haven't found any trace of Walter Livingston, we'll have to assume that he's missing and presumed dead."

He watched her. This time she didn't cry. She didn't wince or frown. More and more she was getting used to the idea that Walter might never again be a part of her life.

"I'll . . . I'll have to think about it. I'm starting to

dread the coming winter. No more picnics, that's for sure. I've heard that sometimes they get fifteen *feet* of snow here."

"September fifteen looks better and better."

When they finished walking the mile back to the saloon, it was not yet four in the afternoon.

"Would you like to see my cabin? It's fixed up quite nice inside."

Liza smiled. "Young man, you know that would not be proper. We'd have no chaperon."

"Don't you trust yourself with me, pretty lady?"

"Oh, yes. I trust myself, and I trust you without question. You would never do anything to me that wasn't proper. But for now, I think it's best to maintain my spotless reputation."

"Then you have heard about it?"

"About what?"

"The newspaper is sponsoring a Queen of the Klondike contest. I've entered you."

"You what?"

"I've entered you in the Queen of the Klondike contest. I took over that picture of you in the beaded gown you wear in your show."

Liza frowned, then it changed to a smile. "You really entered me?"

"I did."

Her smile broadened. "I had heard something about the contest. I guess it's too late for me to back out now. What is it that I have to do?"

"Just be yourself, and sing and dance your heart out. The voting is when the next newspaper comes out. Probably next week. It costs a dollar to vote and the money goes to equip our new fire department. With all these wooden buildings we really need one."

There was more to the contest than that. There

were two fancy dinners and speeches and each of the six contestants paraded on the stage at the Monte Carlo saloon. Five of the six contestants were entertainers in the saloons and dance halls of Dawson.

From the outset there seemed to be a favorite. Liza was everywhere, dancing and singing, shaking hands and doing her famous routine of catching contributions in her skirt. This time they went to the fire department fund.

The votes were counted by the town council and in a big ceremony at the Monte Carlo, Liza was crowned Queen of the Klondike.

Her crown, which she got to keep, was fashioned from more than 50 gold nuggets that had been donated. It weighed a little over two pounds and was said to be worth over $650 just for the gold. Liza cried and smiled and paraded and caught more nuggets and coins and pokes in her skirt.

She was delirious, and had chosen Bryce to be her escort to three dances and a big dinner. Liza was radiant the whole evening. When it was over and he walked her back to the side door of the New York Saloon, she pulled him into the shadows.

"I've decided," she said. "If we haven't found Walter by September fifteen, then I'll wave good-bye to you at the dock. If you be good, I'll even kiss you good-bye. I've got to find Walter or stay here forever searching for him."

Liza kissed Bryce on the cheek, squeezed his hand, and slipped inside the door, and Bryce could only stare at the closed partition and wonder if he would ever be able to marry this woman.

The next morning, Bryce had an agenda worked out. He surveyed his 24 properties. He figured out which ones were paying off and found four that were marginal. Now would be the time he would start to sell off his holdings, but he would do it gradually so not to cause a scare.

He put a notice on the bulletin board next to the claims recorder's office announcing that he would take bids on the four claims. All bids had to be in no later than three days hence.

Then he evaluated the 20 working placer digs that he had left. Four were paying off the best. He had room for more men on the works, and promptly hired six men to work on each of the four claims. In each case they were digging gopher holes and trenches to follow old streambeds. Each of these four claims had a dig boss who was honest and loyal to Bryce. No gold dust would be stolen at these sites.

Next he worked the rest of the afternoon riding a horse he had bought to the rest of his claims. Two of them he shut down and would sell. He moved those men to other claims. Two more he found had struck richer pay dirt than before, and he brought in more diggers there. It was simple to hire men to work by the day. There were at least ten thousand unemployed men drifting around Dawson. Most of them were broke and needed to raise enough money for the passage down to St. Michael on the "outside."

Bryce watched one set of men working his Sugartree Creek claim Four Above. The overburden here was eight feet thick. The frozen ground underneath had some gold in it, but not enough to bring it up, thaw it, and put it through the sluice box.

Down eight feet they found the old streambed and the raw gold was worth working.

The ore had to be dug out by a man with a pick and shovel working in a tunnel often only three feet high. The buckets of ore were dragged back to the shaft, which had a rope, and the buckets were winched to the top.

Each bucket of sand and gravel was taken to the nearby sluice box, and poured in at the right time to keep the water flowing and the gold dust falling into the cross-hatched baffles along the bottom of the sluices.

Too much water and the gold washed away. Too little water coming down and the dirt, clay, and smaller rocks caught in the baffles.

Some claim owners cleaned the gold dust from the baffles once or twice a week. In Bryce's claims, the gold was cleaned out at the end of each working day.

On two of his claims, he had crews working around the clock. There was no time to lose; the winter and the freeze-up would be coming back soon.

Bryce knew how they worked the gopher holes in the winter and stacked the gold-rich ore in piles to be worked come spring and the thaw, and he didn't want to have to do that. They built a fire on a prospective spot for a gopher hole, and when the fire went out they had melted the frozen ground down a foot. That was dug out and lifted to the surface and thrown away. Then another fire was built in the hole and allowed to burn out and another foot of frozen ground was dug out and discarded. This went on until they hit paydirt or solid rock.

If things went right, he would have made his

fortune before the weather got cold enough to freeze up the Yukon.

That week he sold his mining tool store. He made about $5,000 on the sale and had shown a profit when he ran the store. Next he sold his clothing outlet. He broke even on the sale, but had made money while he ran it. Now he could concentrate on his claims from his office on Front Street.

When he got back that afternoon from his circle of claims, he found two offers for two of his claims. He read them. Both were far too low. He put the offers in a stack on his desk. There would be one pile for each of the six claims. He sent one of his hired men to the bulletin board with a notice that two more of his claims were up for sale.

Then he sat back and checked the calendar. Lots of time before September 15. He had to put his best efforts in on those projects which would pay off the most. Already the days were starting to grow shorter. The daylight was down to 21 hours now.

That same day, it was just after six P.M. when Superintendent Irons came into Bryce's small office on Front Street. The moment Bryce saw the man he knew there was some news—good or bad, he didn't know.

"There's been a find up on El Dorado Forty Above. I'm going up to take a look. If you still have that horse, I figured you might want to traipse along."

The policeman wouldn't even hint at what kind of a report he had been given. It took them an hour and a half to work their way upstream and then to El Dorado and over the trail that meandered high on the El Dorado stream.

When they came to Forty Above, there were six men standing around something on the ground. Bryce jumped down and ran to the canvas-wrapped form. He pulled back the cover and stared at a body that had been underground and frozen for many months.

The superintendent came up and knelt beside the remains. He fished in the back pocket under the body and found some papers and a wallet. It was a snap-top-type wallet that so many of the men carried. Everything of value they owned often was inside.

Superintendent Irons opened the snaps and shook out a few coins, two keys, and a letter, still stiff from the freezing. Irons opened the letter, breaking it in half at the fold. On the top half in a clear, feminine hand the address and name could be read:

"To Walter Livingston, Dawson City, Yukon." In the bottom of the letter was the salutation: "All my love, Elizabeth Cromwell."

Bryce looked at the Mountie, who pointed to one of the miners. The man spoke up.

"Two of us just bought the Forty Above. Not a whole lot here. We found this one gopher hole that had been filled in with overburden from another hole. We figured we'd dig it out and try some tunneling. Save a lot of work that way.

"We got down about ten feet and ran into this canvas. When we seen it was a body, we sent for a Mountie right off. We got him dug out and hoisted up, and there he is."

The flesh had not decomposed a whit. It had been frozen from the day Walter had died. The superintendent examined the head a moment and grunted. A large blood-red gash showed on the back of Livingston's head. He had been bludgeoned with something, maybe an ax. No man could live with a deep wound like that.

"The widow shouldn't see this," Bryce said. "I'll take the responsibility for the body. Let's take him down to his claim, Thirty-Seven Above, and bury him there. There's a shallow gopher hole we can enlarge and use as a grave. I'll put up a marker and then bring her out if she wants to come."

The Mountie approved and an hour later, Walter Livingston was lowered into his grave and the hole filled and a wooden marker erected.

Bryce stopped a moment and frowned. He couldn't remember a single stone-cutter in Dawson. There was no undertaker. He had heard of a few men dying from disease. He didn't even know if there was a cemetery.

Bryce checked with the foreman on Thirty-Seven Above, picked up a week's worth of gold dust and small nuggets, and headed back to town with a saddened heart. At least it was over, the waiting, the not knowing. It was finished. He wondered how Liza would react.

He pondered it on the trip back to town, and hardly said a word to the lawman as he tried to figure the best way to tell Liza. He did it a dozen ways in his mind, but none of them seemed to be right. How should he do it? What could he say that would let her down easy?

He still had no idea when he washed up in his office and put on a fresh shirt and jacket. Spur McCoy stopped by with a question and he told the Stateside lawman about finding Water Livingston.

"How can I break the word to her?"

McCoy shook his head. "It's hard, the most difficult task most men ever have. I'll go with you if you think it might help?"

"Please come. We'll go to Josh's office and let him know."

They walked over to the saloon and up to Josh's office. He was sitting in a chair behind his desk when the two men stepped inside. Josh had been well aware that Bryce was closer to Liza than he was, and it had built an irritation between the two men. Now that had washed away.

"Josh, I need your help." Bryce said.

Josh took a long drag on his cigar, stared up at the two men facing him, and nodded. "They must have found Walter Livingston's body."

"Yes. He was murdered on his claim. Hit in the head and dumped in a gopher hole and the over-burden shoveled in on top of him."

"Who?"

"Nobody's thought much about that yet. Shouldn't be too hard to lay it on his former partner. They worked hard just before the first boat got ready to go down the Yukon with the breakup. Then both of them were missing. The partner must have killed Walter, taken all the gold, and vanished downstream on the steamer."

"We know the problem now," Josh said. "Any ideas?"

"A dozen, maybe two dozen," Bryce said. "None of them seem to be right. Maybe you should call her in here and I'll tell her that he's dead and buried with a marker."

Josh squirmed in his chair. "Must be a better way. A kinder one."

"Seeing us all here together, she might figure it out in a second," McCoy said. "We might not even have to put it into words."

Josh called one of the girls and sent her to bring Liza into the office. Bryce stood and held his hands behind his back so they wouldn't shake.

McCoy stood at an army parade rest.

Josh sat behind his desk.

Liza came in the door with a bright smile, but when she saw the three men in the office all with serious faces, her smile faded. Then she wailed and ran to Bryce.

Chapter Twenty

Liza staggered as she ran to Bryce. He rushed and caught her so she wouldn't fall.

"It's Walter, isn't it? Someone found . . . found Walter's . . . his body. He's dead."

"Liza, I'm so sorry," Bryce said. "I hoped this hunt would turn out differently."

Josh brought a chair over and Liza sat in it. Her body went limp, her eyes closed, her hands fell at her sides.

"Liza."

She didn't respond. Josh knelt in front of her and caught her hands and put them in her lap. He covered them with his own and spoke softly.

"Liza, you knew this might happen. You must have been just a little prepared. I'm terribly sorry about your Walter. But we're the living. Would he have wanted you to give up on everything? Is that what he would have wanted you to do?"

Liza opened her eyes and looked at Josh. Bryce doubted if she'd heard what Josh said. She glanced up at Bryce and McCoy, then the tears came.

"Bryce, my Walter is dead!" Her eyes went wide and she gasped. "I've never felt anything hurt so awful before. It's like something smashed me into pieces and I'm floating, trying to put myself back together. I've never known this kind of agony. Help me back to my room, please."

McCoy touched her shoulder when she stood. "Liza, you know the truth now about what happened. It won't make it easier now, but it will in the months and years to come. Your whole life is ahead of you. Remember that. Remember, the dead cry their tears for the living. Ours is still the struggle, the fight. Walter's battle is over."

She watched him a moment, nodded, then went toward the door and toward her room. Bryce helped her all the way.

McCoy left the office. There was nothing more he could do.

Outside, he took a lungful of the clean air and looked around. He was going to ask Bryce about the rest of the whores in town. So far he'd seen dozens of them and their madams and pimps, but there had to be more. A man like Arthur Walling would have one steady whore he relied on, who he confided in. All McCoy had to do was track down that one *puta* and convince her that she should talk about her customer. Money usually did the trick with the fancy ladies. Their loyalty most always was in their pocketbooks.

He had investigated "Lousetown" across the Yukon River. That was where most of the whores operated. But they were the cheapest and worst of the lot. He was more interested in the sub-rosa kind of fancy lady, who might do something else during the day and spend her nights on "confidential liaisons" with the rich and the famous of Dawson.

More and more of the ladies around town were finding that a lucrative way to have a second income. He just had to find the right one.

The most elaborate restaurant in town had a French menu and a cook straight from Quebec. It also had a head waiter who couldn't find you a table without a five-dollar incentive. McCoy went to the establishment. It was not the peak serving hours, and he talked to the elegantly dressed man as he tossed a 20-dollar gold piece in the air and caught it.

The head waiter seemed insulted. "Sir, you think that I would know such indelicate things? That I would have any idea where one of these high-class whores might be found?"

"Damn sure of it. That's why I came to you. I don't begrudge you a bit more profit from your work. Pointing the rich of Dawson toward the right address must be profitable. Right now you could be twenty dollars ahead of the game. I want the five best late-night hostesses in Dawson. I need their names and where they can be found after the workingman's day is done."

The head waiter said to call him Pierre, and

now he looked around. "Let me seat you for some of our special coffee and cakes, and I'll have what you want written down. People are watching. I must keep up appearances."

"Lead the way."

The coffee and little cakes cost him two dollars, and the 20-dollar gold piece vanished into Pierre's hand as well as he slipped McCoy a folded piece of paper.

McCoy held his hand a moment in a tight grip. "Pierre, if these aren't the real fancy ladies I need to see, the best of the high-class whores in town, I'll be back and reduce your height about six inches by pounding you on the top of the head."

Pierre smiled through a hint of pain. "There is no problem, I'm sure. You'll be pleased with at least one of these ladies."

"I'm hunting information about a client, not to get myself serviced," McCoy said. "I only pay pimps. I never pay whores."

Pierre looked shocked as McCoy let go of his hand. McCoy finished the coffee, paid the cashier, and left the restaurant to examine the paper.

It was nearly four o'clock before McCoy found the first address on the list. The name was Maryanne and she had a small frame house on First Street up the slope from Front Street one block. He walked by, then went to the door and knocked.

A tall, slender woman answered the door.

"Maryanne?" McCoy asked.

"Do I know you?" she asked, her face in a slight frown that did nothing to distort the pretty fea-

tures in a face slightly enhanced with a touch of
lip color and cheek rouge.

"Pierre said I should see you," McCoy said.

"Good old Pierre. Come in. I'm not real busy
right now or tonight. Things are a little slow."

Inside it was a typical living room, with a couch,
four chairs, pictures on the wall, and a bearskin
rug on the floor. A small fireplace at one end
would do double duty in winter.

"Did Pierre say anything about how expensive
it is to live in Dawson?" she asked. Maryanne
wore a thin dress of pretty silk fabric that molded
tightly against her slender figure and was cut low
between large breasts.

"He did, but I'm not a regular caller. I want
to find out what you know about one of your
friends, a man who is from London, who gam-
bles, and who is nearly six feet tall and maybe twenty-five or six. Nice-looking chap. Do you
know him?"

She frowned and the illusion was broken. Now
her features showed how sharp they could be
when she wasn't selling. "English you say, with
an accent?"

"He's probably tried to lose it. I'd say in the
heat of passion the real accent would be more
pronounced."

She grinned. "It does happen. Any name?"

"He might call himself Arthur, which is his real
name, or he could be calling himself anything.
Any English regulars."

"Two, but one is short and a bit on the fat side,
but a good tipper. The other one is not over five-
six and slender as a birch sapling. I doubt if either
of them would fit your description."

"I'm afraid you're right." They had been standing, and now she motioned to the couch.

"We could sit and talk a bit more or go into the bedroom. I'd guess you don't want to waste your visit here." She undid the front of her dress and let it slip down off one fine breast, pink-nippled with only a hint of an areola, but so perfectly formed and still with a bit of an upward tilt that he figured she couldn't be more than eighteen or maybe a year older.

"Beautiful, Maryanne, but I'm not buying. I'm trying to find a killer. I do appreciate the offer, though." He bent and kissed the breast, nibbled a moment at the nipple, and straightened in time to see her catch her breath with a small gasp.

Her hand came around his neck and held him. Her eyes turned misty and shrouded for a moment. When she opened them they were star-tlingly green. "I wasn't trying to sell anything," she said. Her voice husky. "It's been a while since I've seen a man as good-looking as you are, and I just didn't want to let you get away." She pulled his hand down to her crotch and spread her legs incitingly.

McCoy tweaked her nipple and stepped back.

"Not this time, Maryanne, but it's an interesting offer. I might stop by some other time. Right now, I'm supposed to be working. My name's McCoy. If you come across a gent like I described, I'd appreciate it if you'd send a note to me in care of Superintendent Irons."

Her brows went up.

"I'm not a Mountie. I'm from the States hunt-ing this hombre and I sure hope I can catch him. Thanks, Maryanne." He went to the door and when he looked back, she stood there as he had left her, legs spread, one breast showing, and a vulnerable, needful expression on her pretty face.

McCoy checked out two more of the ladies of the evening. They had prices from ten to 30 dollars for a one-hour rental, but neither of them knew an Englisher who looked like Walling.

He eyed the fourth name on the list. "Marsha," he said softly. Her address was on Front Street out toward the downstream end, where some houses and a hotel were being built right on the main avenue. He went up and knocked on the door and waited.

He had to knock twice more before he heard anything inside the small house. Then the door opened a crack and he saw a dark eye staring at him.

"Who the fuck are you?" she asked.

"Who the fuck you think I am?"

"Some bastard with a hard-on. Cost you fifty bucks."

"Too much, I just want to talk."

"Another of them weird guys. Go away."

She tried to close the door but his boot stopped it. He eased the door inward. She was leaning against it now, and it took some major force to get it open.

Inside, the window was open and it was light. She darted to the dresser and came up with a hide-out, a small one, probably a crotch-hiding .22.

"Move out the door or I'll shoot," she said.

"Then Irons will have you on the first boat down the Yukon." Slowly he pulled out his own hide-out. "My gun is bigger than your gun. You want to shoot or shall we talk?"

She grinned, then broke up laughing. "Hell, I don't have any bullets for the damn thing anyway." She put it back in the drawer and closed it. When she turned he noticed for the first time what she wore. It was a one-piece dress that had been deliberately cut to form some show-off holes. One breast showed through one of the holes. On her other breast only her nipple showed through a small cutout. Strip holes slanted down each leg in front, but there was a heavy patch sewn over her crotch area.

"Nice outfit," McCoy said.

"Most guys like it. You really not hard up? My titties don't give you a stiff pole in your pants?"

"I'm not fourteen looking for my first bare tits," McCoy said.

She sat on a big bed and lit a cigarette. She inhaled just like a man and blew the smoke out through her nose.

"So, we talk. You want to strip and show me your crotch to pay the tab?"

"Not particularly. My question is about one of your regulars, the Englishman, the one who gets rough sometimes." McCoy was stabbing in the dark, taking a chance. What could he lose?

She laughed. "Yeah, he does get rough and mean now and then but he always pays extra for it. I warned him. Cut him off for three days once and he nearly went crazy."

"Does he talk wild and funny sometimes when he's about ready to make it?"

She frowned. "How the hell could you know that? Damn, you been under the fucking bed or something?"

She scowled a minute more, then shrugged.

"Sure, he talks about England, about how he can't ever go back. He killed some guy. It was more an accident than deliberate. It was in a knife fight and this bloke wasn't any good at all. Happened right after he knocked up the gent's sister and he fucked her to a fare-you-well. She wanted a wedding ring, but he told her to go jump on a runaway freight wagon."

"What about here. He ever get talking about what he's done here?"

"Just once. Something about a hatchet. Sounded like he clubbed somebody with a hatchet in the head. Something like that. He wasn't clear about it and he was humping me like a pile driver. I don't need to prolong that kind of punishment. Not for no twenty bucks a fuck."

McCoy stared out the window. So damn close! "What name has he been using with you? Seems he gets a new name every couple of days in his poker games."

"Name? Same one he's always used with me."

"What is it?"

"We ain't talked about any real pay here, big stud. What's it worth to you to find out? I'm a working girl. I could be flat on my back fucking up a twenty-dollar bill. That's what it's going to cost you, a sweet twenty."

McCoy took a bill from his wallet, folded it, and let her hold the top end. He held the bottom part.

"The name?"

"Figured you knew it before you got here. He's about six feet, maybe an inch under, slender, no more than twenty-five, blondish hair, and an English accent. The name he always goes by with me is Arthur. Arthur Hallifax."

"I'll be damned!" McCoy said.

He let go of the bill, then grabbed it and pushed it in the hole around her bare breast.

"That's to keep the girls company," McCoy said. He turned for the door.

"That's it? You don't want to get chewed or pumped off or nothing from me?"

"What you've given me is more important than you might know. Now I've got some real work to do." He put his hand on the knob. "Oh, forget that I was ever here. I especially don't want you to tell Hallifax that I was asking questions. If he finds out, he'll be down the river on the next boat and you'll lose a good customer. I have your word on your silence?"

She laughed. "Hell, ain't you a shit? You asking a whore to give her word? You think I'm like regular people or something?"

"That's right. I think you're regular people making a few dollars. You'll probably go outside when this rush is over and settle down in Memphis or maybe San Francisco, get married, have three kids, and become a pillar of the community. Now remember, not a word about this little talk to anyone."

Her eyes were wide as he left the place. All he could think of was Hallifax. The son of a bitch was a much better actor than McCoy had ever imagined. Now, the problem was how to prove who he was and that he did in fact kill White-Smith. Evidence, he needed evidence. If Hallifax was as clever about that killing as he had been with everything else, there just might not be a shred of hard evidence that he could present to a court.

Not a chance that he could have the fancy lady

he'd just talked to testify. Marsha was the name he had on the list. Oh, now that would be a picture, Marsha in the dock testifying against one of the English nobility.

McCoy kicked at the hard ruts in Front Street. Now he really had his work laid out for him. He'd better get at it.

Chapter Twenty-One

Bryce put his arm around Liza and helped her down the hall. Once away from the office, he bent and picked her up and carried her. Josh knocked, then opened her door and called as they went in.

Her one roommate looked up in shock, and when she saw Liza crying she nodded and slipped out of the room.

Bryce placed her gently on her bed, and she curled into a ball and closed her eyes. He knelt beside the bed, smoothing back her long dark hair and talking softly to her. He wasn't sure what he said, just comforting, soothing words. He wanted her to hear the familiar sound of his voice.

She cried for five minutes; then he wiped away the tears and she sobbed a few times, then drifted into a troubled sleep.

Bryce sat on the floor beside her, then pulled over a chair. He spread a light quilt over her and she tucked it tight around her as she slept. Liza still lay curled into a protective ball, a fetal position, the classic defense a human uses in time of terrible stress.

After an hour, Bryce left the room. He went to Josh's office.

"She won't be singing tonight for you," Bryce said. "There's a chance she might never perform again. It depends how hard she takes his death. I thought she was prepared for the probability of this, but I guess she wasn't. I tried."

"I had mentioned it to her a few times too," Josh said. "You just can't tell how a person will react."

The two men stared at each for a moment.

"Take care of her, Josh. There's a nurse here in town. See if you can hire her to stay with Liza. I'll pay the cost."

Josh waved away the last idea. "I'll send someone to find the woman."

Bryce nodded and left the room. He walked down to the gambling hall and outside. The sun wasn't quite so bright now. The days were growing shorter. By the middle of winter there would be only two hours of weak light from the sun.

He trudged back to his office on Front Street. What now? What could he do to help Liza over this tragedy? How would she react when her grief was purged? Would she want to dance? Would he have a chance to marry her?

He worked three hours in his office, then saw that it was almost midnight and decided to see if he could get some sleep.

The next morning he went first to the New York

Saloon. Josh was in his office and said that Liza had not come out of her room. He had sent in breakfast but she had refused it.

"She said she didn't want to talk to me or anyone," Josh said. "Mrs. McWhorter, the nurse, is with her. She told me Liza is holding up quite well, considering. She's through crying. Now she sits and stares out the window."

"I want to talk to her," Bryce said. "Maybe she'll see me."

He tried. She told him through the door to go away. She wasn't talking to anyone.

Downstairs, he headed for the hill just in back of the mud flat where Dawson sprawled for two miles along the river. He soon found what he looked for.

The summer wildflowers were still blooming in their short season. He found arctic poppies, blue lupine, yellow daisies, arnicas, and crimson fireweed. He picked a handful of each to make a bouquet and took it back to the saloon. One of the other dancers in the hallway saw him and hurried to get a vase with some water in it.

They arranged the flowers, and the dancer took it and slipped into Liza's room. Bryce waited across the hall. A moment later the dancer came out and held open the door. She nodded and Bryce hurried inside.

Liza sat by the window watching the street. She was dressed, and Mrs. McWhorter sat reading a book.

The flowers were on the windowsill beside Liza. She turned as he came in. Her face was drawn, haggard, her eyes dull and lifeless. She didn't smile. Liza motioned to the flowers.

"Thanks," she said in a whisper.

"You're welcome. Pretty flowers for a pretty lady." The comment went by without her acknowledging it. She looked out the window again.

"My Walter is dead," Liza said. She held out her hand, and he caught it and sat on the floor beside her chair.

"Yes, Walter is gone. He has been for months now. I'm so sorry."

"Yes, my Walter is gone." She turned, and when he saw the terror in her eyes he wanted to put his arms around her and hold her and tell her it would be all right.

"Walter is gone, Bryce. What am I going to do now? I know how Millie felt. I think I understand now how Millie could do what she did. It's all gone. Everything. I feel dead inside. It's like I died along with Walter and just don't know it yet."

Bryce was worried by her talk about how Millie felt. He had to get her thinking along different lines. Business. That might do it.

"Liza, I've decided to sell six of my claims. They aren't paying out and with a deadline approaching I figured I had to work on the most productive."

She didn't hear him.

He caught her hand and touched her shoulder. "Liza. Did you hear me?"

She shook her head but turned to look at him. He went on. "I'm going to sell six of my claims. They aren't producing enough. the E1 Dorado Thirty-Seven Above is still doing well."

She winced but continued to watch him.

"Liza, remember we talked about leaving by September fifteenth. I think that's still a good idea. What do you think?"

Liza shrugged. "It doesn't matter."

"Did you hear how the men called for you last night? When you didn't perform there was nearly a riot. Then Josh told them about the death in your family and they settled down. The show just wasn't the same. They want you to come back and entertain them."

"Why?"

"It's what you do. You're a singer and a dancer. It's how you make your living. You're talented at it, the best in the Klondike. Anyway, you're the Queen of the Klondike."

The hint of a smile touched her face and was gone.

"It isn't important anymore, Bryce. Nothing is important."

"Lots of things are important to me, Liza. In fact, you, Liza Cromwell, are the most important factor in my life. I value you more than all of my claims, my business. You are the best friend I have ever had in my life."

She turned and watched him. "Bryce, you're just trying to make me feel better."

"True, but it's also a fact that you are remarkably important to me. Liza Cromwell, marvelous lady, is the most important factor in my life."

She reached out and put her hand on his shoulder. "That is kind of you to say, Bryce. I'm tired. I think I'll take a nap for a while."

He went back that afternoon with more flowers and she talked to him. She seemed a little more resigned to the fact of Walter's death.

It was the third day before he talked her into going for a walk outside. They went through the side door and along the back of the building into the slopes behind the town. Half a dozen miners saw her and came and told her how sorry they were, and then asked her to please come back and sing for them.

On the slopes, they sat among the flowers and looked down the stretch of the Yukon River. There was a difference in the air. It was still in July but already the heavy heat of summer was slowly easing. Before long it would be cool and then horiffically cold.

"Liza, I'm leaving on the steamer the fifteenth of September. I want you to come with me. There's nothing to hold you here now."

Liza watched his face and she smiled; then she sighed and looked down the waterway. It was the only way to the "outside." "I don't know, Bryce. I'm still so confused. I know I should be singing again, but I can't bring myself to do it." She frowned. "Maybe it would help if I said good-bye to Walter. I've never had a chance to do that. Can you take me out to his grave?"

Bryce rubbed his face and held her hand. "Are you sure? It's just a grave and a wooden marker."

"I know, you told me. But I want to go. I must go up there and say good-bye to Walter. Let's go right now."

At the grave on El Dorado Thirty-seven Above, Liza knelt in prayer for a half hour. Bryce had stopped all work on the claim and it was as silent as death. The men dozed or talked quietly. When Liza stood, she walked to her horse with a quickness that surprised Bryce.

She let him help her mount; then he swung up on his own horse and she glanced at him. Her face looked different. The sadness, the indifference, the hopelessness had been washed away.

"Now, Mr. Bryce Jeferies, I'd say it's past time

that we get back to town so I can do a little rehearsing before the show tonight. I'm ready to work again. You said you wanted to take me with you in September. I'm considering it. You may be right. It might be the right time for both of us to leave. Then we won't have to endure that long, cold winter."

Bryce was so surprised he couldn't speak for a quarter of a mile. Then he told her he was glad she was thinking about leaving. Once started he couldn't stop talking. He told her what he had been doing, pushing the production of the good claims and selling the rest.

She looked at him and with a sparkle in her eye he hadn't seen for a long time, she asked him a question. "Mr. Jeferies, just how much money are you worth right now? When you sell out and get on that boat to St. Michael, how much money would you have?"

Bryce chuckled. "You're a businesswoman again, I see. I don't know how much it would be. I won't until I find out what I can sell the claims for. The secret is to sell them singly and not create a flood of available claims and lower the price. In the bank, I'd say right now that I have about a hundred thousand dollars."

"Glory be! I'd never imagined."

"Some of the Gold Kings of the Yukon made that much in a month on their richest strikes. I was lucky to get some of the better claims."

Liza returned to the saloon and rousted out the girls for a quick rehearsal in the room behind the saloon. That night she was back in form, and the miners gave her a five-minute ovation when she first came out on the stage.

That night she took in more than $50 in gold

dust and coins tossed in her raised skirt.

Bryce talked with Superintendent Irons the next day. He had written an arrest warrant for Frank Davis, who had been the legal partner with Walter in their claim. Davis was from Vancouver and might not be too hard for authorities there to find. He was charged with murder, grand theft, and flight to avoid prosecution.

"We'll find him, and with any luck he'll hang. We Mounties look with great pride on always getting our man. Especially on a murder warrant."

Bryce continued selling claims. He put two more of the smaller producers on the market and both were snapped up by newcomers. He showed that the claims were paying out $300 a week and sold them for $1,500 each.

Two days after Liza began singing again, Arthur Hallifax sent a note backstage to her and she came out to talk to him. She had heard about him and his gambling, but didn't know about McCoy's campaign to find evidence against him.

Arthur had a sarsaparilla ready for her. He was dressed elegantly in a dark blue suit and a gold-trimmed vest with a heavy gold chain spotted with gold nuggets.

He held her chair, and sipped a sarsaparilla himself.

"Thank you for coming back to entertain us after such a tragedy," Arthur said.

She nodded.

"I know you're still a grieving widow, but I want to ask your permission to come courting. I understand that's the proper procedure in even this untamed country."

She smiled. "It's not exactly the fashion, and I'm not ready yet to talk to anyone about courting, but

I appreciate your suggestion. I'll certainly keep it in mind." She paused. "I understand that you're a gambler."

"Yes, I do use the cards to make a living. So far that life has been good to me."

"You do come from England. It's an accent that's hard to disguise. What part of England?"

"North, the lake country, a small town that you've never heard of."

"Then you're not really an earl or a lord?"

"If I were an earl or a lord, I'd be home lording it over my country castle." He chuckled. "I'm afraid I'm only an untitled lad from the old country trying to make his way in the strange and wonderful New World."

Liz smiled, then stood. He rose with her. "Time for me to get backstage. Thanks for the drink." She turned and left wondering just what the tall Englishman had in mind. He was a man who did little without the thought of benefitting himself. How would that apply to her? Liza had no idea. She dismissed him from her mind and hurried to get her costume changed for the next show.

Arthur Hallifax watched the comely lady leave. At first he had thought he might insist that she go with him on the steamer that would be leaving in a week. The craft was the *Benedict* and she was laid up for some repairs before sailing from the dock at Dawson to St. Michael.

He had spent some time with the captain of the steamer, and together they had worked out a plan that could be highly beneficial to both of them.

The captain, Emmett O'Grady, had been working on the plan for months. Both men had decided this was the trip and that Hallifax would be a full partner and supply the additional men needed.

Not just men, but men with rifles and revolvers.

Handguns were illegal in the Yukon, but dozens had slipped through. Hallifax knew how to get them.

Rifles were plentiful. No man could be denied a rifle in bear country. It was for self-protection. The captain had an assortment of handguns he kept on the boat and they were not subject to the Mounties' inspection, unless they were brought to shore.

Hallifax went to the dock where the repairs continued on the *Benedict*. She had unloaded four hundred cases of whiskey after the run up the river. Not as many cheechakos were coming on the boats up the river these days. But there would be a full load of disappointed gold seekers going downstream.

Hallifax met with the captain in his cabin.

"I'd say we go down at least fifty miles before we put the plan into action," Captain O'Grady said. "That will give us time for a good run to the coast before anybody could catch us."

"Sounds about right," Hallifax said. "Only I'd add another hundred miles to the takeover spot, but you're the expert on these matters. You sure the cargo will be on board?"

"Indeed it will. It's been waiting. Going back as defective tools. They've done this before. I happened on it my first trip downstream this spring."

"If the shipment doesn't come on board, you let me know. Me and my men don't want to take a month-long boat ride just to look at the damned scenery."

"I'll let you know, don't worry."

"Will there be any guards?"

"For defective tools? I should think not. It would

ruin the whole secret. There were none used the time before."

Hallifax lifted the cup of whiskey the captain had provided him. "This is a project I'll drink to," the gambler said. "Biggest gamble of my life with the best payoff. I'll supply five men. They already have been hired and I'll start paying them in two days to keep them happy and drinking. You'll have four trusted men to add to the group?"

The captain nodded. Hallifax lifted his cup again. "At last we're on our way to a fortune, Captain O'Grady. Who says the English and the Irish can't work together. Just a few more days and we'll both be stinking, filthy rich!"

Chapter Twenty-Two

Spur McCoy walked his way back to Francine's boardinghouse and went in. He sat by the window and looked out but didn't see anything. He was deep in thought, trying to come up with some kind of idea to make Arthur Halifax confess his misdeeds.

That was a hell of a big order. Halifax was a tough nut, he wouldn't scare easily, and it was doubtful if he could be thrown into a panic and forced to run. The Mounties used to check out every person who sailed to the Outside. He didn't know if they still did or not.

How could he get to Hallifax, make him nervous, maybe even scared enough to upset him, maybe make him blunder into a mistake?

Evidence always worked, but he had none at all from the London crime. He had nothing but the death of White-Smith, which almost certainly had to be laid to Arthur Walling/Hallifax.

What the hell now? He thought over what the fancy lady had said in her house. Hallifax had talked about killing someone in Dawson. Then something she said registered that he hadn't heard fully or ignored. Halifax had mentioned a hatchet.

A hatchet. A hatchet had killed White-Smith, not an ax as the superintendent had figured. A hatchet made a fine weapon, could be concealed and brought out at the deadly moment it was needed.

A hatchet. What could he do with that?

Somewhere in town or in the river was a hatchet that had killed White-Smith. McCoy knew that he would never find it. He didn't even know if the Englishman had been killed in town or upstream or downstream.

It figured that he had been struck down close to the shoreline. It would be easier to pull the body ten feet into the water than to haul it three or four miles from up in one of the claims areas.

Still, he would never find the hatchet.

How many kinds of hatchets were there? Would Hallifax even remember what the death tool looked like? McCoy grinned. Chances were he'd bought it at a store or borrowed or stolen it. He wouldn't have had it in his possession long. Almost any hatchet in general use, doctored up with blood or more likely a generous serving of dry catsup, might be something to grab the killer's attention.

McCoy grinned.

A knock sounded on his door. He opened it and found Francine standing there, a bottle of wine in one hand and a plate filled with crackers and four kinds of cheese in the other.

"Party time?" she asked. She wore a modest dress and her blond hair was braided and rolled into a bun at the back of her neck.

"Any time is party time," McCoy said. "I'm warning you that I'm right in the middle of trying to figure out something."

Francine grinned, stepped inside, and closed the door with her foot. She put down the wine bottle, snapped a waist-high night lock, and smiled at him. "You missed supper. When you came in I figured you might need some liquid refreshment and a whole lot of loving from a good woman to satisfy all of your needs.

"If I can't get your mind off your work and onto something a lot more interesting, then I'll take my wine and go home."

She started by unbuttoning the front of her dress. Her movements caught McCoy's attention and he watched her. She shrugged one side of the dress and let it sag down to expose one breast.

McCoy reached out and caught it, caressing it, working around it and up to the nipple, which surged upward and hardened as he toyed with it.

He would buy a hatchet tomorrow, or maybe two or three. In the meantime he would figure out some ingenious and terrifying ways to bring the bloody hatchet and Hallifax together.

"You have slipped away, haven't you, McCoy? This problem you're working on. Anything I can help you with?"

"What? What was that, Francine?"

She repeated the question.

McCoy grinned. "Yes, you just might be some help. I have to work out some plans and details.

That would really startle him if something happened when I was in sight so he would know it
wasn't me doing any of the wild stuff."

"What are you talking about?"

"You'll find out."

Francine pulled the dress off over her head.
McCoy grinned. This tall, shapely blond lady wore
absolutely nothing under the dress.

"I don't like to be a pig in a poke, so I'll show
you what you get right at the start." She grinned,
and did a little bump and grind for him, making
her breasts shake and her crotch hump forward.

"Now, it's about time we get you as naked as I
am. I get to have the fun of stripping you naked,
big man. I get to rip your clothes off and love
every second of it."

He caught her hands and held them. "Damnit,
Francine. I'm trying to work out an important
problem I have. I need to do some planning and
set up some things."

"Fuck you, McCoy. I've got some highly important plans too, and they concern your naked body.
I've got to get some loving today or I'm going to
explode right here. How would you explain to the
Mounties when they find me splattered all over
your bedroom in about a thousand pieces?"

She moved his held hands down until each
rested on a breast.

"Now, isn't that a lot better place to be working
than on some stuffy old plans? Hey, we can make
plans just how we're going to make love the first
four times."

She pushed in against him and found his lips
with hers. Her whole body trembled as she kissed
him. When she came away from him her arms
went around his neck and she sighed.

"You must know what you do to me, McCoy. You turn me to jelly. Damn I want you right now. Please? Don't make me beg. Let's see if you're reacting to my naked body."

She felt his crotch and grinned. "Hey, you're all business, right? Then what's this ax handle doing in your pants? This birch tree about a yard long? What is that thing?"

McCoy grinned, picked her up, and nibbled on one breast as he carried her to the bed. He held her two feet off the covers and dropped her.

Francine yelped and giggled when she hit, then grabbed him and pulled him down. Her face had flushed and her hips ground against him.

"Fuck it, McCoy, don't even bother undressing. Whip that cock of yours out right now and poke it into me. I need him bad, McCoy. Come on, do me right now before I explode."

He could see she was serious. It surged his hot blood and he pulled open his fly buttons and pushed down his underwear. Before he could do more, her hands were there to pull him free.

"Oh, lordy, what a dandy!"

She pulled his erection toward her crotch and McCoy followed. It took her only a moment to position him; then she put both hands on his rump and pulled him forward.

McCoy thrust slow and easy, moving in as her juices made way for him, and a moment later he was fully inserted and her arms and legs locked around his back and she cooed and sang a little song.

"Oh, I know a girl who lives on the hill, she won't fuck but her sister will. I'm her sister."

She sang it over and over again as they pounded at each other. She met each of his thrusts, and before he gained a full head of steam, she cried out sharply, gasped, and then her body twitched and threshed as spasms hit her, setting each nerve ending on fire, shaking her and shattering her. She moaned and screeched, then wailed long and low, ending on a note so high McCoy wondered how she got there.

One time she stopped and he stroked again, only to set her off on another long series of spasms and vibrations that rattled her.

"Oh, God, oh, God, I'm gonna die. Oh, God, that is fine, so fine. Oh!" She surged into another series of spasms as she climaxed again and again, until she was so worn out she could only sigh.

McCoy sensed her satisfaction and he surged forward, his trigger ready as he powered at her with long thrusts that came almost out of her, then rammed in hard, jolting her up the bed.

Then he sensed his time coming and he shortened the strokes and speeded up until he was one giant pile driver stroking three times a second and inching her back toward the head of the bed.

Before her head touched the top boards, he shattered himself on the rocks below after a long dive that found him soaring off a high cliff aiming at the ocean wave. The wave stopped and sank back toward the next oncoming wave, leaving the jagged rocks with only a foot of water over them instead of the usual 15 feet of green roiling Pacific ocean.

As he collapsed on top of her, he was vaguely aware that Francine was climaxing again. He had set her off. She shook and shivered, and then the series of spasms racked her again before she gave a long sigh and smiled at him, then closed her eyes and rested.

Five minutes later, McCoy came alive again. He eased away from Francine and sat beside her on the bed. A moment later she groaned and sat up beside him.

"I love it when you smash down on me, driving me into the fucking mattress that way. Beautiful."

He caught her face in one hand and turned it toward him.

"Francine, we've got to get serious for a while. Get your clothes on and then we're going to do some planning."

She eyed him curiously.

"Francine, I told you I'm a U.S. lawman. I'm in town trying to catch a killer. Now get dressed and I'll tell you all about it. Then we're going to plan just how we can scare this gent into confessing or make him go mad and kill himself, I don't much care which."

Francine nodded and pulled on her dress and buttoned it up to her neck, and sat back on the bed beside him. Her hand went toward his crotch, but he pulled it away.

It took him five minutes to tell her about Arthur Walling/Hallifax and what he figured he had done and that he had no real way to prove it.

"Scare the bastard half to death," she said.

"Easier when it gets dark. A man alone, at night, can get scared of lots of things. But we don't have that darkness. Got to figure out something else."

"I like the idea of the bloody hatchet. You can use that all sorts of different ways."

Yes, the hatchet, but what else? We don't have a body. We could fake up one, a half-alive mummi-

fied one. But that works best at night too, when
things aren't so clear.

"Get him drunk first, sour his senses," Francine
said. "Then do your games and tricks on him. His
alcohol-fouled mind won't be able to pick up on
your tricks. He'll think it's real."

McCoy reached over and kissed her cheek.
"Now you are talking! Great idea. But that way
will work only once. After that he'll be careful not
to drink too much. He's smart and wary."

They sat, thighs touching and sipping the wine
and working on the cheese and crackers.

"What the hell else?" McCoy asked the room.

He snapped his fingers. "Blanks in his gun and
in mine. Let him get my gun when his won't kill
the 'ghost' of White-Smith."

Francine grinned. "Hey, I get to be around when
you're tormenting this killer? I get to watch?"

"Watch, hell. You'll have to help. I won't be able
to do everything. I might have to hire a couple of
men to help us too. Depends on how elaborate
our tricks on him turn out to be."

"What's first?"

"First we plan out the whole caper from start
to end. We know exactly what we're going to do
and when and how. Then we start to torment Mr.
Walling until he cracks open like a ripe pea pod
on a summer afternoon."

They planned for three hours; then McCoy
seemed satisfied and the wine made him sleepy.
Francine suggested that it was time to get to bed
and before McCoy realized what was going on, he
was hard again and feeling ready and they coupled
slowly, like a pair of oversized hippopotamuses,
and climaxed and came apart and fell into each
other's arms.

The wine bottle somehow became empty, and they both laughed and fell together on the bed, but they were beyond any serious lovemaking and drifted off to sleep holding each other's various body parts, even though the best expectations had degenerated into laughter and impotence and then blessed sleep.

McCoy awoke at 6:30 A.M. as usual. He stirred, and Francine sat up beside him with a start.

"Oh, God. I just dreamed that I was serving drinks at my fancy ball for all of the town's best and when somebody asked for wine, I calmly told them they better drink whiskey because I had pissed in the wine. That brought down the house with laughter and I was the hit of the evening."

"You were the hit of the evening last night." McCoy pushed over and looked at the pad of paper where he had written down the litany of fear and fright they had worked out for Arthur Walling.

"Oh, damn. I'm late. The cook will be mad as a whore with only one tit." She stood, stretched, and looked at McCoy. "Of course I'm not so late that I couldn't heat up for you for a quick morning fuck."

"Business first," McCoy said. "Anyway, you ruined me last night for at least a week. You get breakfast for us all, and I'll be happy to participate. I've got a lot of arrangements to make this morning."

After breakfast, McCoy went to the first hardware store he found. He bought three hatchets that were exactly alike. They were not fancy, cost a dollar each. The same item in a Stateside store would bring not more than 20 cents.

He took them back to his room and laid them

on the dresser top. Francine had left a pint jar filled with catsup. He dabbed some of the bright red sauce on the blade of one of the hatchets and let it sit there and dry.

His second job was to find Walling. The gambler probably worked late and got busy on the next day's gambling about noon or shortly thereafter. McCoy found him about two o'clock on his survey of the tenth gambling hall. This was one of the big ones.

He watched Walling until he was sure he was set up in a long-running game, then hurried out on more errands. He bought a jacket, trousers, a vest, a black hat, a white shirt, and a derby hat—all used. He took them back to his room, where Francine was hard at work converting three old pillows into a dummy. Skinny pillows made the legs, a larger one the torso. They would use sticks for the arms. The head was a problem.

"This gent is going to be a real swell when we get him done," Francine said. "After he serves his purpose, I might sit him in my parlor so the curious will think I have a gentleman caller."

"You don't think he may develop some fatal wounds?"

"Like gunshots?"

"Something like that, maybe a knife slash," McCoy said. "Depends how close the two come to each other."

"What about the head?"

They tried a ball, but it wasn't big enough. Then Francine found a round pillow that worked. With the pillow sewed on to the torso there was no neck, but that didn't matter. The hat came down low, and some charcoal lines and some paint made the pillow into a face that would pass. In the dark. Only it wouldn't be dark—unless they used the inside of a building. Perfect, McCoy decided. That's how he would get his darkness.

With the dummy well underway, McCoy went back to the saloon where he had found Walling. Walling was still in the game, but now there were only three players left. It would soon be over. Nobody likes to play poker with four players, let alone three or two.

McCoy needed to know where Walling lived. A boardinghouse or a rooming house probably. Or a hotel. He had to know. The only way to find out was wait and watch him until he went home. He might not do that for another six or eight hours.

The gamblers ended the game and Walling/Hallifax went across the street for a meal. McCoy found a seat in a corner out of sight, and had some food as he waited for Walling to finish his. Walling was a slow eater.

After the meal, Walling stopped at the bank, then came out and to McCoy's delight, headed away from the games and up to First Street, then down two blocks to a two-story house that evidently had been built as a boardinghouse. Walling went in a side door, evidently having an entry all for himself. A moment later, McCoy saw the shades go up and Walling stared out the window a moment, then went out of sight.

Fifteen minutes later, Walling came out. He was dressed differently now, more like a miner, with a workingman's dirty pants, knee-high boots, an old logger's plaid jacket, and a felt hat that had seen its share of hauling water and being stepped on and lost in a dig or two. This must be his low-stakes poker costume, or just another way

to make the big spenders think they had a sucker
on the string.

Now Walling wore glasses with large wire-
rimmed frames, and a short, stiff mustache
that he must have glued on the way actors do.
It changed his appearance completely.

When the gambler walked down the street and
out of sight, McCoy tried the side door Walling
had just come from. It was locked. He went
around to the front of the house and found a
sign.

"The Welcome Arms Hotel. All rooms now
rented. Try us again in a month. J. W. Lansbarger,
Prop."

McCoy didn't bother going in. He knew the
room. Now he had to work out the details.

Back at Francine's, McCoy found the hatchet
he had "bloodied" with catsup. It had dried and
the catsup looked fairly convincing as blood. He
dabbed on some more, making what he hoped
would be splatters and spray on the head of the
hatchet and some on the handle. Then he let that
dry as well.

It would be tonight. Better get the things in
motion. He spent some more time putting catsup on the other hatchets, trying to duplicate the
first one as best he could. When the first one had
dried, he put it in a stiff paper sack and carried
it with him as he went back to the house on
First Street and found a convenient waiting place.
He was two houses down and sitting against the
stump of what once had been a conifer of some
kind.

He was in the open, and anyone going up or
down the street could see him. But he wouldn't
stand out. Every spare spot on half the streets

in town were filled with men sitting and waiting. Most of them didn't know what they waited for. Thousands of men had no jobs, no chance for jobs, and no way to make any income. They lived on their original 1,000 pounds of food the Mounties made them bring in. The only decision they had to make was "when." They knew they had to give up the gold rush fever, to go back down the Yukon River to the "outside." The thing they had to decide was when.

He saw six other men sitting on the same side of the street as he was along the block to Front Street. Nobody would give him a second look.

McCoy had some of the cheese and crackers that had been left over from the night before. He nibbled on them as he waited. As he did, he worked out plans for the other bloody hatchets. One would not be enough. Three should be about right.

He sat there for three hours, then took a short walk, came back, and hunkered down against the same stump. He was glad some "stump jumper" hadn't taken over his perch while he was gone.

It wasn't until nearly ten o'clock that night that he saw the familiar figure of Walling coming down the street. He did not walk a straight line. The man hummed an old English drinking song as he passed, and now staggered just a little to make him look like a typical comic drunk.

The sky was as light as it had been at noon. The darkening would come sometime after midnight. McCoy was not sure just when. He saw clearly when Walling went to the small house-hotel side door, used a key, and stepped inside.

A few moments later he saw the shade pulled down and behind it the faint flicker of a lamp.

Some people are sticklers for habit. At night you lit a lamp inside, so Walling lit a lamp. McCoy had not worked everything down to the last detail.

On this one there were several little problems. He walked up to the side of the house, and worked around to the window where the shade had been drawn. With a strong heave, McCoy threw the catsup-stained hatchet through the glass window. It powered through easily, punched the shade forward, and landed with a clatter on the wooden floor inside.

As soon as McCoy threw the hatchet, he ran beside the house and past the rear door, then circled around the house next door so he could come out on the same street but one house down.

McCoy looked with caution past the front porch of the next-door house and saw Walling outside his room, near the broken window. He wore only a brown shirt and still had on his work pants and boots. He stood there scratching his head and staring around. At last he shook his head and went back into the side door with faltering steps. The door closed solidly behind him and McCoy eased away from the porch next door, went back to the street, and walked down to Front and then on to Francine's boardinghouse.

She met him as soon as he came in the door.

"So, how did it go?"

He told her.

Francine laughed softly. "I'd love to be a mouse in the side of the room and see the expression on the killer's face when he saw the hatchet with blood on it. He's drunk, you said, so he would be sure it was blood.

"No note, no message, just him and the hatchet that could have killed White-Smith. He'll be thinking: Did someone find it? Did someone see him kill the man and retrieve the hatchet? Will there be a letter about blackmail? Oh, how delicious! Now, what have we planned on to do next?"

Chapter Twenty-Three

Arthur Walling took one more look around the street. He had rushed outside at once when he heard the window break. He had been outside within a few seconds, but there was no one on the street or near the house who could have thrown anything through his window.

He checked again. Three men sat hunched over on the far side of the street, probably sleeping. None of them had had time to throw the item through the window and get back in position before Arthur gained the door and his view of the area.

Arthur shook his head at the mystery of it. Now he wondered why anyone would want to throw something through his window. He would have to pay for the damage. He didn't even see what the object had been. Maybe a rock or a piece of wood or a heavy stick. The item itself might give him a clue.

Back inside, Arthur closed the door and stared at the scatter of glass on the wooden floor.

Then he saw the bloody hatchet.

Arthur stared at it for a moment, then jumped back. He felt his heart race. His face quivered, and he realized his knees shook and wobbled as he took three steps away from the ugly red-stained hatchet and fell more than sat on the bed.

It couldn't be! No one had been there. No one had seen him use the hatchet. No one could know. His head swirled around and it felt light and a darkness half-covered his eyes, and he thought of shaking his head to clear it; instead he bowed it low to his knees to bring more blood to his starved brain cells.

Slowly the darkness drifted away and the lightness ceased and he sat up.

He stared at the bloody hatchet again.

It was a logical impossibility. It couldn't be happening.

But it was.

Someone had just thrown a hatchet through his window. It wasn't just any hatchet, it was one that had bloodstains on it. He bent toward the hatchet, then pulled back as if his hand would be burned.

Someone knocked on his door and he jumped up more frightened than he had ever been in his life. Was it blackmail? Did someone want to kill him in revenge?

The knocking came again, then a voice. It was his landlady.

"Mr. Hallifax, are you all right? Somebody said your window broke."

A wave of relief flooded him and Arthur scurried around the hatchet to the door. He opened it and tried to smile at the landlady.

"Yes, I'm fine. Someone threw a rock through my window. I have no idea who it could have been. Oh, yes, a man lost some money to me in a card game. He must have followed me here and threw the rock to spite me. I'll pay for a new window. Is ten dollars enough? Here, take it. I'll sweep up the glass, you can have the new one installed tomorrow. Oh, could I borrow a broom and a dust pan? Thank you."

The woman lifted her brows. "Some ingrates don't care who they hurt. I'm just glad you weren't injured, Mr. Hallifax. I'll bring the broom right away."

He thanked her and closed the door. He turned slowly and stared at the bloody hatchet. He couldn't remember for sure what the one he had used had been like. The size was about right. How could he ever explain it to the landlady?

But could he pick it up? He took two short steps toward the hatchet, bent forward to lift it, then shook his head. He couldn't touch it.

But he couldn't leave it there!

He moved another step toward the bloody hatchet, and then with a sudden thought, he nudged the handle with his boot. It moved. He pushed it farther away from the glass until he had it all the way under the bed. Now no one could see it.

He breathed a small sigh and sat down on the edge of the bed. She would be back any moment. He couldn't look so concerned. The big question remained: Who had thrown the hatchet through the window? Another one nagged at him. Why did that person throw the hatchet and was it the same one he had used at the river? He scowled thinking about it.

The only logical conclusion was that someone had seen him do in the vicar's son, had searched until he found the hatchet as proof, and now would hound his victim for a few days before he made some arrangements to meet and present his blackmail demands. Yes, that had to be it. The only logical explanation. At once Arthur felt better. He stood and began pushing the larger pieces of glass toward a central point.

A moment later a knock sounded on the door and he opened it.

"I'll do it, Mr. Hallifax. No sense you sweeping up this glass. Now, you just stand back and it'll be done in a thrice. Hope this doesn't worry you any. I'll report it to Superintendent Irons and have him keep watch on the house now and then. He frowns on this sort of hooliganism."

Arthur Walling/Hallifax had recovered somewhat from his fright. He smiled and nodded at his landlady.

"Yes, ma'am, I think that would be a good idea. No telling what some wild-eyed loser might do next. I'd like to catch this one and let Irons make an example of him, but I'm afraid we don't stand a ghost of a chance of finding him out of thirty thousand ruffians out there. Oh, no need to mention my name to the superintendent. It wouldn't add anything and might put me in a bad light."

The woman smiled at her boarder, dumped the broken glass into a basket she had brought with her, and nodded. "Wouldn't think of laying you open to anything like that, Mr. Hallifax. Indeed I wouldn't. There, that should do it. You be careful barefooted in here. I got most of it, but can't say for sure there ain't a shard or two hiding around."

She turned, opened the door and left with a wave of the broom at him.

Hallifax dropped on the bed and shivered. It had been all he could do to put up a normal front for the woman. How could he play poker when his nerves were this on edge? A long walk, yes, some physical exercising always had calmed him down. That's what he would do. At least the low-born who threw the hatchet wouldn't know where to find him then.

He went out quietly, making sure that his hide-out derringer was in place under his left arm and that it was loaded with two .38-caliber rounds. Just wait until he had a confrontation with this blackmailer!

He would walk the length of the town of Dawson four times, that should be eight miles. That would put him in much better shape for the night to come. As he walked, Arthur Walling/Hallifax tried not to remember the sound the hatchet had made when it connected with the side of White-Smith's head and sank into his skull, splattering blood and going deep enough to kill the man instantaneously. It had been a "thonk" like hitting a ripe watermelon with a knife.

"No!" Arthur said out loud. Two miners looked up at him from where they sat on some logs next to the street. He scowled at them and walked ahead. He would not think of anything to do with White-Smith again—ever.

Back in the rented room at Francine's boardinghouse, Spur McCoy watched her put the final touches on the dummy. With just a little light and far enough away, it would pass as a real person, a dead one perhaps, but that was what it was supposed to be. The slash on the left side of the head dabbed with more catsup was a nice touch, McCoy thought.

He snapped his fingers. "One more errand. I want to see if I can find Bryce Jeferies. I hear he can throw a hatchet like an old woodsman."

"You won't be gone all night, will you?"

"Not a chance. I need some sleep. But first, a small task."

He found Bryce at the New York Saloon cheering Liza as she sang her last show.

McCoy sat down and tugged at Bryce's sleeve. When Liza finished singing, Bryce led the cheering; then he grinned and looked over at McCoy.

"Thought you came in. Where have you been last couple of nights?"

"Working. Wondered if you could help me." Briefly he explained who he was and what he wanted Bryce to do.

"Yeah, I know this Hallifax. Tried to get Liza to go out with him. She didn't. You think he's your killer?"

"Almost certain. We'll see how he reacts. Here's what I want you to do."

After McCoy laid out the plan, Bryce grinned.

"No problem. To put the hatchet in his back would be another story, but just in the door is easy."

"First I want to get the same one I used earlier tonight. Further confuse him and set him on edge."

McCoy took out pencil and paper and wrote the message. He had some cord and would tie the letter to the hatchet handle. The two walked near Arthur Walling/Hallifax's rooming house and watched for a light in the man's window.

"Doesn't seem to be in," Bryce said.

"Or he's sleeping, which I doubt. Let's take a look." They walked up to the broken window and looked inside.

"Nobody there," McCoy said. He unlatched the double-hung window and pushed it up, getting the broken pieces of window out of the way. Then he bellied up and inside the opening and dropped to the floor. He struck two matches, and at last found the hatchet under the bed. He came out holding the weapon and grinning.

McCoy slid out the window and pulled it back down, and then they retreated to a safe spot. They tied the message on the handle of the hatchet and Bryce hefted it.

"A little longer handle than I'm used to using, but all I have to do is stick it in the door beside him," Bryce said. "Not a problem. Wish to hell this guy would come home."

They had worked out their little act. Bryce said he needed to be about 25 feet from the door for best accuracy. They found a spot near the house next door that was 40 feet from Arthur's rooming house door. They simply sat down in the midnight sun and waited. McCoy was positioned so he could spot Arthur Walling/Hallifax coming if he walked down from Front Street.

They waited another hour, and then McCoy punched Bryce, who had drifted off to sleep.

"He's coming," McCoy said. "Let's get up and walk toward him and then turn around and walk in front of him a ways, then go back toward him. We're drunk and singing. Now!"

They knew what they needed to do. Both men had been drunk enough to make the staggers convincing. The song was one of the bawdy drinking tunes the miners loved, and it worked. They got almost to Arthur, then staggered, almost fell and turned and walked in front of him. Then they stopped, swayed, and fell down in the street.

Arthur Walling/Hallifax went by them with ten feet to spare and continued on to his doorway. As soon as he was past, Bryce pulled the hatchet out of his shirt and he and McCoy moved up silently behind their victim.

Bryce was 30 feet from the door when Arthur Walling/Hallifax put the key in the lock. He never had a chance to turn the key. The hatchet spun once and the sharp blade sank an inch into the plank door a foot from Walling's head.

By the time he jolted around, all he saw were the two drunks singing again and walking back the way they had come before. He stared at them as they moved past the next house.

Then he realized they were the only ones around, the only ones who could have thrown the hatchet. As he started after them they staggered down the side of the next house and disappeared.

He ran then, but when he rounded the house all he saw was an empty yard where it backed up to the alley near the rear doors of the stores along Front Street. He scurried from one to the next. Most of the stores had mounds of trash and old boxes and cartons behind them from merchandise brought in. He couldn't prowl into each pile of garbage.

At last he gave up and went back to his door. Arthur Walling/Hallifax looked at the bloodstained hatchet sticking in his door and trembled. He grabbed the handle after steeling his nerves, then pulled the weapon free, opened the door, and hurried inside.

Once in his room he dropped the hatchet on the floor as if it were a hot iron. Only then did he notice the paper tied to the handle.

"Yes!" he said softly. "It's the note, the demand that my blackmailer is going to make on me."

He untied the string and read the letter.

"Arthur Walling/Hallifax. I know you killed James White-Smith with this hatchet. It's about time we met again, face to face, and I'll tell you exactly what I want. You will go to the Bryce Jeferies offices tomorrow at ten A.M. There will be a letter there for you in a sealed envelope.

"Jeferies knows nothing of this. The letter will tell you exactly what to do and where to go so we can have another meeting, face to face, and I will accuse you again of ruining my sister and killing my brother. Then I will have my revenge."

The letter was signed James Whitc-Smith.

"Arrrrrrrrrrrrrrrrrrraugh!" Arthur screamed. He dropped the letter and fell to his knees, then crawled to the bed, where he threw himself face-down and beat the covers with his fists.

"Noooooooooooo! This can't be happening. The man is dead. I threw him in the Yukon. I saw his bloated, ravaged body when they brought it up on the steamer. James White-Smith is dead. I know he's dead." Arthur stalked around his room, pacing furiously.

If White-Smith was dead, why was he planning to go for the letter tomorrow and get instructions what to do next? Why? Because a blackmailer was the worst kind of villain. He was cunning and smart and never gave you an even break. The only thing to do was to kill this blackmailer and send him on a long swim down the Yukon as well. That was why he would get the letter tomorrow.

Yes, that was what he would do. Two rounds from his derringer should do the trick. If not, he'd have a pocketful of rounds to reload with. A gun against a hatchet was not a good match.

He felt somewhat better. It had to be a blackmailer. James White-Smith was dead. He couldn't have written that letter. Some very much alive and greedy person wanted to get rich and then be on the next steamer down the Yukon.

Arthur Walling/Hallifax snorted. The blackmailer would go down the Yukon, all right, but not in the way he figured that he would. He would be floating face-down with two bullet holes in his heart or his head.

McCoy and Bryce had eluded the half-hearted search in the alley by Arthur Walling/Hallifax with no trouble. They'd simply shifted around one stack of empty boxes and then another. Once they'd slipped into the back door of a store and left when the killer gave up.

Now they walked back to Bryce's office, where McCoy wrote out the second note. He had planned it with Bryce, who was delighted to be in on the scheme.

"We can use that old storage room here behind my office," Bryce said. "It's forty feet long and half that wide and has a ten-or-twelve-foot ceiling, rafters really. All we have to do is nail a blanket over the one window and keep the back door shut and it's as dark as the middle of January at midnight."

"In Vancouver," McCoy added.

"Can we get the other things we need?" Bryce asked.

"The powder might be the one problem," McCoy said. "Without that we'll have to make our own, maybe with some diluted gunpowder. I'll try in the morning at two stores that might have what we need."

McCoy put the directions for the victim in an envelope Bryce gave him. He wrote Arthur's name on it and they left it on Bryce's desk.

In back of his office, they both looked at the large storage room.

"Used to be a business in front and they kept their stock back here," Bryce said. "I changed things around because I bought the building for a song."

The room was fairly light with the window open. The big doors at the back were closed and let in no light at all. They nailed an old blanket over the window and stood there in the gloom.

"Almost feels like night," McCoy said.

"Will this be dark enough to pull your stunt?"

"It'll have to be. I need some quarter-inch rope, two pulleys, and the hatchet that I have in my room. I sure hope this one works. I'll have Superintendent Irons along for the show if I can talk him into coming."

They parted and McCoy went back to his room. Francine roused from the bed and watched him.

"All this work and no play . . ."

"Enough, wench. Ye who prattle on as a little old woman causes me great pain in mine breast!"

Francine sat up and stared at him. "What the hell was that?"

"You don't know much Shakespeare, I'd say. The trap is set. Now all I have to do is get you to help me tomorrow about six-thirty in the morning so we can be ready by ten. That means we need some sleep now, not some sexy play."

"Fine. I'm sleepy enough to nod off right beside your gorgeous body."

She did.

In the morning, McCoy found what he wanted in the second store, bought enough for three good-sized batches, and listened as the man told him how to use the powder. A match touched to a six-inch row of the powder would be the safest. He found the quarter-inch rope and pulleys to use with it with no trouble. They had spirited the dummy down to the back door of Bryce's office and inside without causing too much attention.

Bryce borrowed a ladder from next door and began rigging the dummy on the rope and pulleys. He tied one end of the rope on the ceiling rafters as high as he could, and the other end of it just beyond the door in back about head high. He pulled the rope as tight as he could to eliminate any sag.

One run-through with the dummy and it worked perfectly. Then he rigged the powder and the powder trails on three wooden boxes along the sides of the warehouse. They were ten feet apart. By nine-thirty he was ready and waiting.

Superintendent Irons had groused about leaving the office, but at last he'd decided he would be there to see what happened. He sat in a chair near the inside door that led from Bryce's office to the warehouse section.

Promptly at ten, McCoy watched through a crack of the open door as a haggard and not well-dressed Arthur Walling/Hallifax came into Bryce's front office.

"Yes, sir, what might I do for you?" Bryce asked.

"I . . . I was supposed to pick up something here this morning."

Bryce frowned. "And who might you be, sir?"

"Arthur Hallifax."

Bryce nodded. "Yes, I found this under my door this morning. It has your name on it. I hope nothing is wrong."

"No, no, just some family business." Hallifax took the envelope, tapped it on his hand, then walked outside. Just beyond the door he tore open the envelope, unfolded the paper, and read it, frowned, then read it again. He began walking toward the end of the block so he could come around to the back door of the Bryce Jeferies offices.

Bryce poked his head in the back room. "He took the envelope. Looks like he's on his way back here." Bryce stepped into the darkened back room and closed the door.

He positioned himself at the second box where the trail of powder lay. Francine was at the last one, and McCoy would do double duty and start the first powder burn.

They waited.

It was nearly five minutes before they heard someone at the back door. Then it opened, letting in a shaft of daylight. A figure stepped in and then the door closed quickly.

McCoy had climbed the ladder and readied the dummy. Now he spoke in a falsetto and quavering voice.

"Are you Arthur Walling/Hallifax?"

There was a gasp from the darkness near the back door.

"Yes, I'm Hallifax."

"You're the man who killed me. I've come to collect your eternal soul to roast it in Hell!" McCoy's voice rose on the end and he fired his derringer, then sent the dummy rolling down the pulley over the taunt rope aimed at the back door. He dropped to the ground and a moment later struck a match and lit the trail of powder.

The sudden bright light from the photo flash powder gave a startling image of the figure floating downward toward the back door holding out a bloody hatchet ready to strike. Then in quick succession the other two flash powders went off in brilliant but brief gushes of light, showing the dummy coming closer and closer to the back door.

They heard a scream from Arthur Walling/Hallifax; then the door rattled as he evidently tried to open it.

"You killed me, Walling, and now you shall die. The hatchet you used is in your room. It's evidence against you. You'll hang, Walling. Hang for killing me, James White-Smith!"

"Nooooooooooooooooooooooooooo!" Walling/Hallifax screamed. He fired his derringer twice at the hanging form of the dummy and just after the second round, two Mounties stormed through the door flooding the area with light. They grabbed Arthur and held him for Superintendent Irons.

He took the man outside into the morning light and stared at him. Arthur Walling/Hallifax had dropped the derringer. One of the Mounties found it.

"Is this your weapon, Hallifax?" Irons asked.

Arthur was so shaken he could hardly speak. He

shook his head. "N . . . no . . . not mine. I thought you fired it."

"I'm arresting you, Walling, on a British warrant and for the death of a British subject, James White-Smith."

Arthur pulled himself up and frowned. "It was all a trick, wasn't it? A sham, a costume ball to make me crack. You have no proof that I have committed any crime whatsoever, Superintendent Irons. I know it, and you know it. You can't prove I owned or shot that handgun, whatever it was. You can't prove that I killed anybody anywhere.

"Now, unless you have some evidence to charge me and arrest me, I think you had better rethink your charges. I'm still a British subject, and the unlawful or false arrest of a British subject brings a stiff penalty, even for a superintendent of the Canadian Royal Mounted Police."

McCoy watched the little drama playing out. He realized that his demonstration and theatrics had not been enough to reduce Walling to a blubbering, confessing killer. Now it looked like even an arrest of Walling was slipping away.

Superintendent Irons scowled. "You may be right, Mr. Hallifax; however, in other matters I do have wide latitude. The weapon, for example. No one else was near the spot where the weapon fired." He grabbed Hallifax's right hand and sniffed it. "I can smell cordite on your hand, which is the result of that hand firing a pistol.

"Therefore I am giving you a blue ticket. You have a week to get your affairs in order and be on the boat that sails a week from today. Since you've done no other damage in this area that we know of, you won't be incarcerated until the ship leaves. I'm releasing you on your own recognizance. You will be on that boat a week from today."

"If I wind up my affairs earlier, may I take an earlier boat, Superintendent?"

"Yes, the Mountie on the dock will record when you're leaving and on which boat. Now move along and tend to your affairs."

When Arthur Walling/Hallifax walked down the alley and out of sight, McCoy went out to talk to Irons. He wanted to see the dummy, so they went back inside and opened both doors for more light. He frowned at the dummy holding the hatchet.

"Hatchet, McCoy? Where did you come up with that idea."

McCoy told him about the fancy lady and Walling's wild ravings about killing someone with a hatchet. "Not exactly testimony for a court of law, but something I thought I could use against him."

Irons smiled. "That's probably what happened. I'm thinking that you're right, he's the killer of the English lad and this White-Smith. But he's right too. We don't have a scratch of hard evidence against him. I'm damned sorry to see him get away, but there's nothing we can do."

Irons turned stern eyes on McCoy. "None of your Wild West eye-for-an-eye justice, McCoy. I've heard about you down there in the States. No cowboy justice, or I'll put you in the dock for murder."

McCoy held up his hands. "I'm mad as hell that he's going to run, Superintendent. But like you say, no evidence, no trial. You don't suppose I could challenge him to a duel?"

"Dueling is against the law in the Yukon," Irons said.

"Figured," McCoy said, and went back into the big dark room and took down the rigging and the dummy.

Francine grinned at him. "What the hell do we do with this dummy?"

McCoy laughed. "I'm giving him to you and naming him Arthur." Despite the laugh and joke, McCoy was in a somber mood. There must be something that he could do to trap the killer, but how? He hated writing a report to the general that he'd found the killer but they couldn't arrest him. He'd think of something. He'd damn well better.

Chapter Twenty-Four

Arthur Walling/Hallifax walked away from Superintendent Irons and out of sight down the alley next to Front Street. He shivered with rage and fright. Never could he remember being so terrified, so at a loss, so ready to give up. That monstrous figure speeding at him through the air with the bloody hatchet raised ready to strike him down had curdled his blood and set his very soul on fire.

The voice had accused him and he'd wanted to run, to hide. Instead he had drawn his derringer and fired twice at the figure. At once he'd known he had made a mistake. Then the Mounties had been there accusing him, badgering him.

He had struck back. He had proclaimed himself a British subject and derided them for having no evidence. The good old British common law had won the day for him. The Mountie knew he had no solid evidence.

So he had held his head high, berated them again, and walked away.

All he'd suffered was a blue ticket. He would be on a boat out of Dawson within a week. He snorted. Plenty of time to get done what needed doing. An abundance of time to make certain arrangements that he needed to take care of.

Timing now was important. He was not sure just when the captain of the *Benedict* would be leaving. That was first on his list of things to get done within the week.

He took a notebook from his pocket and wrote a message. He folded it and on the outside wrote: "To Captain O'Brien of the *Benedict*." Then he looked for a likely messenger.

He asked one man if he could read, and the man admitted that he couldn't.

"But I'm a good worker, strong, and I follow orders good," the strapping youth with blond hair said.

Hallifax nodded. "Just the man I'm looking for." He took a dollar bill from his pocket and tore it in half. "This is not good, just half of it, right?" The young man nodded. "I'm going to give you half of it. Then I'm going to tell you to deliver this message to a ship's captain.

"Find out where the *Benedict* is tied up at the dock and give this note to the captain. Wait for a reply. Do you understand that?"

The young man repeated the instructions word for word.

"Good, here's half the dollar bill. You deliver the message, bring back any reply, and meet me right here. Then I'll give you the other half of the dollar bill."

The blond hulk nodded, took the message, and ran toward the docks.

Hallifax did some pacing up and down on the planks in front of three stores, and used up ten minutes. He saw the young man rushing back a moment later.

The youth looked for Hallifax, and came trotting up to him.

"The captain said thank you and he'll meet you there." The youth hooded his eyes. "I get the other half of the dollar now?"

Hallifax handed it over, and the messenger headed for the first saloon on the street to spend his wages.

Hallifax turned and walked down Front Street toward the place of the meeting. It was a small cafe set out on the edge of the docks, and provided some of the best baked salmon in all of Dawson.

The gambler arrived slightly before the meeting time and went in and to the back, where he found a booth and slid into one side. He waved the waiter away saying he was waiting for a friend.

Captain O'Brien came in moments later. He had a hat on down over his eyes, and Hallifax now adjusted his own black hat so it shielded much of his eyes. O'Brien stopped a moment and said something to the cook and laughed with him, then went on to the rear booth and slid in across from Hallifax.

"So we meet without a hundred watching eyes, Englisher. You have the men we need?" The captain said it in a voice so soft that Hallifax had to lean closer to hear it all.

"Yes, I have the men. When will your repairs be done? Irons has given me a blue ticket, so I have to be gone in a week."

Captain O'Brien nodded, not asking why the

Englishman was being expelled from Dawson. He looked around the empty cafe. Then he went on in his soft voice.

"Our repairs will be done this morning. I've asked Superintendent Irons for a sailing time of just before six o'clock today. He said it would have to wait until tomorrow at noon so he could check all of the passengers and allow any merchants to get freight on who wanted it shipped."

"So it's tomorrow noon."

"Aye, but just so the bank can move its boxes of heavy 'tools' on board. I'd guess they will come about eleven tomorrow."

"Then we sail at noon. Good. I'll have my five men there at nine o'clock so they can get signed off by Irons and put on the ship. Don't try to collect fares from them or tickets. We'll come separately. I'll give each one a piece of cardboard with a number five on it. I'll be the last one on board."

"Sounds good. About the . . ." He looked up and stopped as the cook brought back two plates loaded with baked salmon steaks and all the trimmings. He put down the plates with silverware and came back with heavy mugs filled with coffee.

"Makes it look better if we eat," O'Brien said.

They ate.

During the meal they decided it might be best not to set any time to start their surprise on board. They would just play it as it came and pick the right time and the right place.

The baked salmon with a special sauce on it was the best fish that Hallifax had ever eaten. When the food and coffee were gone, the captain stood and left the cafe. They had no more business to settle. Tomorrow they both would be one step closer to being rich.

Hallifax went to the Gold Nugget Saloon and found two of the men he had hired. He talked to one of them and had him round up the other three. Then he met them one at a time without anyone wondering what he was doing. They sat at a back table with whiskey glasses and spoke in low tones.

"Have you ever killed anyone?" Hallifax asked the first man.

"Ain't about to say," the man answered.

Hallifax grinned. "About what I'd say to the same question. Now, you know what we're planning. Will you be able to shoot a man or two if you need to so you can carry out your assignment?"

"Yeah, sure. You say the payoff at St. Michael is five thousand dollars. Not much I won't do for that kind of money."

An hour later he had contacted all five men. He had given them specific instructions about coming to the ship at nine in the morning ready to travel.

He told them they wouldn't need to bring the usual three weeks' worth of food. "We'll be borrowing enough food from those other passengers who won't be needing it anymore," Halifax said, and each man laughed.

He had given each of the five men $20 as partial payment and told them to have a good time. It would be at least three weeks before they saw a woman or a gambling table again.

Hallifax headed down Front Street to the small house where Marsha lived. Hell, if she was busy, he'd wait until she was free. He was going to have one last good session with her before the ship sailed.

Marsha was a woman he could talk to. She seemed interested in his poker games and his wild stories. Sometimes he said crazy things when he was about to climax, but he never remembered what they were.

He knocked on the door and pushed it open. Marsha stood there in a petticoat so thin he could see through it. The hot blood in his groin surged. She was saying good-bye to somebody.

Hallifax stepped ahead and crowded the man to one side. As the other man left he waved a 20-dollar bill at her and caught her elbow.

"Damn, I was hoping you'd be free."

"You new around here? I ain't never free. For you it's the usual fifty bucks and don't forget it."

"All heart, woman. This is going to be our last time so let's make it good."

"Yeah, I hear you got a blue ticket from Irons."

"You heard so fast?"

"Not much else to talk about. You knew better than to blast away with that derringer when you know you ain't even supposed to have one."

They went into her bedroom and he closed the door and reached for her breasts.

She reached for his wallet, took out $30 more, and then rubbed his crotch.

"So, what are you going to do on the Outside?"

He pulled off the petticoat and watched her beautiful naked form. Hell, what would it hurt. He told her what he had planned for the downriver trip on the *Benedict*.

Marsha's eyes went wide. "Now, Arthur, you're fooling me. That's the wildest story you've ever told me. I don't believe a word of it." That was

what Marsha told him, but deep down, she saw
how easy it would be, and how desperate Hallifax
was. It all added up to the truth. Hallifax was
going to try to capture the ship like a pirate of
old and rob everyone on board. So since she knew
about it, what should she do? Should she tell anyone? Would anyone believe her?

When Bryan Jeferies watched Superintendent
Irons walk away from the alley in back of his
building, he figured the try for Hallifax was over.
He helped McCoy take down the rope and the
dummy and put away the boxes.

"A good try, McCoy. Better luck next time."

McCoy snorted. "Yeah, if there is a next time.
I've got a week to prove he's a killer and there isn't
any evidence."

McCoy walked Francine back to the boardinghouse and Bryan went to work behind his desk.

He had sold two more of his claims. Now he
was down to the 12 that were producing the best
gold dust. All of them were on a two-shift basis,
with the men working 11 hours a day for six
dollars a day. That was two dollars more than
anyone else paid and his men responded by working much harder.

He decided to get rid of his water service and
his bread bakery and route. He sold each to the
men who worked in them. They were to send
him 20 percent of the profit for the next year;
then they would own the businesses.

Next he thought about Liza. She was going to
need a lot of convincing. He went to the New York
Saloon and sent a note up to Liza suggesting a
walk up to the wildflowers. Ten minutes later
Liza came down and found him at a back table.

She wore a polka-dot dress and a sunbonnet, and at first he didn't recognize her.

"Liza, it is you."

She sat down beside him and smiled. "Bryce Jeferies, what a thoughtful, kind thing to suggest. I'll always have a tender spot in my heart for wildflowers, especially those that you brought me that day when my world had collapsed.

"Let's go see if there are any still blooming."

They walked up the slope to where they had been before, and found hundreds of blooms. Some had peaked and faded, but there were all the kinds they had seen before.

Liza scurried around picking arctic poppies and daisies and batches of the crimson fireweed.

They sat and looked out over the river and its passageway downstream.

"Liza, I want you to come to Portland with me. I've got enough money to set up a good business, maybe even launch you in a variety hall of your own, no booze, just a place where people would pay money to come and see you sing and dance."

"Bryce, I don't know. I haven't decided for sure to leave Dawson. I'm making more money here than I could hope to for a few years anywhere else."

"Liza, I'm not just asking you to come along. I want to marry you. Will you be my wife, Liza?"

She stared at him for several seconds. Her eyes went wide, and then a smile broke over her face and she surged forward and kissed his lips. The wildflowers were dropped and forgotten.

He held her tight, hardly believing that she was kissing him. The kiss went on and on, and at last they broke free to breathe. Her smile gleamed like a radiant star in the daylight.

"Yes, yes, yes, Bryce Jeferies, I'll marry you. Tomorrow or next week or when we get to Portland. Anytime. Let's see, Mrs. Bryce Jeferies, or Mrs. Liza Jeferies. Or Liza Cromwell Jeferies. They all sound so wonderful."

Bryce couldn't say a word. He just looked at her and opened his mouth and nothing came out. She laughed and kissed him, and at last he found his voice.

"You just made me the happiest man in the world. I'll scratch up a preacher today and we'll get married tomorrow. Probably not time enough to do it today . . ."

Liza held up her hands.

"Whoa there, horse. Getting married is more than just the preacher. I want a proper wedding. In the saloon, with bridesmaids and a wedding march and invitations and the whole thing. It will take two or three weeks to plan."

She stood, then bent and picked up the wildflowers. "I know I want wildflowers like these for my bridal bouquet. Oh, this is delicious. We have so much planning to do."

He caught her hand and hugged her tightly, then grinned at her. "Whatever you want, but remember, we're leaving here at least by September fifteenth. I don't want to get frozen in up here, even with a beautiful bride like you."

McCoy left the boardinghouse and found the closest saloon and ordered a whiskey. He sat at a table next to the wall and nursed the drink. What in hell could he do that would make Hallifax break? He had taken his best shot with the hatchet. Maybe he should contact the girl again—Marsha?

The more he thought about that, the more it seemed like it would not be productive. He'd used her information on the hatchet and almost won, but lost in the end to the damned English reserve, guts, and logic.

What else was there? Get Hallifax in a big-stakes poker game and win away from him every dollar he had? No, he was too smart for that and he would cheat to win. That was out.

Confront him in a fistfight? Now that might be interesting. Walling didn't have his derringer anymore. Unless he had found a replacement for the one Irons took away from him. A fistfight. Yes, now there was an idea.

Not practical. The Englishman would be careful not to get in any more trouble before his boat sailed. When would that be? A week from today was the last one he could take. Irons would know when he left. That wouldn't be much help.

He could arrange to sail on the same boat that the Englishman did. Now that might be productive. He thought about it, then hurried to the Mountie office and found the Superintendent.

"Mr. Irons, I want to be sure to sail out of here on the same boat that's taking Hallifax. I can escort him down to U.S. territory and maybe there we can detain him on some kind of charges while we try for more evidence."

Irons frowned at McCoy. "I only go by the law, McCoy. I can't dream up these wild ideas to try to convict a prisoner, or even to arrest one." He sighed. "Damn, McCoy, I wish I could sometimes. I estimate there's a ninety-five-percent chance that Hallifax is Walling, and that he killed the

White-Smith gent we buried a week or so ago. But there isn't one solitary, legal thing I can do about detaining him here."

"So I'll sail when he does and hope to get lucky downstream. If nothing else develops, I can always throw him overboard as soon as we get into U.S. waters."

Irons looked up sharply.

"I was only joking, Superintendent. I'd never do that. If he wanted to come at me in an honest gunfight, I wouldn't back down, but I won't put him in a watery grave unless he gives me good cause and I can prove it. I have to write out reports to my superiors too, you know."

"You did have me going there for a minute, McCoy."

"Any boats sailing today or tomorrow?"

"One today." He looked at a listing on his desk. "The *Klondike II*, leaves at six o'clock. Two go out tomorrow, the *Benedict* and the *River Runner*. The first one is set for a noon sailing and the other one for about six-thirty, the captain said."

"Will you know if Hallifax is on board any of those boats?"

"We will. I'll have a man at each gangplank to record the name and hometown of any and all passengers."

"Any idea when he'll be leaving?"

"None. You might check the bank and see if he's closed his account there. It's the best signal we have that someone is about to leave—or to run away."

McCoy thanked the Mountie. "I'll check by at the gangplank at the boat today and both boats tomorrow and have my bag packed and ready to leave. If there are any developments downstream,

I'll send word up on the next steamer."

The two men shook hands, and McCoy walked out of the office and went directly to the bank. He found the manager and reminded him about his lawman status.

"Does Arthur Hallifax still have an account here? Superintendent Irons has ordered him out of town and I'm wondering if he's closed his account."

The banker scowled for a moment. "Well, If Superintendent Irons has authorized it, I guess I can tell you." He went to some accounting books and returned quickly.

"Yes, he was in earlier today and closed out his account taking paper money. I had heard that he had been given a blue ticket so it was no surprise."

McCoy headed for Francine's place and packed up his belongings. She was out somewhere. He took his bag down to Bryce's office.

"Leaving?" Bryce asked looking up from his desk.

McCoy explained the situation. "So I'd like to leave my bag here in case I need to get away in a hurry. He might be sailing today. There's one boat leaving about six I need to check on."

I'll probably be here late. If not there's a key under the welcome mat in front." He stood and came over and shook McCoy's hand. "It's been interesting meeting you, McCoy. Sorry our little sideshow didn't break Hallifax. Maybe you can do some good with him in your three weeks going downriver. Oh, the happy news. Liza and I are getting married. She said yes today."

"Congratulations, it's a good match. You'll be staying here?"

Bryce looked at the door, then shook his head. "Don't say anything to anyone, but we'll be out of here before the freeze-up. Neither one of us want to put up with a dark fifty-below winter. September fifteen is our last day here. We might leave sooner, depending how the claims I still have sell."

McCoy held out his hand. "Good luck with everything, especially with Liza. She's a fine one, you take good care of her. Now, it's time I should check that boat."

McCoy found the boat was a bustle of action. Last-minute freight was being loaded, and passengers were lined up waiting their turn at the gangplank. McCoy found a man with a list at the side of the ship.

The sailor nodded. "You the gent checking our passenger manifest?"

"One of them. Where's the Mountie?"

"He's here. He checked the names on our list against the one we gave him earlier. He seemed to think somebody else might show up."

McCoy asked if Arthur Hallifax had signed to go downstream.

"No, sir. The latest blue ticket? Ain't seen him and his name sure ain't on the passenger list."

"You loaded to capacity?"

"No, sir, room for a dozen more. If'n they got their three weeks of food. I don't plan on sharing my grub with nobody."

McCoy thanked him and wandered over to some boxes destined for a local store and sat on them. He'd watch and wait. It would be just like Hallifax to rush up late and get on just as the gangplank was being raised.

If he did, McCoy would sprint on board as well.

He would buy food from some of the passengers. He'd heard that there was always someone willing to sell food on the downstream trip.

McCoy idled away the last hour before the craft sailed by watching the harbor operation. There was more activity here than he expected. A sternwheeler paddled in from the slow waters near shore and tied up.

"Whiskey!" somebody on board shouted. "We've got a thousand cases of damn good whiskey!"

Before they had finished tying up, there were half a dozen merchants on the dock, and the auction for the cases of booze was set for within the hour.

Passengers began moving on board the *Klondike II*. McCoy walked up and watched them. Hallifax could also use another name and disguise himself if he thought there was some need to. You couldn't tell what a skunk like Hallifax might think he had to do to get away from Dawson clean.

The ship was a half hour late in sailing and Hallifax hadn't shown up to board. There was an off chance he could use a small boat and meet the ship downstream, but it wasn't likely. He must still be in town.

McCoy picked up his suitcase at Bryce's office and walked back to his room at Francine's. She sat on the porch steps waiting for him.

"Moving in or moving out, stranger?" she asked.

In his room he explained it to her.

"Going so soon? We hardly got to know each other."

He petted one breast and kissed her lips softly. "Hey, I think we investigated each other about as much as a couple can. We had some good times. You knew I'd have to leave sooner or later."

"I know, damnit. I just didn't want it to be sooner." She watched him a minute. "You have any supper?"

McCoy shook his head.

"Damn you, I don't know why I bother. Maybe tomorrow you'll be gone and I'll be alone again. Come on, I'll get you something to eat. We had roast beef tonight and there's plenty left."

After he ate, they went back to his room; then she pulled him away and to her room.

"If this is going to be one of our last nights together, I want it to be special. Tender and soft and slow. You know, almost like married love."

It was.

Chapter Twenty-Five

The next morning, Marsha Brown awoke about eight, made herself a quick breakfast, dressed in a conservative, high-necked dress, and walked down Front Street toward the Mountie office. She had on a hat with a veil that concealed her face.

She'd decided early that morning that she had to tell Superintendent Irons what she'd heard last night. Normally she wasn't so public-spirited, but this would be a tragedy if it happened and she knew about it.

That made her partly responsible. Legally she could be held liable if she didn't report it. She had to tell the Mounties.

Half a block later she convinced herself that they wouldn't believe her, that they would laugh her out of the office. She was sure that was what would happen, and walked right past the Mounties' office.

A block later she changed her mind. They would believe her. The superintendent hadn't gained his lofty position by being stupid. He would listen at least, then evaluate. It couldn't hurt to be ready, send along some men posing as civilians but with their arms.

She turned in at the Mountie office, and almost couldn't open the door. Someone behind her opened it for her and there was nothing left to do but walk in. She saw a Mountie at the counter and went up to him.

"I'm Mrs. Brown and I need to see Superintendent Irons."

"I'm sorry, ma'am, but the Superintendent isn't in right now. He's out on a case. Can someone else help you?"

The young man looked no more than twenty-five. What would he know? He'd laugh at her. No, she didn't have to say how she found out about the information, just that she knew.

In half a breath she changed her mind again. "No, no, I need to talk to Mr. Irons himself. Could I wait?"

Marsha Brown sat on the hard wooden bench for two hours waiting for Irons to return. At the end of that time, she quietly stood and walked out the door. She had tried. Damnit, she had tried to tell him what might happen on board the *Benedict*. If it did happen, it wasn't her fault. She had tried.

Spur McCoy had arrived at the docks a little before nine that morning. He had brought

along his one traveling bag, and set it behind
some piling on the dock and sat down on the logs
watching the stern-wheeler *Benedict*. She was a
bustle of activity. A wagon pulled up with two
sturdy-looking teamsters. They backed the rig up
to the gangplank and used small hand trucks with
wheels on the front, and then balanced the load
on the wheels as they started to move 15 heavy-
looking wooden boxes onto the ship.

McCoy wandered over and looked at the last of
the boxes. It was newly made and marked "Hand
Tools" in stenciled black letters. The address on it
was somewhere in Vancouver, B.C. The men who
came back with the hand cart had their shirts wet
with sweat. One of the men looked at the last box
and groaned.

"Holy damn shit, thought we had done the last
one."

"One more," the other man said. "Then we go
get our breakfast."

The box on the hand cart vanished up the gangplank to the curses of the freight men. McCoy
faded back to the piling again.

Not ten minutes later he spotted Hallifax walking up with a traveling bag. Hallifax talked a
moment with the man at the gangplank, then
moved back to the string of 50 men and wom-
en who had lined up to board the vessel.

McCoy felt a surge of emotion. So he had
guessed right. The Englisher was leaving on the
boat today. McCoy thought of buying some food
to take along, but didn't want to let Hallifax out
of his sight. One man came up to Hallifax in the
line, but the Englishman shrugged at the question

the man must have asked and turned his back on him.

Figured. Hallifax was still angry at being banished from Dawson. He'd have to do his cheating and gambling at ordinary towns from now on.

More freight came to the ship. There were large cardboard boxes with names painted on them and destinations. A rocking chair was one of the items, then a grandfather clock with the works all removed, dozens of small boxes, and a few more larger wooden boxes that seemed to be heavy as the crew manhandled them up the gangplank and into the hold.

At eleven o'clock the man at the plank let the passengers on board. No one had minded waiting. They knew it was a three-week trip to get to the "outside," so what was another hour or two in port?

McCoy made sure that Hallifax got on board; then he went over and talked to the man at the rail. He had seen the man selling tickets, and McCoy had out the $110 for the downstream passage. He found himself assigned to a large room that had 40 bunks in it and 50 men. They would sleep in shifts if they wanted to stay below deck.

Six women had a cabin to themselves. There were more men in another large room somewhere else. McCoy looked around to make sure that Hallifax wasn't in his big cabin, then carried his bag with him and went topside to watch the craft pull away from the dock.

It wasn't a large ship, about 150 feet long not counting the huge stern paddle wheel. But it would make good time down the river. He heard the calls of the seamen; then the last lines were cast off and the craft turned lazily a moment with the gentle flow of current next to the docks. As soon as the paddle wheel was clear, the clutch kicked in and the big wheel began to turn as the diesel engines hammered deep in the hold and drove the ship out in the current. They started their journey promptly at 12:30.

McCoy turned to go talk to the captain and came face to face with Arthur Walling/Hallifax. McCoy looked right through him and brushed past his form, seemingly not taking any note of the man.

Hallifax stared at McCoy as he walked away, and McCoy could feel the angry glances as he rounded the cabin and headed to the bow. McCoy wasn't sure if Hallifax remembered him from their conversation about England, or had noticed him the day before in the darkness of the warehouse. He wasn't sure if he would recognize him as one of the drunks who had probably thrown the hatchet into his door. But even if he did, what could Hallifax do now?

Arthur Hallifax watched the man out of sight. He'd seen him before, several times. In the New York Saloon talking with some merchant and with Liza. But somewhere else as well. Yes! He was one of the people in the background yesterday at the merchant's warehouse. He was one of the ones who'd set up the dummy and the bloody hatchet to try to break him while the Mountie watched.

Who was he? Some kind of a lawman? He was probably American. Whoever he was, he was trouble. Hallifax walked up to the top deck and to the captain, who was still with the man at the wheel, making sure he knew this stretch of the river. He saw Hallifax and motioned him into his cabin, then hurried there himself.

"Captain O'Brien, we've got some trouble." He told the sailor about the man on board who had been in a plot to discredit him in Dawson.

"You think the superintendent suspects something? Has he put other men on board in civilian clothes to guard the gold?"

Captain O'Brien lit his pipe and puffed. "Don't think so. If this man's an American, can't figure why he'd be concerned with an English warrant you say is out on you. At any rate, he's just one man. Every hour we make about ten miles downstream.

"We wait two days, we'll be over two hundred miles downstream, and then we'll take over the ship, put the passengers on shore with four of my crewmen, and sail on free as a bird. Right before we take the ship, we bring this McCoy into my cabin, put him in irons, and take him out of the picture before he can stop us."

Hallifax relaxed a little. "Sounds like you've thought of everything, Captain O'Brien. One man against us won't be any big problem."

They toasted their success. Two hours later and some 20 miles downstream from Dawson, Captain O'Brien and Hallifax came boiling out of his cabin. They had heard a revolver shot, then two more. Both the captain and Hallifax had their six-guns in hand as they ran to the wheelhouse.

The regular pilot lay dead on the floor. One of the five men Hallifax had hired steered the ship.

"You blundering fool!" Hallifax exploded. "We're not ready to take over the ship yet."

"The hell we ain't," a second man said behind them. Hallifax turned and saw one of his men with a six-gun aimed at him.

"Now, look, men. This is a little misunderstanding. I guess we just go ahead and take over the ship now that we're started." He shrugged to the Captain. "Nothing we can do now. Alert your men, Captain. Seal the passageways below, keep the passengers below deck."

A crewman ran up. "Captain, what's the trouble? Oh, God, Harley!"

Captain O'Brien shot the crewman in the heart, and his eyes went wild with wonder and surprise as he fell to the deck dead.

"Get moving!" Hallifax shouted at the other of his men. One dashed below to the engine room. One took over the steering, and another left the upper deck to secure the areas on the first deck.

McCoy heard the first two shots. He pulled the twin six-guns from his travel bag, fisted them both, and ran toward the wheelhouse. A shot nipped his upper left arm. He turned and fired once, and a man with a six-gun took the round in the chest, pivoted over the rail, and splashed in the cold Yukon River water.

McCoy jumped the inside rail and raced to the wheelhouse. One man stood there grinning. Two bodies lay on the floor. McCoy cocked his six-gun and the wheelman turned, gun in hand. McCoy shot him in the shoulder, slamming him to the deck. McCoy kicked away the six-gun.

"What the hell is going on?" he demanded.

The pirate on the floor groaned. "You shot me, you bastard!"

"Happens when you point a gun at me. Now what's going on here?"

"What's it look like. We're taking over this scow. We've got ten men all armed and not a damn thing you can do to stop us."

McCoy saw the lever that signaled the engine room. He reversed the lever to "All Stop," then cranked the big wheel so the craft angled toward shore. He saw what he figured was a sandbar ahead. He tied the wheel hard over with a piece of line, then ducked low and waited to see who came to investigate. A crewman ran in first.

McCoy's six-gun aimed at his gut stopped him. McCoy pointed to the deck and the man dropped and lay quietly. A man who looked like a miner ran in with a six-gun. McCoy's shot slammed into his shoulder jolting him sideways into the bulkhead. The weapon dropped from his hand and he bellowed in pain.

"Down or you're dead," McCoy whispered.

As he said it, the bow of the stern-wheeler, drifting now with the shallow currents, hit the sandbar. The sudden jolt threw McCoy backwards. His head battered into the solid wood railing and a deep, dark blackness closed in around him.

When McCoy came back to consciousness, he stared at three weapons pointed at him. One rested in the hand of Arthur Hallifax. Hallifax grinned.

"Well, McCoy, you almost made it, but not quite. About a pair of queens short, I'd say. Oh, yes, I know who you are. I checked your identification. On your feet. You have your choice, jump overboard or have us throw you. You have five seconds to decide."

One of the gunmen was the captain, another the first mate. A captain was pirating his own ship? What was on board that was so valuable?

McCoy staggered to his feet. Both of his weapons were gone. No, all three, including his hideout. He went to the rail and looked down. The stern-wheeler was aground on the sandbar. It led to shore. Not three feet of water covered it.

On shore he saw a bedraggled rabble of the former passengers.

"That's five," Hallifax said, and started toward McCoy. He vaulted over the rail, twisted so he would land feet-first, and hit the three feet of water and plunged his feet into the sand. It jolted him but he stayed erect.

At once the engines pounded, the stern-wheeler's big paddle went into reverse, and for one long moment he hoped that the craft was grounded for good. Gradually the big wheel pulled the ship off the sand, and a moment later it came free and backed into the current.

Two minutes later the *Benedict* swept around a curve and was gone downstream.

McCoy waded to shore and looked over the passengers.

"Anybody in charge here?" he asked.

Everyone looked at everyone else.

"Anyone know for sure what happened back there? I was unconscious part of the time."

"Bastards stole all our gold and our cash and our food and are heading for St. Michael," one man said.

"Ruined me," another man said. "All my dust and my goods. I'm not worth a dime."

"Who took over the boat?" McCoy asked.

"The crew and four or five gamblers and riff raff," a woman said.

"The captain was in on it too. I saw him holding a gun on you back there."

McCoy nodded. "All right. Anybody know the country? How far are we from Dawson?"

One man stood up. His clothes were half dry already. "We weren't afloat more than two hours. That means it can't be more than twenty miles to Dawson right upstream."

"So let's start walking," McCoy said. "We can't do any good here. I want four men to bring up the rear, help anyone who's having trouble. Don't leave anyone behind." He looked around and picked his four men, then got the rest of them into a line. "Keep it four or five across, then you have somebody to talk to."

He sized up the other men, picked out two as the leaders, and got the line moving. There were no small children, and the women all looked solid and strong enough to walk.

Now he went along the line. "Do we have any runners here? Anyone who can run the twenty miles to Dawson and get a quicker start on the chase after your goods?"

Two younger men volunteered. Morgan went to the head of the line and he told the two lead men what he and the volunteers were going to do.

"Keep the line moving. You should be able to get to Dawson by eight o'clock tonight. Take a ten-minute break every two hours. Otherwise, keep everyone moving."

McCoy and the two volunteers took off at a steady trot up the banks of the river. In many

places the water had receded a little and they
could run on the sand and rocks along the shore.
When they cut inland it was harder.

McCoy pushed the pace a little, dropping into
the Indian trot he had learned from the Cheyenne.
He could do six miles in an hour at the pace. At
that rate it would be more than three hours before
they got to Dawson.

He stopped thinking and concentrated on running. They had been at it for a half hour. Another
two and a half hours to go.

At the one-hour mark, one of the two men dropped out. At the two-hour mark the second man
waved at McCoy and started walking.

McCoy pushed harder then. By his watch it was
a little after five-thirty when he checked again.
Shouldn't be far now. He came around another
small bend in the mighty Yukon and saw Dawson.

Twenty minutes later he ran up to the Mounties'
office and pushed open the door.

"Irons," McCoy said panting. "I've got to talk to
Superintendent Irons."

A half hour later Spur McCoy, Superintendent
Irons, and seven mounties armed with repeating
rifles stood on the deck of the *River Queen*. She
had just unloaded and taken on a fresh supply of
wood for her boilers.

"We're commandeering your boat, Captain, to
take us downstream as fast as you can. We want
to catch a pirated river boat, the *Benedict*. She
has a six-hour head start on us. How long until
we can catch her?"

The young captain growled. "Don't know, never raced unloaded before. The *Benedict* can do
about ten knots. We can make better than that.

Might take us a day to catch her. We should
have enough food on board to feed all of us.
Let's go."

The *River Queen* surged into the current, and
Captain Kinney pushed the throttles forward until
the 80-foot craft bounced down the Yukon like a
runaway log raft.

"We must be doing fifteen knots," McCoy said
holding on to the rail. "Now all we have to do is
figure out what to do once we catch her."

Far below on the Yukon, the *Benedict* rode the
current down the Yukon. One of the crewmen
steered the craft from the wheelhouse.

Captain O'Brien and Hallifax went below and
rummaged through the cargo until they found
what they searched for. The heavy boxes marked
"Tools" were near the bottom of the stacks. They
horsed one of the boxes out, and with a hammer
and crowbar ripped the top off it.

Inside, neatly stacked, lay dozens of six-inch-
long leather bags. Most were round. Hallifax
picked up one and opened the top.

"By damn! he shouted. "Look at the gold dust.
What are these, twenty-pound sacks?"

Captain O'Brien opened one himself and
grinned. "Now I'm rich. No sons of bitches
are going to order me around, demand that I
kowtow to them and do what they say! I'm a
rich man."

"For a damned short time, though, Captain."

Hallifax shot Captain O'Brien through his left
eye. He slammed backward, the bag of gold dust
spilling onto his fancy shirt. Hallifax picked up
the bag of gold dust, salvaged what he could, and

tied up the bag and put it away. He covered up the box of gold, and went topside to talk with his crew. He figured they needed four men to run the ship. Which meant the others were expendable. He'd figure out which ones later.

He could afford $5,000 per man now that he didn't have to split up the gold with the captain. The man had been a fool from the start.

Now Hallifax began to face reality. He had the gold, but could he keep it? The passengers would get back to Dawson and spread the word. There was a chance that Irons might send a boat after him. But he would soon be in U.S. waters where the Mountie would have no authority. Would he come anyway or would he turn around?

Hallifax had to prepare for the worst. He took his eight men and showed them where to fire from if they were attacked from upriver.

"Fire over some protection and duck down. They will have rifles too, but aiming from one ship to another on this damn bouncy river will make a fool out of any sharpshooter.

"I doubt if Irons will chase us into U.S. waters, but he might, so we have to be ready. Now, are you finding enough food?"

The men yelled that they were. Some of the passengers had planned on eating well during the trip.

Hallifax went back to the hold. No one had asked about Captain O'Brien. He piled some freight on top of the captain's body and went back up to the wheelhouse.

"How fast are we going?" he asked the man steering.

"I'd say about eleven knots, our usual speed through here."

"Move it faster, I think Superintendent Irons of the Royal Canadian Mounted Police is going to be following us."

Chapter Twenty-Six

Spur McCoy stood next to Superintendent Irons in the small wheelhouse of the *River Queen* as it slammed down the Yukon. Irons looked at McCoy a moment, then spoke.

"You said you found out about that hatchet from one of our ladies of the evening. You never told me which one. Did you get her name?"

"Marsha, that's the only name I know her by. Has a house out on the end of Front Street."

"She told you about the hatchet and that Hallifax was the man who was yelling about it?"

"She did. Said he told her a lot of things about England too, Something about a man being killed and she had the idea Hallifax couldn't go back there."

"I'm in trouble," Irons said. "A woman who called herself Mrs. Brown waited for me in my office this morning for two hours, when I was out on another matter. When I came back one of my men told me about her but said she had left. He said he was sure she was Marsha Brown, one of the fancy women we know in town. She's an expensive one.

"She told the man at the counter she wanted to see me, to tell me something. I'd bet a bucket full of Canadian flags that she knew that Hallifax was going to jump this boat. I bet he told her all about it.

"Why else would she come to my office and wait two hours to see me? She's usually so scared of the Mounties that she crosses the street when she sees one of us. Something mighty important must have happened to make her come in. I'll see her when we get back to make sure."

McCoy nodded. "Could be. Not your fault she didn't wait a little longer. No sense in even reporting it. But what I don't understand is why Hallifax and the captain and at least half of his crew pirated their own boat? What's on it that's worth getting hung for?"

Superintendent Irons watched water spray the wheelhouse window when the boat hit some small rapids. He looked downstream.

"Did you see any freight loaded this morning before you boarded the ship?"

"Yes. Considerable."

"Did you notice one bunch of wooden crates that seemed heavier than most of the rest?"

"I did. Those boxes were marked as tools, going to Vancouver, B.C." McCoy lifted his brows. "Oh, oh. About the heaviest thing around this place is gold dust. I never wondered how the raw gold was taken out of here, but the only logical way would be on one of the steamers."

"Somehow Hallifax or the captain knew it. We've used his boat before and maybe he caught on. We try to keep it as big a secret as we can. Never lost any of the dust before. Send it down as tools for repair or some such and no guards to draw attention to it. The bankers weren't specific, but there is something over a half-million dollars worth of gold dust in those wooden crates. They said fifteen boxes and each weighed a hundred pounds. That's with our black sand gold that's worth about sixteen dollars an ounce."

"So Hallifax had a big motive for taking over the boat. Makes a lot more sense now. He and Captain O'Brien must have had it set up before you gave him his blue ticket."

"If I had listened to Marsha Brown this morning, we could have sent some dummy boxes on board and not risked the gold. Sometimes I get too busy in this job of mine."

Captain Kinney came up with a pad of paper working on some figures.

"You gents might as well have some supper and get a good long sleep. We won't catch them for a time. I worked it out. They have a five-and-a-half-hour head start on us. They should be averaging about eleven knots. That bigger craft can't stand the jolting of much more speed. Meanwhile, we're doing fifteen knots.

"To sum it all up, they left Dawson at twelve-thirty P.M. today. Tomorrow at noon, we should catch them or be within shooting distance of them. We have a little over seventeen hours of fast running yet to catch them."

Soon they saw the line of stragglers hiking along the shore heading for Dawson. The captain tooted his whistle at the hikers and they waved and cheered. McCoy fired his revolver twice into the air and they cheered again.

Five miles later, they came to the spot where McCoy had beached the craft.

The men ate and then slept. It would be a long time until they caught up with the *Benedict*.

The next morning, just before eleven A.M., McCoy sighted another ship in front of them. She was a stern-wheeler going downstream.

"Has to be the *Benedict*," McCoy said. "Hasn't been any other boat on the river heading this direction.

Superintendent Irons went to McCoy. "It's your call, McCoy. We're in U.S. waters now and I have no jurisdiction. Not even when I'm pursuing a criminal am I allowed to leave Canadian jurisdiction. So it's your show."

McCoy placed the seven Mountie marksmen near the bow of the boat and made sure each had a solid barrier to shoot over. Then he waited.

"We'll open fire at six hundred yards," McCoy said. "We might not hit anything, but we'll scare hell out of them. When we get close enough, concentrate your fire on the wheelhouse. If we can put the helmsman down, we might get her beached and dead on a sandbar."

When McCoy figured they were at 600 yards, he gave the order to fire. He and Superintendent Irons shot as well. He saw a few hits on the craft, but couldn't determine any damage. A moment later they took return fire, but none of the rounds hit the smaller craft.

Slowly they closed the gap. At 400 yards they

opened fire again, and now they could see the hits. Twenty rounds slammed into the wheelhouse, and for a moment there was no reaction. Then the craft heeled over toward shore before she was brought back sharply to mid-stream.

Again they unleashed a concentrated fire on the wheelhouse. Now they were taking rounds from the rifles on the other ship. No one was injured. Their own wheelman had crouched well below the window during the attack.

The third time they fired at the wheelhouse the other craft shuddered and angled toward the shore.

They had closed to a hundred yards now, and McCoy saw a man lift up from the bow and start toward the wheelhouse. He tracked him with the rifle sights and fired. The man did a slow dive forward, rolled on the deck, and fell overboard. One less pirate to worry about.

The craft kept angling toward shore; then the engine cut off and the big paddle wheel stopped. The *Benedict* drifted for a moment; then a surge of current drove it toward shore and they saw it jolt, and heard a scraping, tearing crash as the ship grounded against some rocks and a sandbar.

The battle wasn't over. For more than an hour the two ships traded rifle rounds. The smaller ship backed off to 300 yards and the riflemen fired at each other. One more man on the larger ship was hit, and for a time no rounds were fired at them from the pirated craft.

Then they saw two men heave up and throw a third man off the stern into the river. He threshed frantically in the water, sank once, and resurfaced.

A megaphone-assisted voice boomed over the water.

"Cease fire! We give up. If you want Hallifax, that's him in the water. He says he can't swim."

At once the smaller boat raced forward, and found Arthur Walling/Hallifax sinking once more in water near the shore. McCoy jumped overboard, landed in water up to his waist, lifted a floundering Hallifax to his feet, and shoved him toward the shore 50 feet away through shallow water.

An hour later they had it sorted out. Three members of the crew were dead. Three of Halifax's men were missing and presumed shot or drowned. Captain O'Brien was dead, probably shot at close range by Hallifax, but it couldn't be proved. That meant they had three crewmen and two of Hallifax's men as prisoners besides Hallifax himself.

Superintendent Irons and McCoy found the captain's body and the gold boxes in the hold. One had been opened and examined. For just a moment, McCoy ran his fingers through one of the open sacks of gold dust.

"Makes you think, doesn't it, Mr. Irons? Makes you understand just a little why a man like the captain would hatch a plot like this to get his hands on nearly a ton of gold. It would be my guess that the captain had planned a watery grave for Hallifax and his five men just as soon as they got the passengers ashore and were back on the river. Somehow, Hallifax beat him to the double cross."

"Gold," the Mountie said. "I've seen so much of it that it has almost no meaning to me anymore. Like a banker who works with money all day and gets sick of it. But you're right about what it does to men. In the ground or out of the ground, it seems to make men go stark raving mad.

"At least we know this can't last forever. The creeks and valleys are about panned out. The benches will yield gold for another year. I expect that by the end of 1899 most of the gold diggers will be gone from Dawson. It will shrink from thirty thousand men down to two or three hundred. By then I'll be moving on to a new assignment as well."

McCoy authorized two of the Mounties to remain behind on U.S. soil as guards over the hulk of the riverboat and the freight. A repair crew would be sent down to salvage the craft. The gold was lifted out of the hold on pulleys and taken aboard the *River Queen* to move it back to Dawson, where it would be shipped again on another boat heading toward Vancouver. McCoy bet that this time there would be some guards.

Two hours later the smaller boat angled out into the current for the day-and-a-half trip back to Dawson pounding upstream against the current.

Superintendent Irons lit a cigar and put his feet up. He had just taken a nip from his glass of sippin' whiskey and he nodded at McCoy. "I'm taking your suggestion that we move the bank's gold out of town now only with a military guard. We're getting a half a troop in soon to help us control the area. I can see now that one of the important things we need to do is to guard the gold going downstream."

The two men looked over at Arthur Walling. He sat in a heavy chair and was bound to it by chains

with padlocks on them. Two of the miners swore
that they would testify that he had killed Captain
O'Brien and that he had shot one crewman and
one of his own hired hands.

The five modern pirates were chained together
in one of the forward cabins. They were prisoners of the United States Government until the
ship made it back into Canadian waters. Then
they automatically reverted to the custody of the
Mounties, who would prosecute.

Walling would pay the price in Canada and
London would be notified.

"So, mission accomplished, Mr. McCoy. What's
your next assignment?"

"First I have to get outside and down to Seattle
so I can wire my office. That's going to take up to
two months. Never can tell what might happen in
two months."

Back in Dawson the next day, McCoy carried his
suitcase to Francine's boardinghouse. He went in
and rang the bell and she came out all efficient
and proper. When she saw him she dropped a
book she had been reading, screeched, and ran
into his arms, holding him like she would never
let go.

"I was wondering if you had any rooms available," McCoy asked when she stopped kissing
him.

She shook her head. "Sorry all full. But maybe
I can find a place for you."

She took his hand and led him into her private
rooms, then to her bedroom.

"Don't say a word, just strip off your clothes,
lay down on my bed, and relax."

The next day, McCoy checked out the sailing

imes. A ship was set to leave the following day. It was a larger stern-wheeler with six cabins available. He hurried in and booked one of the cabins. The other steamship company had refunded him his money for the *Benedict* ticket he'd never used.

He went from the steamship company to the New York Saloon and found Bryce there talking with Liza. The two congratulated him on the final apprehension of Arthur Walling and the upcoming trial.

"There's been a trial set for next week," Bryce said. "My guess is that Walling will be the center of a necktie celebration within another week. Couldn't have happened to a more deserving bloke."

Liza held on to Bryce's arm. She looked at him as if she never wanted to let go.

"When's the wedding?" McCoy asked.

"Two weeks, just two weeks," Liza said. She bubbled as she told McCoy all about the arrangements.

" . . . and I'm going to have five bridesmaids, all of the girls in the dance troupe. It's going to be the biggest, fanciest wedding that Dawson has ever seen."

"Sorry I won't be here," McCoy said. "I'm sailing tomorrow for St. Michael."

"Oh, no!" Liza wailed.

"You'll live. One of these days I'll travel out to Portland and come and watch you dance and sing. I hope you do get your own variety hall there."

Then it was time for Liza to go backstage for a rehearsal. She came over and kissed McCoy on the cheek and hugged him for the first time ever.

"Spur McCoy, you be good, and don't go getting yourself shot. I'm looking forward to meeting you again in Portland. Give us a couple of years to get going down there."

Bryce gave him a hearty handshake and McCoy headed back to the boardinghouse. He didn't miss supper that night. It seemed more special than usual.

After they ate, he told Francine he'd be leaving. She wasn't as upset as he figured she might be. She shrugged, and said he could play some poker that evening in one of the saloons. She had some important business to take care of. She didn't say what it was or how long it would take.

The next morning he said good-bye to Francine. She simply kissed him, told him to take care of himself, and waved good-bye. McCoy was surprised but pleased that she was taking it so well. He carried his suitcase down to the Mounties' office, where he wrote out a deposition covering his part in the capture of Arthur Walling/Hallifax. He signed it and Superintendent Irons signed it, and it would be used at the trial if necessary. Irons said they probably wouldn't need it.

Irons walked McCoy to the ship. They said good-bye at the gangplank.

"Next time you get to the States, send a wire to Washington, D.C., and find out where I am," McCoy advised. "I'd be proud to show you around some of the States."

The Superintendent said he had no idea where his next assignment might be. "It's been interesting working with you, McCoy. I like the way you do business." They shook hands, and McCoy boarded before the other passengers because he had a cabin. He was shown which one by one of the crew. He backed through the cabin door holding his suitcase in hand, and before he turned around he sensed someone was behind him.

It was too late to draw his hide-out. He turned slowly. Francine jumped into his arms and smothered his surprised face with kisses.

"Where the hell have you been? Don't you know it's almost sailing time?"

He frowned. "I don't quite understand. I thought you had the boardinghouse to run."

"What do you have to understand? I'm going to Seattle with you. I'm tired of the North Country. My important business last night was to sell my boardinghouse. A man has been trying to buy it for two months. I decided, why not. It's sold. I got his check this morning and cashed it at the bank, then told the captain I was traveling with you. He grinned like a fool and let me in about a half hour ago.

"Food? I brought enough to last us two months. We can eat great or just nibble on each other. Damn, I have you all to myself for two months. You're going to be worn down to a nub by the time we get to Seattle."

She offered him a cigar. He nipped off the end and lit it on the match she struck. Next she handed him a tumbler full of some amber liquid. He tasted it and grinned.

"Tennessee sippin' whiskey," he said with a sigh, and settled down on the wide bunk. "Now this is living. All this and a two-month ride back to the Outside. I think I'm going to like it here. Somehow it doesn't seem so important to get back to Seattle."

That's what Spur McCoy, Secret Service agent said. Deep down he wondered what kind of an assignment the general would have for him as soon as he hit Seattle. It was something to ponder for a while. In the meantime all he had to do was eat, drink, and pay attention to a pretty lady. Life was getting tough, but he could take it.

KANSAN DOUBLE EDITIONS
By Robert E. Mills

A double shot of hard lovin' and straight shootin' in the Old West for one low price!

Showdown at Hells Canyon. Sworn to kill his father's murderer, young Davy Watson rides a vengeance trail that leads him from frontier ballrooms and brothels to the wild Idaho territory.
And in the same action-packed volume...
Across the High Sierra. Recovering from a brutal gun battle, the Kansan is tended to by three angels of mercy. But when the hot-blooded beauties are kidnapped, he has to ride to hell and back to save his own slice of heaven.
_3342-9 $4.50

Red Apache Sun. When his sidekick Soaring Hawk helps two blood brothers break out of an Arizona hoosegow, Davy Watson finds a gun in his back—and a noose around his neck!
And in the same rip-roarin' volume...
Judge Colt. In the lawless New Mexico Territory, the Kansan gets caught between a Mexican spitfire and an American doxy fighting on opposite sides of a range war.
_3373-9 $4.50

SPEND YOUR LEISURE MOMENTS WITH U

Hundreds of exciting titles to choose from—something for everyone's taste in fine books: breathtaking historical romance, chilling horror, spine-tingling suspense, taut medical thrillers, involving mysteries, action-packed men's adventure and wild Westerns.

SEND FOR A FREE CATALOGUE TODAY!